Donna. L. Jones

Donna L. Jones is a new author, who lives in Wales with her husband, two children and Springer Spaniel. Her debut novel *The Rise of Global* will be followed by the sequel *The Rise of Global: Label.*

For Wyn, Georgia and Levi.

Donna L. Jones

The Rise of Global

A CIP catalogue record for this title is available from the British Library.

ISBN 9781786292711 (Paperback)
ISBN 9781786292728 (Hardback)
ISBN 9781786292735 (E-Book)
www.austinmacauley.com

First Published (2017)
Austin Macauley Publishers Ltd.
25 Canada Square
Canary Wharf
London
E14 5LQ

Acknowledgments

Thank you to Aileen, Sam, Liz and Jo. A special thank you to Lorainne for her encouragement, prayers, proofreading and more proofreading!

Thank you to my family and especially my mother for always reading and telling me stories when I was a child. For buying books that inspired me and which made me want to become a writer.

Above all, I would like to thank my heavenly Father for giving me a love of writing and the vision for *The Rise of Global*.

As you read this book, please take time to consider the giver of languages, the Lord God himself. The story of The Tower of Babel can be found in the Bible:
Genesis 11: 1-9.

Glossary

GL – Global Language
GS – Global Standard
MT – Mother Tongue
MLWA – Minority Languages World Association
GPC – Global Protocol Committee
GSPC – Global Standard Protocol Committee
GSW – Global Standard to the World

1

Apollos sat at his kitchen table waiting for Nastan who was late, as usual. Their soup bowls and spoons were set ready, waiting. 'Ten minutes late,' thought Apollos, checking the time firstly on the grandfather clock that chimed reluctantly, then on his wristwatch that ticked wearily to the beat of his pulse.

'That boy is getting later every day,' he thought to himself impatiently as he turned off the stove before the soup became pulp. He moved to his comfy chair with the window view, so he could look out for Nastan. Another five minutes passed and Nastan appeared, sprinting up the hill, his arms in perfect motion and his knees lifted high to gain pace.

Nastan stood breathless by the kitchen sink. He looked over to Apollos whose head was down looking at his wristwatch. The grandfather clock listlessly struck 4:15 pm. Apollos cast him a disappointed look. In between hurried gulps of water, Nastan asked him in Global, 'Papa, can I go to the lake with Grigor? I'll be back in time to walk with you to the meeting, I promise.'

Apollos looked at Nastan dejectedly. But his sad look wasn't because of Nastan's thoughtlessness, because he was late or because he had already eaten with Grigor and his family.

Nastan continued speaking in Global, 'Papa, the soup won't waste, we can have it tomorrow. Grigor's mother has invited us to supper with them. She said to tell you she has plenty of lamb soup, kozinjak and baklava leftover from yesterday. You don't usually skip her Easter Sunday meal. She told me to tell you she missed you yesterday and …'

In their own language, Apollos interrupted Nastan and said pointedly, 'Speak in our own language Nastan, speak in our beloved Mother Tongue or this old man will not be able to understand you.'

Nastan's insistence in speaking a foreign language that Apollos could not understand which had no place in their home - that was the real disappointment. That hurt him more than the soup spoiling, or being absent from meals, or being late.

'Speak in our own language,' he repeated, feeling perplexed by how self-assured Nastan had become in speaking Global. Nastan's lips were moving, his voice was familiar, but his words were not.

'Papa, no-one can hear us. No-one cares if we speak Mother Tongue anymore,' continued Nastan, in Global.

Apollos cast him a scolding look.

Reluctantly, in Mother Tongue, Nastan repeated, 'Papa, no-one cares about speaking Mother Tongue.'

'I care Nastan, I care,' he replied, his voice diminishing. 'Mother Tongue is your first language; Mother Tongue is who you are. Global plays no part in our lives. I cannot understand you and I have no desire to understand you, except in our own language. You may be speaking Global perfectly for all I know, but your accent gives you away, Nastan.'

But Nastan was tired of having to speak Mother Tongue, a minority language that no-one of *his* generation cared about. He knew his Global was far from perfect, but he was so tired of his grandfather's stubbornness to accept that Mother Tongue had no place in *his* future. He was tired of their daily routine and soup and having to be on time. He wanted a new routine – he needed a new routine.

Frustratingly, in Mother Tongue, Nastan replied, 'No Papa, Mother Tongue is who you are and who your parents were and their parents before them.'

'So how do you propose *we* talk to each other if you do not speak Mother Tongue?' enquired Apollos.

'I could teach you Global. I am sure you could learn it,' replied Nastan.

Apollos laughed mockingly.

Haughtily, Nastan said, 'I want to speak Global fluently. I want to speak Global so well that there is no trace of Mother Tongue in my accent. I want to be the same as my friends and their parents and the majority of our country now. None of my friends speak Mother Tongue at home, so, why do I have to?'

Defensively, Apollos replied, 'None of your friends Nastan? I think you are forgetting about Grigor and his family. They still speak Mother Tongue. They still value Mother Tongue as their language.'

'Well, they are the only family in town, who still do,' he replied indignantly.

'I think you are exaggerating Nastan. There are many families in town who only speak Mother Tongue. There are many families who are upholding their duty. We all have a duty, Nastan, to be language upholders. We all have a duty to pass our ancient language down to the generations, so that way it will always be spoken.'

'Spoken by who Papa? It is only your generation and Grigor's family who really care about it. These other families you speak of, it is only the parents that talk with you in Mother Tongue, which is out of respect for you, not for the language itself. How many young people in

our town do *you* speak Mother Tongue to except Grigor? I have heard the old women who come down from the mountains; the *only* language they speak is Mother Tongue and because they have *never* learnt Global, they are unable to communicate with their own grandchildren. Why have they never learnt Global? Why won't you learn Global? What use is a minority language when it is just dividing people, dividing families?'

Apollos replied, 'Because it is *our* language Nastan; because it is *our* language gift from God. It is not the fault of the older generation that the young people are not speaking Mother Tongue. If the language was being passed down as it should, there wouldn't be a problem. Grigor doesn't seem to have an issue with talking to me in Mother Tongue. Why can't you be more like him Nastan? Why can't your generation be more like him? Now he's a real language upholder.'

Nastan hated it when his grandfather did that – comparing him to Grigor, comparing him to his best friend. Grigor would sit and talk with Apollos in Mother Tongue, while, lately, Nastan would spend as little time as possible with him so he didn't have to speak his own language. But Grigor had a different spirit to Nastan. Grigor had a contented spirit. Grigor knew where he belonged, Nastan wasn't so sure. Nastan didn't know why he felt this way about Mother Tongue; why he felt this way about Global - it was as if he was living in someone else's body. Now they were reaching their teenage years, their sense of belonging was being tested.

Their opposing views of Mother Tongue were dividing their friendship.

'Isn't Global a language too? Isn't Global also a language gift from God? Why are you so opposed to me speaking Global?'

'Because Global is taking the place of Mother Tongue,' he replied solemnly.

Apollos had watched Global, the *super language*, creep into their country, into their town, into their lives. He had been waiting for it. He had been expecting it for a long time. He had seen it spread into other countries where it didn't belong; countries which had so readily adopted it as their official language, forsaking their own Mother Tongues. But he wasn't about to let Global take the place of *their* Mother Tongue. Speakers of *their* language were strangers scattered throughout the world, who, like him, had upheld their vernacular. A language that, even though it was only spoken by a "minority people", was legally protected by the Minority Languages World Association (MLWA). His Mother Tongue had stood the test of time. His generation was living proof.

But every time one of his fellow language upholders, each time another brother or sister of his generation left the earth, the threat of a lost language, the threat of a lost culture went with them. Apollos knew that if Mother Tongue became extinct, it would be the middle generation who were responsible. The majority of the middle generation were neglecting their duty to pass it down to their own children.

Apollos poked the fire angrily and the sparks danced around as if they were agreeing with him. He picked up a few sheets of old newspaper, crumpled them and threw them on the fire. Among the newspaper was the notice that all Mother Tongue citizens had received about the meeting. He retrieved it and held it in his right hand, shaking it irately.

'You see Nastan; this is what is happening in our town. This … this Global language is the very reason we need to hold onto Mother Tongue with our very being,' he said vehemently.

But Nastan couldn't share his grandfather's view. He was looking forward to the day when Global would officially replace Mother Tongue. Nastan reached out to take the notice off Apollos but in disdain Apollos threw it onto the fire and Nastan watched as the word "Global" turned to ashes before his very eyes.

'People are saying that Global is going to be the language of the whole world. I don't think burning a piece of paper is going to change that. Anyway, what is so wrong about wanting to be like everyone else? What is so wrong with speaking Global instead of Mother Tongue? I've heard that in the International School in the city it is taught as a first language and has replaced Mother Tongue.' Nastan continued, 'Why do I still have to study my native language and learn other Taught Tongues in school when other children are allowed to study and speak Global properly. Why do we have restricted Global lessons in school? Why …?'

'Enough,' Apollos shouted, placing his left hand on his chest, trying to relieve the dull pain that was radiating in his fingers. 'I will not tell you again. I do not want that killer language spoken in this house. Be thankful that I have not excluded you from those restricted lessons. Global is spreading like a disease. People want to be careful or they will have a second *Babel* on their hands,' he said, agitatedly. 'But this time maybe God won't be so merciful.'

The Tower of Babel was a story Nastan knew extremely well. It had been *their* story, *their* bedtime story. It had been that way since Nastan was little, since he had found the story in his grandfather's Mother Tongue Bible. Apollos had taught him how to turn the pages carefully because they were so fragile, if they tore, he wouldn't be able to repair them. When they had turned to the page in Genesis and Nastan saw, for the first time, the illustration of a city with a tower, which to his young mind, looked like a huge birthday cake, with layers and layers that reached up to heaven, he had wanted to look again and again. Surrounding the tower were the people of the whole world, living happily together as one big family.

But, as Nastan got older, they had gone from just looking at the illustration to Apollos telling him what had actually happened at Babel...

'Many years ago, there was a mighty warrior named Nimrod who wanted to be in charge of the whole world. He thought he was as important as God. In fact, he thought he could be God. Nimrod went from place to place, rebelling against God and building great cities. When he came to Babel, Nimrod and the people set out, not only to build another great city, but also a great tower. They wanted this to be the place where they could live together and from there rule the entire world. They wanted to make a name for themselves by building a tower so big, that it would reach heaven. They wanted the tower to bring glory to themselves and not God. The people were blatantly mocking God. But God was watching very closely.'

'The people who were living at that time spoke *a* common language that everyone shared. This made it all the easier for them to plot and scheme against God. But instead of punishing the people, God came down from heaven and confused their tongues with languages that they had never heard or spoken before. Not only did God give new languages to the people, he took away their rebellious tongue, so they were unable to speak to each other in the *one* world language. Their plans to build a tower were abandoned. Then, in their family groups, God scattered the people over all the earth, taking their allotted language with them. The scattering of the people fulfilled God's original plan which was that the population should spread over the earth, not bunch together in rebellion at Babel...'

Apollos poked the fire once more. This time the sparks didn't dance around in a bright warm glow, they clung lifelessly to the ashes from the newspaper. Apollos sat back in his comfy chair, staring out of the window.

'Go to the lake Nastan,' he said pensively. 'But do not be late; I need you to walk with me to the meeting,' he added, trying to hide the tears in his voice.

'I promise Papa. I'll be back on time,' Nastan replied, compliantly in Mother Tongue and left, not wanting to agitate him any further. Nastan didn't want to run the risk of his grandfather excluding him from the limited Global lessons he had in school. Nastan didn't know how, after he had forged his grandfather's signature to receive the lessons in the first place, how he, hadn't pulled him out. Apollos had been mortified when Nastan's school teacher had praised him for having an open mind to Global. Apollos had closed his mind to Global many years ago. But now it would seem that Nastan's fraudulent activity, his deceitfulness, his lack of respect to ask for permission, had quite unexpectedly brought Global back into his life. Apollos knew that he should have told Nastan's teacher what he had done. But pride had stopped him from informing the school that his grandson, whom he had raised to honour and obey, was capable of such deceit. Apollos had thought that after a few lessons, Nastan would have decided he did not want to learn Global. But, that certainly had not been the case.

Apollos placed his walking stick in his left hand and prized himself out of his chair. His strength was failing. Each day he was finding it much harder to get out of his chair even with the stick as his aid. He stood crouched in his doorway as he watched Nastan walk energetically away. He slumped back down in his chair with his treasure chest on his lap. He unlocked it and pulled out the newspaper cuttings that he had hidden from Nastan. They still tore at his soul, each time he looked at them.

He stared lovingly at the photograph of his son, Stephen that was on the mantelpiece. It had faded over the years, but his memory of him was as strong in his heart as it had always been. The older Nastan became, the more like Stephen he became, in ways, which Apollos hadn't anticipated. Apollos closed his eyes and in Nastan, Stephen came alive again. Apollos locked the treasure chest and hid the key in its usual place. He sat back down, deciding that he would rest his eyes until Nastan came home to take him to the meeting.

2

Nastan got to the lake to find Grigor already there. This part of the lake was unofficial. It was off the tourist trail. The fish and the tourists were across the lake, in the authorised zone, where you pay to catch fish. Grigor sat in silence, concentrating. His fishing rod was in the water and he was pretending to fish, practicing his technique as usual. Nastan sat down and joined in the silence, noticing the contented look on Grigor's face. Nastan looked at the fishing rod that Grigor had brought for him and wished he felt contentment from something. He wished he felt happiness from pretend fishing. He longed to tell Grigor that he wanted to go to the International School and study Global. But even though their friendship was solid, Nastan knew there was a limit to what he could share with Grigor and preferring Global over Mother Tongue exceeded that limit.

Nastan often thought that Grigor should have been born into his family. He had more in common with his grandfather than he did. Grigor loved their town. He made no secret that his ambition was to be mayor one day. How could Nastan share his future ambitions with Grigor when they didn't involve him?

'I'm going to dive in and wake these fish up,' said Nastan, in Global.

Grigor didn't respond. Nastan wondered if he had even noticed he was there.

‘I’m going to dive in and wake these fish up,’ repeated Nastan, but this time in Mother Tongue.

‘You do that and I will cook you for tea,’ replied Grigor. ‘Anyway, the water will be so cold underneath that it will stop your heart from beating,’ he replied sarcastically, wondering why Nastan pushed their friendship by speaking to him in Global. ‘Is it to annoy me? Is it to show off? Nastan knows my feelings concerning Global. Why else would I have made a stand and refused to take part in learning Global at school, even though the lessons are paid for, as part of the Technology in Education Programme. If it isn’t compulsory, then I have no intention of learning it. Yet, my so-called best friend insists on invading my free time with a foreign language I do not care for,’ thought Grigor.

Sensing Grigor’s hostility, Nastan replied in Mother Tongue, ‘Are you trying to put me off diving forever?’

‘Forever is a long time Nastan,’ he replied, trying to recall when Nastan had become someone he didn’t recognise.

During the summer months, the unofficial section of the lake became the place for the unofficial summer sport, diving. It had become a tradition amongst anyone, who was willing and able to dive. Nastan had spent many frustrated years sitting and watching as fathers taught their kids to dive off the worn plank of wood into the depths below. Apollos never came to the lake to watch the diving. He had refused to teach Nastan, claiming it was dangerous and that he didn’t understand how parents could be so irresponsible and allow their children to dive into such deep water.

Apollos had told Nastan that he was not to dive. His father wouldn't have liked him to do it. So for years, with no father to teach him, and no way of knowing if his father would have approved, he had obeyed his grandfather's wishes and just sat and watched. Even when Grigor's father had offered to teach Nastan and reassured Apollos that he would take care of him, the answer had still been 'no'. But Nastan had had enough of watching and in five months exactly, on the twenty first of August, he would be fourteen years old and this was going to be his summer to dive, whether he had his grandfather's blessing or not. After all, he was practically a man now and he needed to start making his own decisions in life.

'You do know there are no fish in this part of the lake Grigor? You could sit here until you are an old man and you'll never catch a thing,' said Nastan, tired of the silence.

'I'm not stupid Nastan. I know there are no fish. You know I'm practicing my technique for when I go with my family to the real fishing lake this summer. You wouldn't believe how fierce the competition is, even at our age. This year I'm going to catch a fish so big it will take at least five men to reel it in.'

Grigor's father had told him that to buy a fishing licence to use in their town was a luxury that only the tourists could afford. It just wasn't possible for regular people like them. But when they go to the "real lake" in the city, they become the tourists; so paying to fish is acceptable. This confused Grigor because what it cost them to fish and to go on holiday for three weeks each year (even though they stayed with his grandparents) would cover the cost of fishing at home all year round!

But Grigor had no money of his own, so all he could do was sit and practice and wait for his holiday.

Nastan hated it when Grigor went away with his family because for him it was the loneliest three weeks of the summer. But at least this year he could join in the diving at the lake. This year he would be the same as the rest of the boys and hopefully wouldn't miss Grigor so much.

'I don't believe it! They cannot be serious! Who do they think they are?' demanded Grigor loudly, breaking his own silence.

Nastan looked up to the scruffy old plank. There they were, the Global boys, standing on the edge, messing around and throwing stones deep into the water.

'I'm going to pound them so hard that their swollen lips won't be able to speak that stupid language,' said Grigor, full of rage.

'Just ignore them. It's what they want. The attention,' Nastan said calmly.

'Listen to them, speaking Global outside school,' said Grigor, packing away his fishing things.

'Are we leaving?' Nastan asked, disappointedly.

'Yes, because I cannot bear to be around those language traitors and besides, I have to go to the meeting in the museum. Don't you have to walk Papa Popov there?'

Unwittingly, Nastan responded, 'Papa, museum, yes, I forgot. I'm going on ahead. It takes him ten times longer to walk anywhere these days. I'll see you there.' Nastan hurried away, hoping that he would bump into the Global boys one day, when Grigor wasn't with him. He hadn't realised before today, just how much Grigor detested Global.

Grigor continued to pack up his things, infuriated by the language traitors. He hated their arrogance, their air of superiority; the fact that they were speaking a foreign language in their own town. They were just like him – well, nearly like him. They were rich and he was poor. They went to the Global International School and he went to school in a shed. Grigor hated that Global was being used in their country and even in their town to divide people. It was only because those boys' parents were rich and language traitors themselves, that they got to go to the International School. Grigor decided there and then that when he was mayor, Global wouldn't form any part of education in their town, not even in the private schools. It would be banned altogether and Mother Tongue would be the only language that mattered. The poorer kids would get to use the International School but it would be paid for by the State and everyone would be equal. Global would not be used as a means to get ahead, not when he was mayor!

3

Apollos was still sitting in his comfy chair, waiting for Nastan, who, despite his promise to be on time, was five minutes late.

'I'm here Papa,' said Nastan in Mother Tongue, trying to appease his grandfather, knowing he was late.

'It's five minutes past. Punctuality defines a man, Nastan,' said Apollos, pleased that Nastan seemingly had decided to respect his wish not to speak Global at home.

'Sorry Papa, but me and Grigor were fishing, well Grigor was fishing and I was just watching and those boys from the … anyway, that's why I'm late.'

'Now we are at least ten minutes late with all your yapping.' Apollos motioned for his walking stick, so Nastan helped him to his feet and placed his stick in his left hand.

They made their way through the side streets that were still paved with branches from the Palm Sunday celebration of just over a week ago. As people walked past each other, they exchanged the Easter greeting 'Christ has risen', 'Truly risen'. There were red dyed eggs displayed in people's windows - the symbol of Jesus' resurrection and the defeat of what Apollos referred to, as the final enemy – death. Apollos told Nastan each Easter and Christmas time that you couldn't have Christmas without Easter and you couldn't have Easter without Christmas, as they are equally important.

Nastan noticed that Apollos was struggling to walk more than usual.

'Are you okay, Papa?'

'Yes, but I fail to see why this meeting couldn't wait until after we have observed the ascension,' he said. 'I did say so, but nobody listens to me anymore. What is the point of being the chairman if I have lost my voice? Maybe it is time for me to retire. I am feeling old today Nastan.'

'Retire, you, never!' said Nastan in disbelief, taking his arm. It was only when his grandfather was out of their home that Nastan realised how old he was getting and how he needed him – how they needed each other – it had been just the two of them all his life.

A group of people noticed Apollos and Nastan struggling to get through the crowd that was blocking the museum entrance. 'Make way for Papa Popov,' someone shouted respectfully in Mother Tongue. 'Make way for Papa Popov,' another person reiterated, causing people to stand to one side so Apollos and Nastan could enter the museum. Nastan felt overwhelmed by the respect the people in their town had for his grandfather. He loved that they affectionately referred to him as 'Papa Popov'. He decided that he, too, should show him equal respect and obey his wishes to speak their Mother Tongue. That was the right thing to do.

Apollos made his way to his usual seat that Grigor and his family, who were already seated, had ensured was kept for him. Grigor motioned for Nastan to sit by him. Inside, the museum was overflowing with Mother Tongue citizens of all ages. The young were there because they had no choice. The middle generation, to whom Mother Tongue had been passed down, were there out of duty. If most of them were honest, their standards had slipped and they didn't use it as they should.

Now the older generation, they are the real language upholders. To them, Mother Tongue is everything. It is everything they live for and with their dying breath they will fight to keep their ancient language alive.

Nastan listened to the chattering around the building. He was listening out for Global. But, for the sake of appearance, everyone seemed to be speaking the correct language. Nastan wondered what his parents' view of Global would have been. He wondered, as millennium parents, whether they would have been lax, or, for the sake of his grandfather, would they have been strict about upholding their language? Nastan felt a sad shudder flow through his body, realising that was something he would never know.

Nastan stared at people's mouths, watching the different shapes and expressions they made from talking. The younger generation weren't really talking at all. The middle generation were moving their mouths quickly, trying to get in as many words as they could. The older generation talked slowly and with consideration, taking time to be heard. Nastan was still in his mouth-watching gaze, when the meeting was called to order. He was annoyed that he hadn't caught anyone out. He was sure that given more time he would have.

'Mother Tongue citizens,' the Mayor began. 'It is with a heavy heart that I stand here this evening. Our beloved language has been the subject of an evaluation without our knowledge. Our beloved language has been discussed by the MLWA as to whether it should acquire "extinct status" with a plan to phase it out of education over the next twenty years.' He took a deep breath. 'What is the reason behind this?' He breathed out slowly. ‘The status of Mother Tongue has been downgraded to “definitely endangered”. His face became red with frustration as he carried on.

‘It would appear that the very organisation which is supposed to work with us to protect our language, is making a case that we are not upholding our Mother Tongue by speaking it at home and,’ he took another deep breath, let it out slowly, then continued, ‘that we are not passing it down to our children. They are claiming that it is no longer valued by the middle generation and suggest taking it out of our education and legal systems altogether.’

His speech got louder and stronger. ‘That would mean, no longer would our ancient language be taught in our schools. No longer would we hear it being used in our courts of law and no longer would legal documents of any kind be written in it.’ He quietened down slightly and spoke more softly. ‘Our brothers and sisters in our capital city are also meeting to discuss this travesty as we meet here. Answers are needed as to whom in our own government has allowed The International School in our city to only teach Global to our children, which in itself is a travesty.’ His speech and gestures became louder and bolder again as he began to point his finger accusingly at the crowd. ‘These are troubling times for us. We owe our heritage to a language that is as ancient as the Bible itself.’ The finger pointing continued. ‘We need to be heard by the MLWA and they need to know that our language is as alive as it has always been. They need to hear from each and every one of us that, as long as we are on God’s earth, then our language will be used and proudly passed from generation to generation.’ He finished, hoping for a few cheers or applause, anything, to show unity.

The people sat in silence, waiting for the Mayor to continue. He hadn't crashed down his hammer onto the podium so they knew there was more to come. In a softer tone, with a huge smile, he said, 'With that in mind, I am very pleased and excited to announce that our Minority Language Council will be putting a scheme in place, which will allow the younger generation to get involved and be our voice in the upcoming MLWA meeting. We are looking for a young person to lead the way to ensure that all school age citizens are backing our campaign.'

Apollos looked at Nastan with anticipation, hoping that he would be the one to lead the younger generation. Nastan felt Apollos look his way but couldn't look at him. He knew if he did, he would be compelled into doing something in which he didn't believe. He couldn't be the one, but he knew who could.

Nastan looked at Grigor. His face was alive with energy and longing for this cause. Grigor turned to his father, who, as the Deputy Chairman of the Minority Language Council, expected nothing less from his son. He beamed Grigor an approving smile and patted him on his shoulder. Grigor hadn't even needed to speak. His father just knew that his son would be the one to lead his generation.

His son would be the one to uphold their Mother Tongue. Nastan felt resentment surge through his body as he witnessed this display of closeness between father and son.

The Mayor continued, trying to sound upbeat. 'I am asking each one of you to sign a petition that I will personally be taking to the next minority language meeting at the MLWA. If you are under the age of twelve, then your parent or responsible adult can sign for you. However, I am asking each one of you to sign your name on the petition document so we can send our united voice to uphold our language and to ensure it is not replaced by Global,' finished the Mayor, crashing down his hammer on the podium and slumping into his chair, almost simultaneously.

Nastan heard people behind him whispering. They were speaking in Global, not Mother Tongue. He turned to see who it was but by the time he could match the words to a mouth, the offender had already stood up boldly to address the Mayor.

In Mother Tongue the offender shouted, 'Global is the way forward. Even in our own country the best paid jobs are given to Global speakers. Look, here's the proof,' the offender added, producing the job page from the *City Times*. 'It's here, in black and white, "an increment is payable to Global speakers"'.

There was silence in the museum, while everyone waited for the Mayor to respond. Nastan thought about the boys at the lake. Their allegiance was with Global. They were language traitors but they didn't seem to care. In fact, their assurance as Global speakers gave them an air of self-confidence.

In a firm tone, the Mayor responded, 'Presently, Global has no official status in our town, city or country. The few jobs where it is of use, are purely for administration purposes, so we can attract tourists,' said the Mayor in defence. 'We have made no secret of the fact that we need to attract a high number of tourists and, yes, Global does play a minimal role in this. We are blessed with our snow-capped mountains that offer wonderful skiing conditions and each of us knows the hunting and fishing is bountiful. But it is not enough for us to take advantage of. We have to generate tourism to remain an independent state,' replied the Mayor.

'Global should replace Mother Tongue; that is the way forward. That is how we will all prosper, ' someone else added to the Mayor's disbelief.

Before the Mayor could respond and much to his surprise, Aphia Joan, a well-loved grandmother within the community, joined in, 'Make Global available in all our schools, so our grandchildren can be the next generation of communicators with the outside world. If we don't, then they will be left behind. Why have Global speaking outsiders come into our town and into our country, when we all have the intelligence to learn it?'

'I do not want to learn Global. I am too old,' came another voice protesting.

'So let everyone who wants to, learn it, and make it available in all our schools as an official second language, not just the International School in the city,' she added. 'What good are minority languages except to communicate locally?'

Other voices were trying to interrupt so the original offender stood on his chair to ensure he could be seen and heard once more. 'We need to ask ourselves why the most powerful Global speaking nation in the world, is investing stacks of money to make us the first completely wireless country on the planet? What is the point of having all this Wi-Fi technology if we still cannot communicate in Global with the rest of the world? Now is the time to grab these opportunities before the investors move onto more agreeable countries that truly recognise the benefits of Global. They will not give us a second chance if we refuse their help now.'

'Global is the future not just for us, but for the whole world. Think of how much easier it would be if each world nation was able to speak *one* common language. *One* common language that would create equal status for all, ' the offender finished earnestly.

Apollos looked over to the speaker on the chair who was commanding so much attention. There were voices nattering all around him, which were getting louder and louder. Some other people also stood on their chairs, deciding this was the best way to be heard. As Apollos sat and watched this display of traitorous behaviour, his memory went instantly to Stephen. Apollos felt dizzy and his eyesight became blurred. He thought he could see the traitorous men turning their chairs to face him. He thought he could see their faces altering. Their noses, their eyes, their hair, their mouths, all mirrored Stephen's; their gestures, their expressions, their talk of Global replacing Mother Tongue, transported him back to the last time he had seen his son …

4

Morning of August 21st 2001

'Stephen, please reconsider. These changes in which you are involved will have massive repercussions on our culture.'

'I know change is hard for you Papa, but we have to embrace Global as the future. If we do not, then we will be left behind. Is that what you want for us, for our country, for Nastan's future – for us to become the poor relation to the rest of the world? Global will never take away who we are. It's all about communication Papa. It's the language of technology and education, that's all. We need Global to communicate with the outside world. We need it to prosper.'

'But what about Ba ...?' Apollos had muttered, unable to finish his sentence.

'Enough about Babel, Papa, please. Its 2001, not the Dark Ages, Global is the way forward. We cannot refuse this offer being made to us because you are acting like an eccentric old fool. There have been other world languages before Global. Are you going to worry about every major language for fear of it taking over? Papa, I am going to the conference and I am going to make my presentation as planned and Lydia and Mama will enjoy a lovely day out.'

'But Stephen …' Apollos had protested.

‘Do you want Nastan to come with us? Lydia is feeling guilty about leaving him on his first birthday as it is. If it is too much for you … if you are not feeling well …’

‘I never said I was not well, Stephen. Nastan’s one, that’s hardly a baby. He’s walking and babbling. Of course I want to have Nastan, today of all days.’

‘Okay, then we really must go so we can get back to celebrate with him.’

Apollos had been bitterly disappointed in Stephen and had been unable to watch him drive away. Nastan was gurgling away oblivious to what was going on and Apollos was grateful that he was too young to know what disappointment and betrayal felt like. Apollos had held Nastan close, thankful that at least Stephen respected his wish that Global wouldn’t be spoken in his home and that, as long as Apollos had a breath in his body, Nastan would be fully aware of his Mother Tongue heritage.

Nastan had toddled over to his toys and picked up a book. Apollos was amazed at how advanced he was for his age. He had been walking for two months already and was chirping away constantly. Apollos was convinced that he would soon say his first word. Apollos had sat in Lydia’s chair in Nastan’s bedroom, hoping that a story would remind him that it was nap time – he had seen Lydia do it many times and it never failed for her. Apollos had picked up a baby book, one that Lydia was reading to him and had begun to read aloud as Nastan lay in his cot, wide awake, legs kicking, contented, knowing and accepting this was his routine, despite his mother not being there.

He had decided to look for one of Stephen’s old Mother Tongue baby books. He opened the cupboard where they usually were but couldn't find any of the books that Damaris, his wife, had kept all those years. He opened the wardrobe, thinking they must be in there. He saw some books pushed to the back of the shelf under some clothing, so he reached in and pulled them out. He couldn't believe what he saw - a Global language baby book. He reached in again and pulled out more books - they were all in Global. He rummaged frantically around the wardrobe and found building blocks with the Global alphabet, an octopus toy that *sang* the Global alphabet and a play mat that was illustrated with "baby's first Global words".

Enraged, Apollos placed all the things he had found on the floor. This was his house. These were his rules and the rules of his house were NO GLOBAL. Not now, not ever. Defiantly, he had left the things on the floor, wanting an explanation from Stephen and Lydia. He had wanted to know what part Global played in his grandson's life. He had hoped with all his heart that Damaris knew nothing about these things; that would be the ultimate betrayal.

Apollos had sat at the kitchen table feeling weary and deflated. Nastan had fallen asleep. He noticed that Stephen's briefcase was by the front door. It was more like a small suitcase than a briefcase. Apollos had never owned a suitcase. He had never left his country, except during his army years, but he hadn't needed a suitcase for that trip. He could not understand how Stephen would have left without it. It went everywhere he went. It had a retractable handle and wheels. Apollos picked it up. It was surprisingly heavy, so he pulled out the handle and wheeled it to the kitchen table. He unzipped it and looked inside and saw pages and pages of documents.

There was a separate compartment with the zip open, revealing more papers.

Apollos pulled them out and to his surprise, found himself looking at Stephen's presentation. There were two copies; one in Mother Tongue and one in Global. He began to read; unable to pinpoint the day when his own son had become a language traitor. 'Mother Tongue Phasing-Out Plan,' he exclaimed, woefully. 'Who does that son of mine think he has become?' he shouted, full of rage.

He had sat at the kitchen table, waiting for Stephen to return to collect his briefcase, wanting him to come back, so he could confront him about all things Global. One hour passed and they hadn't returned. But Apollos knew that Stephen was more than capable of memorising his presentation, word for word, error free and would manage without it in whichever language he planned to speak. Apollos placed both manuscripts back in Stephen's briefcase. He had thought about burning them and the rest of the papers, wondering what it would feel like to see Stephen's research disintegrate before his eyes. Apollos thought how ironic it was that Stephen was spearheading a technology programme, yet, his research and presentation was handwritten and stored in this briefcase. 'I could burn it all now, before they come home. Who would know?' he had thought, calculatingly. But, he had been unable to bring himself to be so deceitful. *'I answer to God, not man,'* he had told himself, steadfastly. He put the briefcase in Nastan's bedroom, with the pile of other Global paraphernalia.

The day passed by quickly, thanks to Nastan's playfulness. Apollos had forgotten how tiring was the attention demanded by a one year old. Apollos had been glad that Nastan had softened his mood; until Stephen got home, at least. But six o'clock passed and they still hadn't returned. Apollos looked at the first birthday decorations he had put up and at the layered birthday cake that sat, invitingly, waiting to be devoured.

'They will miss your birthday altogether if they are not home soon,' he said to Nastan.

Eight o'clock passed and Apollos had been unable to keep Nastan awake so had decided to put him to bed. Apollos had moved to his comfy chair, waiting for Stephen, Lydia and Damaris to return. He had fallen asleep.

'Apollos, Apollos,' he had heard his neighbour calling despairingly, letting himself in. 'Apollos, put on your TV. There has been a bombing at the city monastery. Isn't that where your family were going today? Are they home?'

'No, I have been waiting for hours for them to return,' he had responded, realising that it was now ten o'clock. Apollos switched on his TV to a news report of the carnage the bombing had left. The city monastery and its grounds had been totally destroyed.

5

The days that had passed after the bombing were unbearable for Apollos. He could not believe that they were gone. He had hoped that by some miracle they had made it out alive. That Stephen had made his presentation early and they had gone into the city, away from the devastation.

But, deep down he knew they were gone. Otherwise they would have telephoned him. They would have driven home, the same day - shocked but alive. But, there had been no word from them.

Apollos had been told by the authorities that the bomb had exploded at ten thirty am. Apollos knew that was the exact time Stephen was due to give his presentation. He shuddered at the thought of Stephen standing there, waiting to speak and despite Apollos' feelings concerning Global, Damaris and Lydia, looking on, proudly. Damaris had told Apollos that she was proud of her son and she would support him; she would not let Global cause a division within her family. But sadly, Apollos could not feel the same way about the "devil's language".

'It would have been quick and painless,' Apollos had been told by the investigating officer, who had driven from the city to see him and Nastan personally. 'I am told by Stephen's colleagues that he had dedicated the last three years to his research and he would be devastated that his life's work was also destroyed. They told me that he would have wanted his plans to proceed, even without him. He was very well respected within his area of work. I hope that will be of some comfort to you in the coming days.' Apollos had dismissed the officer's accolade 'well respected within his area of work', as he thought about how little respect Stephen had had for him and his heritage.

His "area of work" had killed his son and daughter-in-law. His "area of work" had killed his wife. 'Damaris, my Damaris, best day of my life,' he thought solemnly, remembering the day they had met. 'Damaris, Damaris,' he cried out, 'worst day of my life.'

Apollos had gone into Nastan's bedroom, into the wardrobe where he had put Stephen's suitcase. The other Global items were still in a pile on the floor. He had thought about contacting the investigating officer to tell him that there was some good news after all. To tell him that Stephen's "life's work" had not been destroyed because he had never taken it with him. For some bizarre reason, for some illogical reason, it had been left behind. But, he had decided against it. He had decided that as long as it was just himself who knew the whereabouts of Stephen's "life's work", Mother Tongue would be protected against the language traitors who had agreed to it becoming a "phased out" language …

But, it seemed, all these years later that protection was coming to an end. Apollos leaned on his walking stick and struggled to his feet. He wanted to confront all the Stephens in the room. He wanted to confront his fellow citizens with their bold statements. A statement that, unknown to Nastan, his own father had laid the very foundations of. He wanted to see the real faces of these language traitors.

‘What are you doing Papa?’ Nastan asked, taking his left arm. ‘Let me help you. Are you feeling okay?’ Apollos didn’t answer. Nastan looked at his grandfather’s face, which was troubled and pale. Nastan had seen this troubled look before, many times. He knew when he was deep in thought because the wrinkles on his forehead melted into his eyebrows until the moment passed and then his wrinkles rested again. But the paleness and sweating, he had never seen this before.

‘Papa, please sit down,’ Nastan said, pleading. But Apollos was fully out of his chair and Nastan knew that he wanted to speak. He knew his Babel speech was about to take place. Apollos held tight onto Nastan, determined that the language traitors in the room would hear him. Apollos’ grip on Nastan’s right arm tightened as he prepared to speak. He opened his mouth, moved his tongue but no words would form. He knew what he wanted to say. He parted his lips to prepare for the words, but still nothing. Nastan knew this was not right. His grandfather, old as he was, was never lost for words.

The Mayor noticed Apollos was on his feet and motioned for silence by crashing down his hammer forcefully on the podium.

‘Please, let us have some quiet for our dear Papa Popov to have his say,’ he said. The language traitors, reluctantly, sat back down.

Apollos opened his mouth once again but his words came out so faintly that they couldn’t be heard around the building. The Mayor was deeply concerned; this was not the Apollos he knew and loved. The Apollos he knew and loved was a strong willed, opinionated, intelligent man of faith, who spoke his mind no matter what. Apollos swayed slightly, causing his walking stick to fall to the floor. Nastan picked it up and held it out for his grandfather to take but he couldn't move his left hand. Nastan indicated to his grandfather to grab it with his other hand but he was unable to release his right hand from its grip on Nastan's arm.

Grigor's family and the Mayor looked on anxiously as their dear friend was failing before their very eyes. They were his closest friends and knew what their status as a people with their own ancient language meant to him.

Apollos, unable to stand any longer, collapsed back into his chair and started to whimper quietly, 'Killer language, killer language.' That's all he could manage, that's all the breath he had left.

A few people around the room started to ask each other in Global what it was that Apollos was saying. The Mayor thumped his hammer on the podium once more, trying to bring back order to, what was supposed to be, a peaceful meeting, and what was supposed to be a united people. 'If this is the behaviour of Mother Tongue citizens themselves who aren't capable of upholding their own tongue in a public meeting, then what chance do we have of saving our language?' he thought to himself, crushed in spirit.

The Mayor struck his hammer repeatedly until the voices around the museum began to dissipate. In the ensuing silence only Apollos' faint voice could be heard repeating, 'Killer language, killer language,' over and over.

The Mayor, fearing the worst for his esteemed friend and patriarch, with one more crash of his hammer, ordered everyone out of the museum.

'I will get Doctor Mitrov,' Grigor offered, racing out of the nearly empty building.

The crowds of people outside the museum were asking each other what had happened. A group of people made way for Grigor, as he hurtled frantically passed them.

'Grigor, what has happened?' one shouted after him.

'It's Papa Popov, he is unwell. I'm going for Doctor Mitrov.'

'But he will be here, somewhere in the crowd.'

Grigor stopped and caught his breath.

'Help me find him,' said Grigor, 'please, quickly, before …'

'Okay, don't worry, we will find him. Just call his name as loud as you can and I will tell as many people as I can to do the same.'

'Doctor Mitrov,' Grigor began calling at the top of his voice. Voices in the crowd echoed his call, but Grigor didn't know that by the time the call for help had reached the doctor's ears it was too late for Apollos.

6

Nastan looked on helplessly as his grandfather clutched at his chest with his left hand as he had done so many times. Nastan knelt on the floor in front of him looking up at his face.

'Papa, don't go, it's just you and me, please don't go,' he said, squeezing his grandfather's right hand that was slippery with sweat.

Apollos looked at his grandson, the boy he had raised since a toddler. He had been his grandfather, his father, his mother and his grandmother, his friend, and his teacher. He couldn't bear the anguish on his face. He couldn't bear that he would be alone. Apollos knew he was going. He knew he was leaving this world and there was nothing he could do. He prized his left arm from his chest and placed his hand on Nastan's head. Nastan's head became instantly warm from the heat that was running through Apollos' body.

Apollos jerked suddenly causing Nastan to get up off his knees. His grandfather's head was hanging backwards and his eyes were staring upwards. Apollos gasped and wished that Nastan could see what he could see. Nastan stood motionless as he watched his grandfather's last moments on earth.

Apollos gazed, unmoving, as he saw heaven opening and Jesus standing at the right hand of God, just as he had expected it to be. 'If only Nastan could see what I can see then he would be rejoicing. If only Nastan could see what I can see he would believe that death is not the end. It is just the beginning.'

Apollos' head fell forward and his arms loosened and fell to his side. The disturbing, awful paleness went and was replaced by a healthy rose pink glow and the clammy, sweaty film that had clung to his hands and face dried up instantly. He was gone. Nastan placed his grandfather's head in his hands and gently pushed it up until he could see his whole face. Nastan was mesmerised by what he saw. His grandfather's wrinkles were gone and his face looked like the photographs he had seen of him as a young man. Nastan touched his face remembering how they had joked that Nastan was able to put his fingers into the deepness of his wrinkles. But now, his face was smooth. His face was beaming as if he knew something wonderful. His face didn't look like death, but like life, like he had just fallen asleep.

7

Even though Nastan had lost his parents and grandmother at a young age, his grandfather had made up for this in many ways. He had helped him find a balance, a spiritual awareness and a belief that even though they would never know why God had allowed his parents and grandmother to be taken out of his life at just one-year-old, everything in life happened for a purpose. That even though the hurt would never go away, he would come to a point in his life that he could live with it. Nastan had truly believed this and had been waiting for that day as long as he could remember. But now, without his guardian, without his protector to turn to, he couldn't see there was any reason in believing that anymore.

Nastan felt frustrated with Apollos and wished that he hadn't told him about his parents and grandmother. He wished that Apollos had just left his recollection of them in the grave so that way he would have grown up with no stories about them. All his life he had grieved for his mother, father and grandmother, of whom he had no real memories.

He had second hand tales from a man who had loved them so deeply that Nastan felt his mother's arms around him. He heard her voice singing him to sleep, he heard his father saying how proud he was of him and the smell of his grandmother's pispilita that made his mouth water. His parents and grandmother had become perfect characters formed by someone else's memories and Nastan would never be able to see them any other way.

Nastan's fourteenth birthday came as quickly as his grandfather had left and for the first time in his life, Nastan visited his parents' and grandparents' graves alone. Visiting their graves on the day Nastan shared with death, was a yearly tradition. But now, he had no one with him to remember the day they had died, at least no one whose heart was breaking. His grandfather, who was the newest addition to the grave, was usually the visitor and Nastan wasn't sure if he could carry on the tradition alone. For some it may have seemed a morbid and strange, custom. But for Nastan and Apollos, it was something that they did together, quite naturally, year after year. Grigor's mother had kindly offered to accompany Nastan on his visit to the cemetery; she had even suggested that this year he shouldn't go, thinking it would be too much for him to endure. But Nastan would not let his grandfather down. He would not undo their yearly homage. Besides, he wanted to ensure that Apollos knew he intended to visit their graves, as usual, and how would he possibly know this if he didn't go to where his grandfather was buried.

Grigor's parents had agreed to take care of Nastan as they were the closest thing to a family he had. Nastan didn't care who he lived with, or where he lived. He especially didn't care about diving and wished that his grandfather was there to tell him not to do it, because he would have listened to him with all his heart. If only he was there to tell him. He didn't care about fishing and that he got to go with Grigor on their family holiday.

The home that he and his grandfather had shared was sold to another family, while Nastan was away with

Grigor. The new owners stripped the house of all its belongings, stripped it of the memories, the smells, the furniture, the photographs, the damp on the outside wall, the creaky gate, the swing that was a plank of wood and ropes full of notches that held the plank in place. The new family had replaced it with a new gate, a new swing, new paint inside and out, new furniture, new photographs, new smells and plans to create new wonderful memories.

Nastan's memories were now in two boxes in Grigor's living room.

In between the boxes was Apollos' walking stick. Apollos' clothes and shoes had been given to the aid shop, bedding had been thrown away and any half decent kitchen utensils had been included in the sale.

'So what are we to do with him? He is a lovely boy and Grigor is very fond of him. But we are full to overflowing already,' said Grigor's mother to Grigor's father.

'If we hand him over to social services Grigor will never forgive us,' Grigor's father replied.

'And when is he going to talk again? It has been over five months,' she said, frustrated. 'I don't think we realise the effect all this is having on Grigor too – Nastan won't even speak to him. Grigor is taking it to heart thinking he has done something wrong.'

'There must be some money. What about from the house? Apollos owned that didn't he?' said Grigor's father, dismissively.

'I don't know how much he owed to the bank. Probably more than the house is worth. We are not family so how are we going to find out? How will it look if we ask?' she complained.

'We must go to the authorities and find out where we stand. We cannot take him in for free. There must be some kind of payment we are entitled to,' Grigor's father said out loud, feeling ashamed that his private thoughts had escaped his lips.

8

Nastan woke to an unfamiliar knock on Grigor's front door. Grigor and his four brothers, who slept in the same bedroom, didn't flinch. Nastan crept down the stairs and stopped in the middle. He sat and listened to the Mother Tongue voices, annoyed that he couldn't see their faces.

The first stranger said, 'Mr Popov's estate has been settled and we are grateful for your patience.'

Grigor's mother was taken aback by this statement, as Apollos lived like a pauper and she didn't think he had anything to leave.

The second stranger whom Nastan noticed had a slight Global accent said, 'Yes. Thank you. In the absence of other family members, it is always better that a bereaved child is cared for by someone who has a connection to them and a connection to the person they have lost. It gives them an inherent sense of security.'

Nastan, even though he was intrigued by the Global accent he could hear in her voice, felt angry that she was referring to him as a "bereaved child".

Grigor's father asked hurriedly, 'Is there any money to take care of Nastan? We love him like a son but …'

The first stranger replied, 'Money, yes, there is plenty of money. It seems as if Mr Popov had not spent a penny of the compensation money he received after the death of his family at the monastery bombing. It has been set up in a trust for Nastan when he reaches eighteen, or in the case of education, he can access the money before. He will not want for anything, financially, that is, of course.'

Nastan froze when he heard this stranger speak of the bombing. His grandfather had told him what had happened on that day just once. He had told him that his mother, father and grandmother were in the city shopping and while they were there they visited the monastery and that a bomb, fired by rebels, had killed them and everyone else visiting the site. He had refused to talk about it again. He had said there was nothing else to add or take away from what had happened so there was no need to talk about it more than once – once was enough.

'So where do we stand now? Should we make it official by way of adoption?' Grigor's mother asked, to her husband's surprise.

The second stranger continued, 'Well, that would be up to Nastan. Adoption is one route, but there may be other routes for Nastan to consider.'

'Such as?' asked Grigor's mother.

'Well, are you certain that Nastan does not have a living relative anywhere else? Maybe an aunt or uncle somewhere?'

'No, his mother was an only child and his father's brother died a long time ago, so no.'

The first stranger said, 'We will make our own investigation to be sure, but as I said, it would be up to Nastan to agree to you adopting him and, from what I can gather, he is not really up to making that kind of decision yet. I understand that he hasn't spoken since his grandfather died?'

'Yes, poor child,' said Grigor's mother.

'Well, hopefully, Angelina, who will be Nastan's bereavement counsellor,' said the first stranger, pointing to her colleague, 'will help him come to terms with what has happened and when Nastan is ready, we can discuss adoption further. But, in the meantime, here is a backdated carer's payment and you'll receive a set amount each month for as long as Nastan stays with you,' said the first stranger.

Grigor's father looked at the bank order, quite happy with the arrangement.

'I am ready to discuss it now,' thought Nastan, leaving his hiding place.

'Nastan,' said Grigor's mother startled by his sudden appearance at the bottom of the stairs. 'We were just discussing … well it seems that your grandfather has left you a wealthy, young man.'

'I heard your discussion,' Nastan replied curtly in Mother Tongue.

Grigor's mother was shocked by the tone of his voice. She knew he was grieving and was relieved that he was talking again but she didn't recognise the voice that had emerged from a child she had known since birth.

'Hello Nastan,' said Angelina, 'it is a pleasure to meet you, I will be …'

Nastan didn't care who she was. All he cared about was leaving this town and going to the International School.

'I want to go to the city. I want to go to the Global speaking school,' he interrupted confidently in Global.

'Nastan, what are you babbling about?' Grigor's mother asked him apprehensively, not realising he knew any Global. She had assumed that Nastan, like Grigor, had refused to participate in Global lessons at school.

'He is saying in Global that he wants to go to the International School,' confirmed Angelina. Nastan looked at Angelina. He couldn't believe that there was at last someone in his life who was a Global speaker. Not a secret Global speaker, an actual Global speaker who even had a slight Global accent – he was elevated.

Grigor's parents were dumbfounded as they wondered how Global had entered their home.

'Of all the places on earth why would you want to go there Nastan? What about Apollos? What about your grandfather? What would he have thought about his grandson being educated in that foreign language? A language that he despised; the very language that took his life?' she asked angrily.

Nastan looked at these adults standing in front of him that were now in charge of *his* life.

'Nastan, I'm sorry, but why would you want to do this? I do not understand,' she said, trying to amend her angry outburst.

Nastan looked at Grigor's parents wondering if they were genuinely concerned for him or was it the bank order in which they were more interested? And these strangers, what business was it of theirs? Why should anyone have a say in his future? It was his future and he would decide.

Nastan slowly repeated again in Global, 'I want to go to the International School.'

'He is saying …' began Angelina again, interpreting Nastan's words. Nastan looked at her in awe. 'That's what I want,' he thought, 'I want to be able to speak Global freely.'

'I get what he is saying, but I cannot understand why?' repeated Grigor's mother in disbelief.

But Nastan felt no guilt; he had been practicing that sentence for a long time, longing for the courage to tell his grandfather, but worrying that it would be the death of him - something he no longer needed to worry about.

9

Grigor found it hard to accept that his best friend would rather live with the language traitors than with him. Nastan seemed to have a different spirit these days and Grigor felt as if his best friend had become his enemy. He didn't understand why he wanted to leave him to go to that school with those boys from the lake. Had Nastan forgotten how they had taunted them, each time they had come to the lake? What about the names they had called them – minority orphans, gypsies, poor, stupid, ignorant? Did Nastan think that the taunting would stop? Did he think the name calling would stop? Did he really think he would be their equal just because he was going to that school? He really was being stupid, ignorant, call it what you want, if he thought they would accept him as their equal.

'Do not be so sad Grigor,' his mother comforted him. 'Nastan has his own feelings to work through and once he has, he will be back where he belongs, you'll see.'

But Grigor was not so sure. He had heard him talking Global with Angelina, his bereavement counsellor, at every opportunity. Going out places with her and not inviting him. Since Apollos' death, Grigor had become invisible to Nastan. He had watched him forming a bond with Angelina, a Global language bond and even though she was an adult, even though she was a kind of guardian who had to visit him every day, she had taken his place as Nastan's best friend. Nastan lived for her visits; learning as many new Global words as he could to impress her. Grigor had looked on helplessly, as their relationship disintegrated week after week.

10

'This one's been here a long time,' said the bank clerk, filling out the paperwork for the delivery driver. 'Would you believe I can remember the day the owner brought it in to deposit. It was such an unusual name, comic even and then I remembered reading that Stephen Popov and his family had been killed in the city bombing. Apollos Popov was his father you know. How quickly thirteen years has gone by. After all the people I have seen since that time I can still see that poor man's grief stricken face. I had to hold back my own tears. He was so sad. He had his grandson with him, the poor mite, left without parents at that age. The little boy kept saying Papa in Global and I remember thinking that he looked too young to be able to speak and especially to be speaking Global. It didn't seem to please his grandfather too much and he kept correcting him, telling him to say Papa in Mother Tongue. He seemed quite overcome when I spoke to him in Mother Tongue. I don't know what language he was expecting me to speak. It was so surreal that the little mite was saying Papa when his Papa had … well, you know. He's the youngest Global speaker I've heard in our town to this day.'

'I can't be doing with that Global. Head office is trying to get me to learn it all the time. They're even offering to pay for the lessons,' replied the driver, checking his watch.

'He left precise instructions too,' said the clerk, producing another sheet of paper. 'It's here look. "Upon my death the briefcase is to be delivered to …" Oh no, of course, you know what this means, don't you?'

'No. What?' he asked, glancing at his watch again.

'Well, it's obvious isn't it? That poor man has died, leaving his grandson, who would still only be about thirteen or fourteen, leaving the poor mite an orphan.'

'Are we done now?' he asked, not wanting to get involved in anyone's bereavement issues.

'Yes, we are,' said the clerk snappishly, affronted by his lack of concern.

The driver picked up the briefcase and said to the clerk, 'I'm sure that whatever is inside will bring the boy some comfort,' realising how heartless he had sounded.

'I hope you are right,' replied the clerk, feeling a bit better. Surprised by its weight, the delivery driver pulled up the retractable handle and wheeled the briefcase to the van.

The delivery driver pulled up outside Grigor's house; looked at his list and realised this was *the* delivery – *the* bereavement briefcase. He wished he hadn't had the family history from the clerk because now he felt obliged to say something appropriate if the young boy answered the door. He wished it could be just like any other delivery, 'sign here please' and that was it, job done.

But now he had all this information surrounding his last delivery of the day.

He hoped no one was home and he could perhaps leave the briefcase with a neighbour or in a shed or something. Anything but look a bereaved child directly in the eyes without saying something compassionate.

He opened the doors to his van and there it was, all alone. He put the paperwork in his left hand and wheeled it with his right hand. He made his way down the garden path hoping that no one was in.

He put the briefcase to rest and knocked lightly on the door. No answer. He knocked again, slightly harder, knowing that it would cause him a lot more paperwork if he had to report that he'd delivered it to a neighbour. Or worse than that, if he couldn't make the delivery today, he would have to try again tomorrow – he was in a no win situation.

'Better to get it over with today,' he thought, practically.

He knocked again, louder still and waited a few seconds. He was about to give up and leave when the door opened and a teenage boy stood there staring at him.

'Parcel for Popov,' the driver said, not in his usual hurried tone.

'Yes, I can sign for it.'

'Are you Nastan Popov? It has to be signed for by Nastan Popov,' he asked patiently.

'Yes, I am Nastan Popov.'

'Okay, if you could sign here please.'

The driver observed him, impressed that this boy, who was now an orphan, staying at a "care of address", seemed so together with his emotions.'

'I'm very sorry for your loss,' he muttered, before walking quickly up the path and jumping into his van for safety.

Grigor stood in his doorway, looking at the briefcase that was addressed to Nastan, thinking how odd the delivery man was. He told himself that he had done the right thing, lying that he was Nastan. Otherwise, the delivery driver would have taken the briefcase back to the depot and it probably would have been days before re-delivery. Or worse than that, his parents would have had to traipse to the depot to claim the parcel for Nastan and that would have been way too complicated. Yes, he had done the right thing.

Grigor gripped the handle and wheeled the suitcase through the hallway to the kitchen table. He noticed the sender was City Bank. He looked closer at the writing on the label and saw that Apollos' name had been recorded as the sender. Grigor felt himself welling up at the sight of Papa Popov's name.

He sat with his elbows securely on the table. He placed his chin on the pyramid shape his arms and hands had formed which took the weight of his head. He stared at the briefcase wondering what it contained. 'It must be official to come from a bank,' he deliberated. 'I wonder if I could just have a peep inside while no one is home.' Slowly, he unzipped the side pocket and tried to peep inside. 'Just a little look,' he thought 'and then I'll zip it back up.'

'What on earth*?'* he thought, as he stared at a document that was in a protective, transparent covering. 'I need to get a proper look at this,' he thought, intrigued.

On the cover page, in bold, large type, in Mother Tongue, was written:

"'DON'T BE LEFT BEHIND INITIATIVE' BY STEPHEN A. POPOV."

'Popov,' he thought confused, 'that's Nastan's and Apollos' surname.'

'Stephen Popov,' he deliberated, 'that was Nastan's father's name.' He turned the page to see an index which read:

INDEX

Section 1. Global Facts
Section 2. The Benefits of Global
Section 3. The Benefits of replacing Mother Tongue with Global
Section 4. The Global Wi-Fi Technology and Education Programme
a.k.a. – "Don't Be Left Behind Initiative"
Section 5. Arguments For and Against
Section 6. Research and Statistical Analysis
Section 7. Mother Tongue Phasing Out Plan
Section 8. Presentation – Overview of Above
Section 9. Funding and Partners
Section 10. Global on the World Map
Appendix 1 – Global Translation of Sections 1 - 10

'Mother Tongue Phasing Out Plan; phasing out of what exactly?' thought Grigor, turning the pages frantically to Section 7. He continued to read:

"Ladies and Gentleman of the International Translators Conference; for those of you who do not know me, my name is Stephen Popov and it is with great pleasure that I find myself here today. I am absolutely delighted to have been selected as Global Language Ambassador. The future for our country is truly one of prosperity and excitement. But, before I get too carried away, I would like firstly to explain the two Global language programmes that are strategic to the 'Don't Be Left Behind Initiative'" ...

Grigor was completely confused. 'Nastan's father, Global Language Ambassador for our country - it makes no sense,' he thought, perplexed.

Inside the briefcase were more papers, pages and pages in Mother Tongue and Global. Handwritten, scribbled and rushed. Different coloured pens had been used – red to highlight and green to correct. There were also meticulously hand drawn diagrams and graphs with codes. There was a scrolled item that Grigor opened – he recognised it was a map of the world but the names of the countries as he knew them had been taken off; they had been replaced by abbreviated codes and colours. There were five countries labelled GL, which were colour coded black.

Grigor noticed that their country was labelled *MT* and colour coded orange but he did not know what this meant. He observed that within one of the black *GL* areas, a smaller section had an orange hue and was labelled *MT*. The orange stood out eerily against the black.

The presence of the colour black on the world map sent an unnerving shiver through Grigor's body. The map seemed as if it belonged to a different era. 'What does this mean and why would Apollos be sending this to Nastan?' he pondered further.

'Grigor, we are home,' his mother's voice echoed as she came through the front door. 'Is Nastan with you?'

Grigor looked at the briefcase and the papers on the kitchen table wondering how he was going to explain himself.

'No, he's out with Angelina, as usual,' he shouted back to his mother. He quickly rammed the papers inside, pushed down the handle, grabbed the briefcase with both hands and ran upstairs. He stashed it in his wardrobe, wanting to have another look, knowing that he had to find a secret hiding place, one where he wouldn't be disturbed. For now, the briefcase and its contents would remain in his possession. If Nastan couldn't be in to take delivery of his own parcel, if being out with

Angelina was more important, he could wait a while for his package.

***

'Nastan, are you sure?' Angelina asked him in Global.

'I am sure,' he responded in Global. He didn't speak Mother Tongue any longer. There was no need now that Apollos was gone.

'This is a big step that you want to take. Why not do a term first and then decide?'

'I am sure,' he repeated again in Global, grateful that Angelina had come into his life. Grateful that it was her job to want what was best for him and that she wouldn't judge him. Nastan had made up his mind. He wanted the International School to be responsible for him and if that meant they had to adopt him, then, so be it. To him, there was no going back.

***

Saying goodbye to Grigor and his family had been easier than Nastan had expected. Grigor's mother thought it best that, as he was leaving on a Sunday, they should say their farewells and then go to church as usual. One by one, Grigor's brothers said goodbye to Nastan as he stood in Grigor's living room. When it was Grigor's turn he said to him in Mother Tongue, 'Goodbye my best friend, I will miss you.' Grigor couldn't hold back his tears. He didn't wait for a response from Nastan but rushed out of his house and walked ahead of his brothers.

Nastan's father and mother stood together in front of him. Grigor's father placed his right hand on Nastan's left shoulder while Grigor's mother held his hands in hers and said the blessing in Mother Tongue, 'May the Lord bless you and keep you and cause his face to shine upon you.' Grigor's father gave him a manly tap on the back and left.

'Nastan, when you are ready to come home, we will be waiting for you,' she said, the tears cascading down her cheeks.

***

'Where is Grigor?' his mother quizzed his father, realising they were missing one son from their church pew.

'I don't know. He left the house before us, after he had said goodbye to Nastan. I assumed he would come straight to church,' replied Grigor's father.

'Where is your brother?' she asked her other sons, who just shrugged their shoulders, unknowingly.

'He will be okay. He has probably gone for a walk. He was very upset,' said Grigor's father, understandingly.

Grigor sat by the lake, alone, wondering what he would do without Nastan. 'Who will I pretend fish with? Who will I argue with? Who will I go trekking in the woods with? Who will I talk to?' he thought, dismayed. There were other boys in his school class, but Nastan was his best friend. They understood each other; at least, they used to.

Grigor stared blankly into the water. It was calm and glistening, just the way he liked it to be when he was "pretend" fishing. The sunlight caught an auburn glow in the water and for a moment he thought he saw a fish. 'There are no fish in this part of the lake,' he told himself, hearing Nastan's voice reminding him of the fact.

The calmness of the water slowly turned into a ripple. The type of ripple a school of fish make when they are swimming up-stream. Grigor stood up so he could peer more deeply into the water. The slow ripple suddenly turned into a maelstrom and beautiful, bright, orange fish were jumping in and out of the water. There were hundreds of them. Grigor couldn't believe his eyes. 'What are hundreds of goldfish doing in our lake? Where have they come from? How could they have got here? Goldfish are usually taken to the tourist lakes and used as feeder fish,' he thought, bewildered. He was mesmerised by the sight of so many fish.

'There are fish in our lake, Nastan. There are fish in our lake,' he shouted aloud, invigorated, looking around and remembering that Nastan was not there.

He heard laughter; loud, annoying laughter. He looked up to the diving board to see the Global boys, mimicking him. He felt stupid, he felt embarrassed that they had heard his outburst, that they had witnessed him calling out to Nastan.

'Nastan, Nastan,' he could hear them saying, mockingly imitating him even further. How he loathed them. How he loathed the very sight of them, the very sound of them. They picked up a few stones, threw them at the water and left, their irritating Global ridicule trailing behind them.

Grigor looked at the lake. The fish had gone, disappeared without a trace. He ran all the way home. He was too angry to cry. He was too old to cry. He went to the briefcase and grabbed the Mother Tongue file.

Outraged by the Global boys and at the thought of who Nastan would become in their company, he opened the door to the wood burning stove, he set the pages free from their binding and threw them one by one into the flames. He watched callously as the papers turned to ash before his very eyes.

He seized the Global version. He looked at the excited flames that were inviting him to feed them once more. He looked at the Global documents in his hands and hesitated. 'Let Nastan have his inheritance from his father,' he thought, calculatingly. 'He deserves to know who his father was; his traitorous father who was prepared to sell his soul to Global. Let him spend all his time and energy trying to translate and make sense of these documents; trying to become his father, whilst I wait in anticipation as his ambition becomes his downfall.'

He picked up the briefcase and decided that while everyone else was in church he would move it. He had thought of the perfect place.

11

The drive to the International School in the city was a journey Nastan thought he would never make. As they drove through the town, Nastan rolled down the car window to hear the church bells ring in unison. The town was almost deserted as the people flocked to their places of worship. Nastan had always been fascinated by the churches and had often asked his grandfather why they had thirteen churches in one town.

Apollos had always given the same reply, 'The church is just a building Nastan. We are the congregation; we are God's people. Churches can be destroyed, but our soul can never be destroyed.'

Apollos' words came alive in Nastan's mind, 'Churches can be destroyed but our soul can never be destroyed.'

'Stop,' Nastan cried out, causing the driver to slam on his breaks.

'Whatever is wrong Nastan?' asked Angelina, startled by his behaviour. 'Have you changed your mind? Do you want to go back home?'

'I would like to visit the graves of my parents and grandparents before we leave,' he said, solemnly.

'Of course, which graveyard are they in?' she asked sympathetically.

'The one just at the edge of town. It is on our way.'

Nastan stood looking down at the grave that his parents shared and at the grave his grandfather now shared with his grandmother. Both headstones had a dove inscription, the symbol of the Holy Trinity Church where they worshipped. Apollos had taught Nastan about the history surrounding the church. Each church in their town honoured a historical event from the Bible and their church honoured the day of Pentecost. As a small child Nastan had been quite startled as his grandfather had told him dramatically, with actions, about the day of Pentecost.

'You see Nastan, all the believers were together in a room when, suddenly, the wind - now this wasn't just a gentle wind, the type that messes up your hair - this wind had strength, this wind was powerful, the kind that makes your body sway and fall around and you need to grab onto something for fear of being blown away.'

'This wind filled the room and then came the tongues of fire.' At this point Nastan had been frightened and confused but Apollos had not stopped to reassure him or explain. He had been so enthused. 'The tongues of fire were in mid-air and they came and touched each apostle and then, Nastan, then, the apostles were able to speak in languages they had never spoken before. Imagine that Nastan, imagine opening your mouth, moving your tongue and out comes a language that you haven't had to spend time learning. It just comes out of your mouth, naturally.'

Nastan felt miserable as he remembered snuggling into his grandfather for comfort.

'There is no need to be frightened Nastan. There are many wonderful, mysterious stories in the Bible, but we are not to be scared of them. God wanted people of all nations to be able to hear the gospel being preached and this is how he did it – he gave the gift of languages to the apostles so the people could understand what was being said in their own Mother Tongue.'

Nastan thought back to the museum, to the meeting where Apollos had been chanting killer language. Was this the reason his grandfather had thought that Global was a killer language? Did Apollos believe that the spread of Global would hinder people hearing about God? When he was younger he had heard Apollos preach about Babel being the "day of confusion". Nastan was confused and didn't know what to think. He was living for now and Global was for now. Global was his ticket out of this town with all its disappointments and heartache. Global and the new school would be his purpose now. After all, his grandfather had left him enough money to succeed and how many times had his grandfather told him that all things happen for a purpose.

Nastan knelt by his grandfather's grave and ran his finger over the newly engraved inscription:

"Apollos Popov fondly known as Papa Popov to all who knew and loved him".

There was also an inscription of his favourite Bible verse:

"I see heaven open and the Son of Man standing at the right hand of God

Acts 7: 56".

As Nastan stood alone and looked at the graves before him he had a strange thought that, if what his grandfather believed was true, if it is all about your soul departing from your body and receiving a new heavenly body, then what was in the graves before him? The rotten, decomposing bodies of his parents and grandparents were just bones. They didn't know he was there. They didn't know that his hands were sweating, that his stomach ached like it had been kicked and that his heart skipped beats then had ten beats in a second that felt as heavy as a drum. They didn't know that he had not eaten in days and that he felt like collapsing to the floor and never getting up again. That he was not allowing the tears to flow from his eyes until one day they would escape and fill the lake.

Angrily he thought, 'It's okay for them, they all believed the same thing. They are happy in their new heavenly bodies while I am stuck here in this decaying, unhappy, lonely shell. Why should I be alone? Why is this fair?' Nastan felt like screaming at the graves, like screaming to God, *why*? What was the purpose behind this? Nastan made his way back to the car knowing that he would never visit their graves again – there was no point.

Angelina waited patiently in the taxi for Nastan. She didn't want to hurry him but she didn't want him upset either. Since she had been caring for young, bereaved people, she had never met anyone as emotionless as Nastan and this worried her. Even though she had used the same methods as with her other bereaved children, Nastan had not shed a tear. He had not shared a memory with her. There was nothing. They had created a memory book, which was still blank. They had tied an empty message on a balloon and let it float up to the sky. He had refused to take ownership of a bereavement bear because, after all, he was nearly a man. They had created a worry box but Nastan had not put one worry into it. It had taken a number of weeks for him to start to trust her, to start to talk to her, but he didn't want to talk about his grandfather or his family.

Angelina was anxious because the very thing that had enabled them to form a bond, the very thing that had started him talking, was that she was able to speak Global, which, she knew was a language Nastan's grandfather had detested. She didn't know why and it was not her job to pry but this fascination Nastan had with Global was a concern. It was as if Nastan wanted to erase his grandfather's memory by becoming someone that Apollos wouldn't have liked.

But, that was her opinion. She was not a child psychologist just a bereavement counsellor. As long as Nastan was engaging with her in some way, then whatever else she thought was immaterial.

Nastan sat in the back seat of the taxi with his two boxes of belongings and his grandfather's walking stick. Grigor's father had offered to keep the walking stick in their house but Nastan wanted it with him. Angelina sat in the front, chatting happily to the taxi driver, trying to act like this was just any other day. She was fully aware of how distressing today was for Nastan, despite his insistence that this was what he wanted. She knew that at some point in his life the last few months would catch up with him - she'd seen it too many times. Children and adults alike who can't cry, who won't cry, the moving on quickly, the getting on with the everyday – it catches up with everybody in the end, quite unexpectedly in most cases. It lurks around corners, comes out in a stranger's voice, a stranger's smile, a smell, a word, a film, a song. It's always there, waiting for the moment. For some, when it comes, it's a sense of relief, a joy that they can at last move on, for others it's the road to destruction.

Angelina turned to look at Nastan sat amongst his pitiful possessions that he wanted close to him, staring blankly out of the window as they left his world behind. She prayed that when his moment came, it would be filled with wonderful memories of a dear grandfather who loved him beyond all measure and that would be enough to keep him on the right path for all his life.

'It's just around this corner, Nastan,' said Angelina, as the car bore right.

Nastan sat up, turning his head left to right, not knowing what he was looking for.

'On the left,' said Angelina, watching him from the wing mirror.

The taxi driver indicated left, drove through two whitewashed pillars and followed the drive to the main school entrance.

'I'll be right back,' said Angelina to Nastan as he watched her disappear into the school.

Nastan got out of the taxi and looked around at his new home. The taxi driver motioned to Nastan that he would return in a moment too. From the tobacco smell wafting behind him, Nastan knew where he was going.

Time seemed to stand still. The school was eerily quiet. Nastan looked at the huge wooden door, which had creaked when Angelina pushed it and then creaked again before it slammed shut. To the right of the door was a coat of arms with an inscription in Global "*Knowledge itself is power*".

'Knowledge itself is power,' Nastan said out loud. He looked around at his surroundings and felt a new surge run through his body. He felt empowered. He felt thrilled to think that when he had gained a proper knowledge of Global, he would use this new understanding to give him power over his own future.

‘Nastan,’ said Angelina, ‘Nastan,’ she called again, breaking his trance. ‘Come with me,’ she said, taking him by the hand and leading him through the creaking door.

The taxi driver unloaded the car of Nastan’s belongings. As he opened the boot, he remembered that Nastan had put all his possessions on the back seat.

‘Who put this in here?’ he wondered, surprised to find a briefcase with Nastan’s name on it, care of the school.

Two boys appeared from behind the creaking door able and willing to take Nastan’s belongings to his room, as instructed by Mr Law, Nastan’s housemaster.

‘There’s one more,’ said the taxi driver in Global. ‘It’s quite heavy,’ he said, pulling the briefcase out of the boot and handing it over to one of the boys.

‘It’s okay,’ the boy said, obviously struggling, but not wanting to admit it was too heavy for him. He lugged it slowly up the stairs and was glad to put it down on the new boy’s bed.

12

As dusk set in, giving warning that it would soon be night, Nastan became overwhelmed with loneliness. He knew this was a loneliness he would have to get used to because, despite Apollos' stubborn ways, Nastan knew what it was like to have been truly loved and he knew that no one would ever love him in that way again. What scared him more than being alone was the uncertainty of knowing if he could ever give love to someone the way that Apollos had loved him?

Nastan locked his bedroom door, unlocking it only once to the insistent knock of his housemaster, Mr Law, who had brought him dinner on a tray.

When Nastan had not gone down to eat and had not opened his door to the boys Mr Law had sent to welcome him; boys he was sure he would get along with because they, too, came from his town, he remembered how he had felt on his first night at school all those years ago. He knew that Nastan was best left to work through whatever emotions would manifest themselves during what would probably be, one of the loneliest nights of his life and he would either wake the following morning, pleading to return to his old life, or, as he had, embrace this wonderful new beginning and the excitement of what the future held.

But Mr Law knew that Nastan had been through a great deal and he wasn't here because he had been sent away by people, who are supposed to love you; he was here because the person who had loved him most in the entire world had gone away for good. Mr Law had met with Angelina and was fully aware of the circumstances that brought Nastan to the school. What Angelina hadn't known until that very day was that the school employed their own welfare officer, so all of Nastan's needs would now be met by the school – she would no longer be involved with him.

When Angelina had said goodbye to Nastan earlier that day and had said to him, 'See you tomorrow, bright and early as usual,' she had felt like a trickster. She had cried all the way home. She had been unable to tell him that she would not be seeing him tomorrow or the day after that or any day soon in the foreseeable future.

Nastan looked at his watch which showed it was just eight pm. Despite it being dark already it was too early for bed. He looked at the two boxes on the bedroom floor and the mysterious briefcase, which actually looked more like a suitcase that had found its way to his new home. He hadn't felt ready to open the boxes all the time they had stared at him in Grigor's house. He knew they contained his grandfather's possessions and he wouldn't allow himself to cry.

'But the briefcase, what could possibly be in that?' he wondered curiously. 'Has Angelina left it for me? Surely she would have mentioned it? Maybe Global language books to help me with my studies,' he thought positively.

He moved the briefcase around full circle, looking for a clue as to where it had come from but there was no sender information. He checked the address label thinking he had been sent it in error but, sure enough, his name and address, care of the school, were printed clearly. He unzipped it hoping to see books from Angelina but what he saw just didn't make sense to him at all.

'What on earth?' he thought, as he stared at a document that was in a protective, transparent covering. 'I need to get a proper look at this,' he decided, intrigued.

On the cover page, in bold, large type, in Global, was written:

'DON'T BE LEFT BEHIND INITIATIVE' BY STEPHEN A. POPOV.

'Popov,' he thought, 'that's my name, that's my father's name – Stephen Apollos Popov.' He turned the page to see an index. The very same index, that, unknown to Nastan, Grigor had illicitly seen.

Struggling to understand all the Global words, he scanned the index again and picked out the words his mind could process. He recognised Global, map, world, Mother Tongue, Wi-Fi, Technology and Education.

These were words that he was used to seeing in his Global lesson at school. He then noticed in smaller print another word he recognised, "translation".

'Great,' he thought, 'if I'm right, there should be a Mother Tongue translation; now that, I can read.' He pulled out the presentation, but couldn't find the Mother Tongue version. He looked in the briefcase amongst the other Global papers but still couldn't find it.

'Who would have sent this to me? What did my father have to do with this? Where is the Mother Tongue translation?' he wondered, pulling out sheet after sheet, desperately. After he had looked at every piece of paper his heart sank, accepting that the Mother Tongue translation was missing. He looked bewilderingly at the pages and pages of official looking documents. He knew just by glancing at them that they were way beyond his capability of understanding. He knew his Global skills were limited to every day words that he used for general conversation.

'Only a native Global speaker would be able to comprehend these documents,' he thought, sorely. His eyes were drawn to Apollos' walking stick, which was leaning against the wall. He remembered how he had rested it every night up against his bedroom chair so he could get hold of it himself if he needed it. He recalled the treasure chest that he'd kept on his bedside table. It was constantly locked. 'The treasure chest,' he thought, 'where is the treasure chest?'

Nastan picked up the other boxes; one was much lighter than the other. He decided that the heavier one must contain the treasure chest. He broke the seal and opened the lid to find it inside. He rummaged around the box looking for the key but it was not there.

Frustrated he broke the seal of the other box, believing that the key must be inside. As he reached inside, his hand froze as he recognised the touch of Apollos' worn Mother Tongue Bible.

Nastan clutched the Bible to his chest, breathing in deeply, taking in every smell of the cover and the pages inside. The pages tumbled open to Genesis, to the story Apollos had read him over and over – the Tower of Babel. Nastan felt a pain in his throat; an overwhelming pain that made his throat ache as he heard Apollos' familiar voice reading to him. The pain moved up onto his tongue and then filled his mouth, causing his lips to part. The tears and uncontrollable sobbing came together and Nastan felt they would never stop. But stop they did. When he had cried enough tears to fill the town lake, his tears stopped. Nastan put the Bible on his bedside table, remembering that he was looking for the key. He didn't know what had just happened but he hoped it would never happen again.

Nastan pulled out the rest of Apollos' belongings from the box, things that he had never seen before: an old passport dated 1941, service medals, including a 50th Anniversary medal for the People's Army, black and white photographs of Apollos and other men in army uniform and a nurse standing in the middle of the men. On the back of the photograph was an inscription: "*Damaris, best day of my life.*" Nastan felt his throat going again as he realised that this was his grandmother.

There was also the familiar photograph of his father as a teenage boy. Apollos had kept it in a frame on the mantelpiece and had dusted it every day. There was another Bible; a Global language Bible. Nastan opened the cover and there was an inscription written in Global:

"To my dear husband Stephen, as you embark on this Global language adventure, do not forget the giver of languages, the Lord himself. Your loving wife, Lydia, August 1st 2001."

'So my mother knew Global too,' he pondered, unable to understand why Apollos would have kept it; deciding that it was probably because it was a Bible, despite the language in which it was written. He couldn't see him keeping any other books in Global. He looked through the pages, realising this was the first time he had seen a Global Bible. But more than that, he realised that his mother's hands had held it too. His mother's and father's hands had once held this Bible that was now in his hands. He turned the pages, hoping to find photographs, notes, passages underlined, anything that would give him a sense of closeness to them. He fanned his way to the back of the Bible and found a handwritten

Mother Tongue to Global dictionary. He recognised his mother's writing in words upon words of translation.

He looked again in the box and the last items that he found were a sober reminder of the past - three death certificates. Emotionally exhausted by what he had seen, Nastan at last found the key to the treasure chest. He put it in the lock and turned it slowly. His throat felt strained and his shoulders heavy. Worried that he would become overwhelmed once more, he asked himself if he should leave it for another day. But before he could make a decision the treasure chest lid sprung open.

Nastan placed his fingers underneath the lid and lifted it fully. He looked inside to see newspaper cuttings from *The City Times* Mother Tongue newspaper.

'Is that it?' he asked himself. 'Why did Apollos keep these locked away?'

He pulled them out and placed them on his bed not really knowing what he was looking at and not really knowing which one to read first. Nastan glanced at a few and then realised that they were newspaper clippings about the city bombing – the most significant event in Nastan's life that Apollos had spoken of just once.

The articles described the devastation the bomb had caused and also gave details about a peace treaty that the Rebel Army had decided to ignore. Nastan read a few of the articles in more detail. Once again, he felt cheated that all this information had been kept from him for all these years. He picked up a newspaper cutting from the bottom of the pile, which was folded in half. He opened it and read:

"City Times 22nd August 2001:

Stephen Popov, Global Language Ambassador, was killed yesterday whilst attending the International

Translators Conference. Popov, who was spearheading the Global Language in Technology and Education Programme, known as the 'Don't Be Left Behind Initiative', was due to deliver a presentation outlining the enhancements this scheme would bring to our country.

Sadly, his presentation was never heard as the Rebel Army bomb that obliterated the monastery and grounds left no survivors. The bombing, which is being described as a 'war crime', was allegedly instigated by the Rebel Army on, what was supposed to be, day one of the Peace Treaty Agreement. Our government has yet to offer an official response to the bombing. The International Translator's Conference has been held in the City Monastery since 1779. Sadly, Popov's wife, Lydia and mother, Damaris, were also killed in the carnage. It is believed they had accompanied Popov just to enjoy a lovely day out and to hear him make his presentation. Popov and his family were expected home to celebrate their son Nastan's first birthday. Nastan was at home with his grandfather, Apollos Popov, who has been unavailable for comment and is said to be 'inconsolable'. Mr Apollos Popov is well respected within the Mother Tongue community and is the chairman of the Minority Language Council. He is fondly known as 'Papa Popov' in his home town.

Stephen Popov had been researching Global Language Development in Education and Technology for the past three years and it is believed that his "life's work" was destroyed in the bombing.

For his sake and for the sake of his son answers are needed as to how this could happen on the very day the peace treaty was due to begin."

'My parents and grandmother killed because they were at the International Translator's Conference; killed, because my father was going to make a presentation in support of Global replacing Mother Tongue. Killer language, killer language,' he thought poignantly, realising that Apollos' last words in the museum were referring to Global as *literally* being a killer language.

'It wasn't just about Babel,' thought Nastan; realising now that Apollos had attributed two reasons for his hatred of Global.

'His life's work destroyed in the bombing.' Nastan puzzled over these words. He looked at the papers that formed a blanket on his bed. He felt scared and excited about what he now knew (even though it didn't make much sense to him). He looked again at the Global documents. 'If only I could fully understand these,' he thought frustrated.

'If only my Global knowledge was better. Are these documents his life's work thought to be annihilated in the bombing? If so, who has sent them to me,' he thought, vexed.

He pondered what he knew so far. His father, his father whom he had never known, who'd had no influence over his desires or ambitions, had been Global Language Ambassador for their country. Global, the very language that Apollos hated, his father loved. Global, the very language that Apollos hated, Nastan loved. Nastan took great comfort from this. It made his second-hand memories of his father come alive as he saw an intelligent man, with a desire, but it wasn't a secret desire, like Nastan's. His desire had been real. He had made it real. He had achieved his ambition, despite the opposition that he would have had from Apollos, the Minority Language Council and the Mayor. His father had had a vision for their country, a purpose and he had sacrificed himself to try to bring that vision to completion.

He looked at the photograph of his father as a teenager. How happy he looked. How alive and full of ambition. He looked at himself in the mirror and held the photograph of his father up to his face. He was struck by how alike they were. A father he had never known whose face was his face. A father he had never known whose smile was his smile. A father he had never known and they shared a love for a language that wasn't their own. How could this be if it was not for a reason, not for a purpose?

His stomach felt strange, but good. His mind was racing with questions; the answers he knew were in the Global language papers. He needed to learn Global, properly and quickly. The Global he had learnt so far in school and his extra secret study wasn't nearly enough for him to translate these documents. He needed to excel at Global and was elated that he was in the International School – where better to achieve this. If these papers were his father's "life's work", he could use them to give himself power over his own future. The work his father had begun, he would complete. That was his purpose from now on.

13

As dusk set in giving warning that it would soon be night, Grigor became overwhelmed with loneliness. For the past five months he had seen his best friend every day. He had shared his home with him. He had shared his family with him and now he was gone, leaving an ache in Grigor's heart. He felt as if he was going through his own bereavement. He felt as if he had lost a brother.

His real brothers came noisily into the bedroom they all shared, jumping on the beds and on Grigor. But for once, he wished he had his own room, he wished he had his own space, somewhere he could run to for peace. How could he feel so alone with a houseful of annoying brothers?

He sneaked out of the house into the cold evening air, sure that his mother wouldn't miss him for an hour or two, sure that she would assume he was upstairs with his brothers.

He thought back to earlier that day and how happy Nastan had seemed to be about leaving. He felt so angry with him for wanting to be in that Global school. He felt angry with Nastan's father, a man that he had never even met, for somehow passing down to Nastan a desire for Global.

'Is it in our genes,' he wondered? 'Are our desires the same as our parents? How else would Nastan have this desire for Global, the same desire his father had, a father that he didn't even know?' 'Agh! The box,'

Grigor thought suddenly, 'I didn't put the box away.' He ran as fast as he could to the Mayor's office and snuck in through the open window as he had done over the last few weeks.

He crept down the hallway, not putting on any lights. He opened the door to the Mayor's office and fumbled his way in the dark, passed the Mayor's desk to the den where he had left the box. He froze when the lights came on, not wanting to turn around to face whoever was there.

'Hello Grigor. What are you doing here so late?' the Mayor asked calmly. 'Do your parents know where you are?'

'Yes,' he lied, turning around, feeling his neck and face catching fire. 'I left my jacket.'

'So you snuck in like a thief in the night. That doesn't sound like you. Is there anything else you left behind?' the Mayor asked.

'No, that's it; I should be going, see you tomorrow for our meeting.'

'Your coat, where's your coat?' asked the Mayor.

'I couldn't have left it here after all,' said Grigor, desperately needing to leave.

'Take a seat Grigor. There's something I need to discuss with you.'

Grigor sat down opposite the Mayor. He hated lying to him but he didn't want to have to explain about the box. He wished he hadn't tampered with the briefcase but given it to Nastan the day it had been delivered. What if the Mayor had found the box? Is that what he wanted to talk to him about? He looked over to the door that led to the den which was closed. He was almost certain that he had left it open when he'd departed earlier that day.

The Mayor got up, opened the door and went into the den, the place where Grigor had hidden the box or so he thought.

'Tell me, Grigor, is this what you are looking for?'

Grigor could feel the fire on his neck and face intensifying.

'I can explain,' he blurted out, feeling relieved to be talking about it.

'I'm listening,' said the Mayor, sitting back in his chair.

'I was so angry with Nastan for wanting to leave, for replacing me with Angelina and most of all for wanting to live with those language traitors. One day, when it was just me at home, a briefcase, well it was actually more like a small suitcase, was delivered for Nastan. The label read City Bank and the sender's name was Apollos so I thought it must be something important. It must be something that Apollos wanted Nastan to have, something of value. At first, I just wanted to take a look at what was inside. But then, after I looked, I couldn't understand or believe what I was reading. I needed more time to read the documents, so I hid the briefcase, thinking I would keep it for a while and Nastan would never know I had looked inside.'

'So where is this briefcase?'

'The briefcase has left with Nastan today. I copied most of the documents and transferred them into this box. I sneaked the briefcase into the boot of the taxi just before they left. I am sure the taxi driver would have found it. I took off the sender information and put on a new label with Nastan's name, care of the Global International School, so he wouldn't know where it came from.'

‘Such meticulous planning. But why Grigor? Why would you not want him to know that the briefcase and its content had come from Apollos?’

‘I don’t know,’ said Grigor, regretfully, ‘I wish I didn’t know any of it.’

The Mayor was silent.

‘Have you looked inside the box?’ Grigor asked him quizzically. ‘Did you know about Nastan’s father?’

‘Grigor, there are some things in life that are better off buried. There are some things in life that we are not supposed to know,’ replied the Mayor, implying that he had.

‘But I do know and I wish I didn’t. How could Nastan’s father have been Global Language Ambassador for our country? Apollos hated Global. It makes no sense. How doesn’t Nastan know any of this?’

The Mayor got up from his chair and looked out of the window. There was an awkward silence.

‘Because Apollos was ashamed and worried,’ said the Mayor emotionally.

‘Worried about what?’ asked Grigor, sensing the Mayor had kept this secret for a long time.

‘Babel,’ the Mayor replied in a choked whisper.

‘Babel? The story from the Bible? What do you mean?’

Clearing his throat, the Mayor said, ‘It was more than just a story to Apollos. He held a very strong belief that Global was, is, the “super language” that will take over the world and bring about a second Babel; the “devil’s language” he called it, along with other names. When Stephen was chosen as Global Language Ambassador, Apollos was devastated and Stephen was overjoyed. Stephen loved his job and loved the new super language he had to learn.’

'Killer language,' said Grigor. 'The day Apollos died he kept muttering killer language. Was this because of Babel?'

'Partly, but also because of something else he never recovered from.'

The Mayor went to his book shelf. He moved a book and put his hand deep into the shelf.

'Because of this,' he said, giving a file to Grigor.

Grigor opened the file which was full of old newspaper cuttings. The Mayor sat in silence while Grigor read…

'So Nastan's mother, father and grandmother were in the city the day of the bombing because his father was supposed to make a presentation about Global replacing Mother Tongue and they were all killed by the bomb.'

'Yes.'

'Killer language,' said Grigor poignantly.

'Apollos truly believed that Global killed his family. He believed that if they hadn't been at the translator's conference, if Stephen hadn't been involved with Global, they'd still be alive today. The day at the museum was too much for him with all the talk of Global replacing Mother Tongue. It was as if his two worst fears were coming to fruition before his very eyes. Plus, he had lived with knowing that his own son had been instrumental in the Global language initiative that has slowly begun creeping into our schools.'

'You said he was worried and ashamed. Ashamed about what?' asked Grigor.

'As chairman of the Minority Language Council, he was ashamed that his own son was so openly opposed to Mother Tongue. That he was prepared for it to be replaced with Global.

Of course the powers that be in our administration were devastated by Stephen's death and even more devastated that all his research was destroyed in the bombing. When they thought they had shown enough respect over his death they launched the Wi-Fi and Education Initiatives. They didn't need his research for that. They wanted to name the initiatives in memory of Stephen but Apollos made it clear he didn't want Stephen's name involved. He said it would be too painful to see his son's name everywhere but the real reason was his hatred of Global. People do not even mention Stephen anymore. They haven't for years, so it was easy for Apollos to keep his past a secret from Nastan and just tell him the bits he wanted him to know.'

'So if the research papers were destroyed in the bombing, what are these?'

'I'm not sure, I have never seen any of these papers before today. There is another thing I do not understand,' said the Mayor.

'What is it?'

'There should be a Mother Tongue translation of the papers. Look, it states it here "Appendix 1 – Mother Tongue translation of sections 1 – 10" but I have looked and looked in the box and there is no translation. It's all in Global.'

Grigor looked sheepishly at the Mayor.

'What have you done Grigor?'

'It was the boys at the lake. They were taunting me in Global. They threw stones at the fish. We had fish in our part of the lake, can you believe it? Actual fish in our part of the lake. They were standing there in their posh uniforms, looking at me, judging me. All I could see was Nastan standing there with them, taunting me too. I was so enraged. I ran home, grabbed the documents from the briefcase and before I knew it the Mother Tongue version was going up in flames on the woodstove. As I watched it burn I suddenly remembered that I hadn't photocopied it. But it was too late, it had already turned to ash.'

'Why Grigor? Why burn the Mother Tongue version and not the Global? Why leave us with a version that we do not understand? How could you have been so careless?'

'It was my intention to burn all of it. The day it arrived I was going to destroy it all. But when I had the Global version in my hand I decided that it would be Nastan's punishment, it would be his shame to know that his father was a traitor to our language, to our culture and to our country. I knew that translating the papers would consume his very being. His Global obsession will become his downfall.'

The Mayor felt saddened that Grigor did not seem to realise that he had his own obsession too.

'Oh Grigor, it will take us months to translate the Global into Mother Tongue, when you had it in your very hands.'

Grigor felt ashamed by his actions. 'I'm sorry. I don't know what got into me, I …'

'We could give them to someone we trust who can speak Global,' interrupted the Mayor. 'Hopefully, they can translate them for us in just a few weeks.'

'But who is there with such knowledge of Global in our community?' asked Nastan.

'You'd be surprised how many closet Global speakers there are in our town Grigor. People you would never imagine to be Global speakers that have kept it a secret for fear of being seen as a "language traitor", as Apollos called them.'

'Well I don't know any closet people,' said Grigor, 'do you?'

The Mayor looked at Grigor, hoping he hadn't realised he was referring to himself.

'Just leave the box with me Grigor. I will make subtle enquiries. In the meantime, do not mention this to anyone. I have a suspicion that what we have here would do much harm to our beloved Mother Tongue.'

'And to the memory of our dear Papa Popov,' said Grigor. 'But what about Nastan? He has the same Global papers. What do you think he will do with them?'

'I'm not sure. His Global knowledge is not fluent, just what he has learnt at school. Plus, I cannot imagine him showing this information to anyone and, don't forget, he doesn't know that we have it too.'

'Yes, of course.'

'But, we need to translate these papers quickly so if Nastan does decide to give this information to someone to translate, then, we are one step ahead of any plans that will endanger Mother Tongue.'

'Do you really think it will come to that?'

'Who knows Grigor, who knows?'

Grigor left the Mayor's office with a sense of relief that he had intercepted the briefcase that day, even though he had made their situation worse by burning the Mother Tongue version. He thought back to the day at the museum and how Nastan had had no intention of being part of the Mother Tongue Youth Movement. If Nastan had come forward that day, if he had come forward with him as the next generation of language upholders, then maybe Apollos would still be alive. As far as Grigor was concerned, Nastan had killed his own grandfather – he killed him by not speaking out when he had the chance, by not reassuring Apollos that, no matter what, he would uphold their language. He would uphold their culture and that, as long as there were Mother Tongue citizens on God's earth, their language would be spoken and passed down from generation to generation.

Grigor thought back to Nastan's teasing about how they had been born to the wrong families and how Grigor should have been a Popov because he was Mother Tongue through and through just like his grandfather.

Grigor felt enraged by Nastan, by his selfishness, by his lack of loyalty and decided that he would make it his goal to develop the Mother Tongue Youth Movement. He would make it his goal to ensure that Mother Tongue would always be spoken in their town and their country. 'If Nastan wants to try to change that, if he wants to follow in the footsteps of his father, then I will be ready and waiting,' he thought, vehemently.

14

Nastan woke to a cooing noise coming from outside his window. He looked at the papers that surrounded him and couldn't remember falling asleep. He opened the curtains, pleased that it was morning. The cooing noise was made by two mourning doves that were perched happily on the window ledge. Nastan opened the window, to let in the air, something that Apollos had taught him to do. Come rain or shine, the first chore of the morning was to open the window to let in the day. The doves didn't seem to notice Nastan and carried on with their morning routine.

Nastan gathered all the documents, along with the newspaper cuttings and put them back safely into the briefcase. He placed the Bibles on his bedside table and put the briefcase and boxes in his wardrobe. He put on his new school uniform, fixing his tie the way Apollos had taught him, their "Sunday ties" he had called them because that was the only time they ever wore them.

He laced up his shoes and did up the buttons on his blazer. He looked at this new image of himself in the mirror and saw his father smiling at him. He felt like a burden had been lifted from his soul and that, for once in his life, he knew about his past and he knew about his future.

He followed the smell of bacon until he came to the Great Hall. Mr Law was already sitting down eating his breakfast, wondering if he should go and check on

Nastan. He was the only pupil not present. Mr Law was about to leave his seat when the grand doors swung open and there was Nastan. He looked different; he looked as if he had become a man overnight. His shoulders were square and his head was held high.

Nastan stood tall in the doorway, taking in his first school scene. He scanned the room noticing there was an empty seat by the boys he recognised from the lake. Mr Law gave him an approving smile and walked over to make formal introductions. Nastan sat down next to the boys he so admired, next to the boys he so wanted to be like. But as one of them spoke to him, he saw Grigor's face staring back at him. He looked sad as if he wanted to cry. Nastan blinked quickly to get rid of Grigor's image from his mind. The other boy joined in the conversation but as he spoke, Nastan saw Apollos' face staring back at him. He too looked sad as if he wanted to cry. Nastan felt overwhelmed. He felt like running. 'What is happening to me?' he wondered in despair. 'Am I losing my mind?' He looked around at the other pupils who seemed oblivious to Nastan and were eating as they usually would.

Nastan tried to listen to what the boys were asking him but their words seemed faint as if someone had turned the volume down. Grigor and Apollos stared at him and their sad faces turned to anger. Their mouths moved voraciously but Nastan couldn't hear what they were saying. The room was spinning and Nastan desperately wanted it to stop. He wanted them to stop.

Nastan lowered his head into his hands. 'Nastan, are you okay?' one of the boys asked. 'Nastan, Nastan…' he could hear them calling repeatedly.

He looked up to see Mr Law holding him firmly by his shoulders. Nastan looked at the boys who were now themselves again.

'It's okay, Nastan. The first day at a new school is always overwhelming,' said Mr Law, reassuringly. Nastan looked at him intently and took comfort from the tight grip he had on his shoulders. A firm reassuring grip that said, 'I understand.' 'Don't worry, everything will be okay.' Nastan looked closely at his face. He had a bold face, the same boldness he was sure his father would have had. For the first time since Angelina, he felt approval and acceptance. He felt reassured about the future.

'Law, that's a good name,' thought Nastan. 'That's a good, strong, Global name. Law will be my name. I will change my name to Law, Stephen Law. I will make a name for myself and people will know me and hear me, because there is a day coming when I will legislate concerning Global. I will pass a new law in memory of my father. One day I will return home and I will make the city the capital of Global. I will make my headquarters there and I will construct an edifice so fine that it will house one superpower, one super language. A structure so magnificent that it will reach up to heaven itself and every eye in the city will see it and all people from every nation will aspire to emulate it. Global will be THE LAW in every nation of the world. Global will be spoken by all the citizens of the world, under a new world order, which will be attributed to me, Stephen Law. Nastan Popov will cease to exist. Stephen Law will rise in his place.

15

Ten Years later …

The Mayor sat at his desk for the last time, taking comfort from the fact that by this hour tomorrow, his worthy successor would be sitting in his place. Ten terms in office, ten terms of unwavering support from the people of his town. He knew others who'd had ambition to be mayor, others who had run for mayor, but, for some reason, for all these years, the people had wanted him.

But now it was time to step down and let the next generation take over. Most of his rivals were long gone. The people that were left of his age group were more than happy to pass the Mayorship onto the man of his choice. A man whom they were certain would protect the statutes of the municipality without fail. A humble man, whom, the Mayor hoped would accept the Mayorship, even though he would protest that he was not worthy.

The Mayor's office was overflowing with boxes as he packed away his paraphernalia from the last four decades. Grigor had offered to help him. He didn't know how he would have managed without Grigor over the last few years. But packing up his office was something he needed to take care of himself. The sun had begun to rise, changing the office interior to a warm orange glow. How he loved the sun rise heralding the start of a new day and how he loved the peace and quiet of his office to gather his thoughts before he had to listen to everyone else's views on policy, business, planning, tourism... 'How odd tomorrow morning will be,' he said aloud doubting his own decision.

He looked to the corner of the room where Grigor's desk sat, knowing that he would soon be at work. He too was an early starter. He pushed on, wanting to get things done before Grigor got there, knowing it was going to be an emotional day for both of them.

He went into the den thinking it best to start in there and work his way out. He couldn't believe how many coats and jumpers were on the coat stand. 'That's where you got to,' he said loudly, putting them into a box. He picked up his trusted torch wondering if he should leave it for his successor for late night working. He felt amused that he had lost count of how many times the electric had tripped and he had fumbled his way in the dark for his companion. 'Yes, I will leave it,' he said aloud, again.

He grasped the worn handle of a small cupboard that was almost hidden in the corner of the den. He pulled on the handle but the cupboard wouldn't open. 'Strange, I cannot remember locking it. Now where would I have put the key?' he muttered to himself. He rummaged around his desk drawers not really remembering what the key looked like. He emptied the contents of the top drawer into one of his boxes and did the same with the contents of the middle drawer. He opened the bottom drawer and there, by itself, was the key. He recalled it was the key because of its odd formation. It was about four inches long and the grooves formed a right angle.

The key fitted into the lock with ease but it wouldn't turn. The Mayor bent over slightly and peered into the mechanism to see if there was something blocking it. He turned the key to the right several times but it wouldn't budge. Then, he remembered there was a technique to getting the lock to open. He pulled the key back slightly and turned it again while pulling it back and fore until he felt a tight fit. He turned the key sharply and at last the cupboard unlocked. 'Better get a new receiver fitted,' he said aloud, 'or one day the key will just snap off in the lock.'

He opened the door and what he saw sent a pendulum of emotions crashing through his body. 'How could I have forgotten about this?' he wondered, ashamedly. But he knew how, because it had been a long time since he had lied to save the future. The years that had passed had been good years and he had convinced himself that what he had done had been for the benefit of his town and its language.

If he had involved anyone else, then who knows what their Mother Tongue community would look like now? - If indeed there was still a Mother Tongue community to look at. He had done what was necessary. A selfless act that had maintained prosperity and peace and which had saved jobs and families. There were only three people who knew about the contents of the box and he was certain that if the third person had any plans to use the contents, then they would have heard from him by now.

Over the last few years the Mayor had tried to locate Nastan. He had visited the Global International School in the city to ask if they knew his address. But his request had fallen on deaf years. 'We do not give out information on the whereabouts of former pupils. If Nastan Popov wants you to know where he is, then I am sure he will contact you,' he had been told curtly, in Global. The Mayor had of course dismissed the Global response, insisting that he did not speak the language and asking for someone who could converse with him in Mother Tongue.

He hadn't located Nastan, but, he had gained a treasured possession.

'I'm sorry, but as my colleague has already explained, we are not at liberty to discuss past pupils but you can take this with you,' said a very helpful Mother Tongue speaker, producing Apollos' walking stick. 'It was left behind when Master Popov vacated his residence. If you do ever find him perhaps you could reunite him with it?' she said, her tone and demeanour much softer and warmer than the unhelpful Globalist.

The Mayor had been delighted to take it. He had been ecstatic that this treasured object that symbolised glorious memories, happy and sad, had found a new home in his hands.

However, his quest for Nastan's whereabouts hadn't solely been because of the contents of the box and the danger the documents could pose. He had been plagued with guilt because he had not cared enough all those years ago to see Nastan as a grieving child, incapable of making a grown-up decision and not as a threat to his cosy world. He had not fulfilled his duty to his dear friend Apollos, to ensure the well-being of Nastan and reassure him that, despite the choices he had made as an emotional teenager, this was his home and he would always be welcome. But now he feared it was too late to offer an olive branch and wondered, all these years later, what type of man Nastan had become.

When Nastan had left town, the Mayor had invested all his time and emotion into ensuring that Grigor, as leader of the Mother Tongue Youth Movement and then later as his understudy, was ready to counteract any threat the future posed to Mother Tongue.

Grigor's father had of course backed him all the way, seeing the opportunities this would give his son in the future; hoping that one day he would be the head of the town's administration and possibly mayor. His vision for his son couldn't have been more accurate.

The Mayor went into his office and to the bookshelf. He moved a book out of the way and placed his hand deep into the back of the shelf looking for *the* file.

He sat on his old chair, which he had put in the den not wanting to get rid of it for some silly, sentimental reason. The file and the box brought abruptly back, memories of his dear friend Apollos and the awful day he had died in the museum. 'I should have told Grigor the truth,' he said out loud, his voice tinged with despair. 'I should have told him ...'

Grigor stood in the den doorway, disturbed by the sight of the Mayor sat in the corner on his old chair, repeating, over and over, 'I should have told Grigor the truth.'

'Mr Mayor, sir, what are you doing sitting in here? What do you mean you should have told me the truth?'

The Mayor, startled by Grigor's sudden appearance, swivelled around slowly; his chair creaking from the weight of the objects he had placed on his lap.

'It has no place in my heart, Grigor, you must believe me.'

Grigor recognised the box that the Mayor was holding. He had not thought about it in such a long time. He had not thought about Nastan in such a long time.

'What has no place in your heart?' he asked, not thinking for a moment he was referring to past events.

'I had no choice. There was no one I trusted well enough, which was wrong I know because there were others who could have translated the documents but I had to take care of it myself.'

'Let me take those things off your lap and help you out of the chair,' Grigor said, wondering if he had taken his pills this morning. His memory had become a lot worse over the past twelve months, which is why he had, at last, relented to step down as Mayor. But this pitiful figure, this pathetic version of the Mayor that Grigor saw in front of him was nothing like the man he had been conversing with just yesterday.

'Let's go back into the office and have a coffee and I can help you ...' said Grigor, reaching down to take the box.

'Don't touch it. It's a box of evil. It makes you do things you don't want to,' he said, looking up at Grigor with tears in his eyes.

Grigor didn't know what to do. He didn't want to belittle him but he knew he needed to bring him back to normality.

'Should I get one of your pills? Have you taken one today?'

'We should burn the box and everything in it. That's what we should have done all those years ago. That's what you should have done. Why didn't you destroy it all? Why didn't you destroy Global when you had the chance?'

Grigor attempted to take the box off his lap but the Mayor held onto it even tighter. Grigor recognised the file too, it was the one the Mayor had shown him all those years ago that had the newspaper cuttings about Nastan's father.

'If you give me the file, then I can help you pack your things away.'

'The file needs to be destroyed. It has destroyed me over the years.'

Grigor didn't understand how seeing these things again could have such a strong impact on the Mayor. They had spoken often of Apollos and it was the Mayor who had raised money to have a bronze sculpture of him placed outside the museum.

'He's disappeared off the face of the planet,' said the Mayor.

'He hasn't disappeared, he passed away, remember?'

'Of course I remember. I'm not talking about Apollos. I'm talking about Nastan. I've tried to find him, to know that he is okay; I abandoned him all those years ago, just like your parents did. We shouldn't have let him go. He was just a child, a grieving child and we all let him go.'

'What do you mean you tried to find him?'

'I've been to the school. They wouldn't tell me anything. I've put notices in different newspapers hoping that he would see them, hoping he would get in touch, but nothing.'

'But why would you want Nastan to return when you have always seen him as such a threat to Mother Tongue? Even when he left you said he was ambitious and not to be trusted. You said that if he did return one day it would be to fulfil his father's ambitions and that would be a sad day for our town.'

'Because I was wrong; he was just a child and I was wrong. If anyone is deceitful it is me.'

'You, deceitful, you are the most trustworthy person in our town.'

'You wouldn't think that, if I told you that I had done something that goes against everything we stand for and I have kept it secret all these years.'

'What have you done? What could you possibly have done that is as awful as you are making out?'

Frantically he confessed, 'It was me. I was the translator. I know Global. I practically used to be Global.'

'What? I don't understand? How could you know Global?'

'When I was fourteen, the same age as Nastan was when he left town, my parents sent me away to a Global International School where, little by little, they chipped away at my culture. They practically stripped me of my knowledge of Mother Tongue and turned me into a Global academic. I hated it. I was so lonely. My parents never visited me. My grandparents were back here. They wrote to me regularly but I didn't see any family all the time I was there. Just as I finished my final exams my parents died suddenly. They were in some obscure country and contracted an awful illness and just died. They couldn't send their bodies' home for burial because apparently there wasn't much left of them to send back. They were buried together in an unmarked grave. Despite their wealth and status, they were buried in an unmarked grave, like nameless paupers. After finishing my exams, I came home and lived with my grandparents. I can't tell you what it was like to be with my family again. I never spoke Global after that. I re-learned Mother Tongue. My grandfather was Mayor; did I ever tell you that Grigor? My grandfather was Mayor for forty years, the same time as me. He chose me to follow in his footsteps, the same way that I am choosing you to do the same!'

Grigor was unsure what to say. Which revelation should he address first? The Mayor was the translator or the fact that he had chosen him to be the next Mayor? The Mayor looked at him longingly, waiting for him to comment.

'Closet Global speakers, that's what you called them. I've never forgotten and have spent the last fifteen years labelling people yes or no. But you just said you never spoke Global again when you came home. How could you translate the documents if you hadn't spoken Global for all those years?' asked Grigor.

'Because as soon as I looked at those papers an unused part of my brain switched on, and it was as if I was back in school, in an examination room. Translating those papers was the most important examination of my life; I had to translate them accurately to know what the potential danger was.'

'But why didn't you tell me back then? I would have understood. I would have probably empathised with you being sent to an alien land to learn a foreign language. What about the death of your parents? Why did you never tell me about that?'

'Because it was in the past and I wanted to protect the future. That's why I did it. You cannot believe the bad taste that Global left on my tongue.'

'Yes I can. I can believe it. I can still remember how those boys from the lake used to make me feel when Nastan and I would hear them speak in Global. Nastan, of course, must have felt differently about it because he couldn't wait to leave to become Global. He was good at hiding his feelings. He had me fooled.'

'So you forgive me?' asked the Mayor in a childlike voice.

‘Forgive you? Forgive you for what? For using an awful experience and turning it into good; you have told me often enough that sometimes the things we experience in life are just for a season and the time you spent in that school was your season. If you hadn’t, we would have had to involve outsiders. You have done nothing wrong. You have ensured that for the last fifteen years we have been able to monitor Mother Tongue. You have made sure that we know what the potential danger is from Global within our own country and from outside. You have been the language keeper for a long, long time and it is an honour that you feel me capable of carrying on the work and being the future keeper.’

‘So you forgive me and accept the Mayorship?’ the Mayor asked through his tears.

‘Yes and yes, wholeheartedly,’ replied Grigor.

Grigor took the box and file off the Mayor and put them back in the cupboard.

‘No one can ever find these documents Grigor, especially my handwritten translation; if anyone ever recognised my handwriting... and no one can ever know any of the things I have just told you. The damage it would cause in our Mother Tongue community would be irreversible.’

‘I understand. No one will ever hear anything from my tongue that will bring damage to our cause,’ replied Grigor, hiding the key in the bookshelf.

‘Now, Grigor, let us go over tonight’s ceremony, so you know what is expected of you,’ said the Mayor, feeling unburdened.

16

'Mr Mayor,' said Monica, 'Doctor Mitrov is here to see you. Should I send him in?'

'Doctor Mitrov? I'm not expecting him am I?' asked Grigor.

'No, he says he just needs a minute of your time.'

'Yes, of course, ask him to come straight in, thank you. And Monica, please call me Grigor, not Mr Mayor. You have known me since I was a boy and it sounds odd.'

'Okay, but just so you know, on formal occasions, I will always address you as Mr Mayor. Just because you are the youngest mayor in the history of our town and probably in the history of our country, there is no need to let modern ways take over tradition, don't you agree?'

'Yes, I quite agree,' said Grigor, compliantly.

Doctor Mitrov entered the room looking quite perplexed.

'Doctor Mitrov, it's good to see you, please sit down. Are you okay? Would you like a coffee or …?'

'It's the Mayor, Mr Mayor. Not you, but the Mayor, your predecessor,' he said babbling.

'You mean our dear old friend Jakov.'

'Yes Grigor, I mean our dear old friend Jakov. I have just left him and well, let's just say he is making no sense at all. Today, he is literally not making any sense at all. He is unintelligible.'

‘So the dementia is progressing, just as you thought?’

‘Yes, the dementia is progressing. But I can’t really say that from a clinical point of view it is progressing the way it should.’

‘Well we both know that he is a feisty, old soul. He isn’t going to fade away that easily.’

‘He doesn’t seem to be fading away at all; that is part of the problem.’

‘Well, we don’t wish him dead just yet do we, Doctor Mitrov?’ said Grigor, with a wry smile.

‘Fade away, dead, no that is not what I mean Grigor. You need to see for yourself,’ said Doctor Mitrov, rising to his feet.

‘What now?’

‘Yes. Now, before we have a rebellion on our hands.’

‘Okay,’ said Grigor, getting his coat from the den, ‘but I was only with him four days ago.’

‘A lot can happen in four days Grigor,’ said Doctor Mitrov, leading the way.

***

‘Grigor, my boy, I am glad to see you. The doctor here has gone mad and has taken to locking me in his house. I nearly escaped out of the window, but thought better of it. Doctor Mitrov, are you feeling quite yourself? I hope you don’t make a habit of placing your patients under house arrest. It is a good job that we are old friends or you’d be heading for a thick lip.’

Grigor stood aghast.

‘You see what I mean? Do you see what I mean?’ repeated Doctor Mitrov, his tone getting louder.

'How could this be? Has he spoken to you in Global before?' asked Grigor, wondering if Jakov had confided his secret to the doctor also. 'Can you understand him?'

'No, he has never spoken Global to me before now. How do you think I can understand him? I do not know Global. I know that he is speaking Global but I do not comprehend the language. I have no intention of knowing it. How on earth does he know how to speak it?' asked Doctor Mitrov, hoping Grigor could provide a logical answer.

'Do you know Global, Grigor? If you do, now would be a good time to confess. I won't hold it against you; I would take it to my grave, it would just be good to know what he is saying.'

'I certainly do not know Global,' said Grigor. 'I have nothing to confess.'

'So how does he know it? How does a man with dementia suddenly start speaking a language he has never spoken before?'

'I don't know,' said Grigor, hesitantly. He didn't understand the workings of the brain, or the workings of dementia, but what he did know was, this wasn't the first time that Jakov had spoken Global. Also, what he knew was that he had promised never to divulge his secret.

'So what are we to do? I cannot keep him locked up. But can you imagine if he wanders into town and starts speaking Global with the people? The retired Mayor and keeper of the Mother Tongue language, the famous Mayor who has lobbied relentlessly over the last ten years to keep Global out, has practically become Global overnight. What are we going to do Grigor? What are we going to do?'

Grigor was stumped. He didn't understand how Jakov was not speaking Mother Tongue.

‘Jakov,’ Grigor said to him out loud. ‘Jakov, it’s Grigor. Can you speak to me in Mother Tongue? Please Jakov, speak to me, please.’

Jakov looked blankly at Grigor and started to speak in Global again. Doctor Mitrov went into his medical bag and started to fill a syringe.

‘What are you doing?’ Grigor asked horrified.

‘Saving our town,’ he said, while injecting a sedative into Jakov’s arm. ‘That will give us some needed time to figure this out.’

***

‘Hello,’ said Grigor, answering his phone.

‘Jakov is not far from death, Grigor. I have to call the Pastor. Jakov would want him to pray with him,’ said a very subdued Doctor Mitrov.

‘Has he returned to his normal self?’ asked Grigor, aware that Doctor Mitrov would know exactly what he meant.

‘No. He is the same as he was.’

‘So he won’t be able to understand the Pastor and, if he talks, the Pastor won’t be able to understand him.’

‘Not given the current situation, no.’

‘And if he should speak while the Pastor is there what are you planning to tell him?’

‘I’m not planning on telling him anything and even if he does speak while the Pastor is there what does it matter. He is a Pastor, he is Jakov’s Pastor. He is your family’s Pastor. We can trust him. Maybe he will think he is speaking in tongues, eh?’

Grigor was silent.

‘Grigor, he has to have the blessing. I will not deny him that. It is more important …’

‘Yes, you’re right, I’m sorry. Of course he has to and yes we can trust a man of God. But aren’t you forgetting something?’ asked Grigor.

‘What?’

‘How are you going to explain that Jakov is in your home under sedation?’

‘He is not under sedation all the time Grigor; just when he has Global episodes.’

‘But still, how are you going to explain that to the Pastor; you alone know how unethical it is.’

‘You don’t have to remind me Grigor of how unethical I am being. In one sense I would have rather let him wander down to town and let the secret out. I will have this on my conscience for ever.’

‘You have to protect yourself, too. If you feel he hasn’t got long then maybe we should take him home and we can take it in turns to watch him. At least then people will see you coming and going and they won’t be shocked when he goes.’

‘And if people want to visit him to pay their last respects?’

‘We will allow them in when he is asleep, so to speak.’

‘How did I ever get caught up in all this?’ said Doctor Mitrov. ‘Once this is over, I am bringing my retirement forward before I am “struck off” or sent to jail.’

‘There won’t be any talk of jail. You are his doctor. You can issue his death certificate and there will be no need for a post mortem.’

‘Have you heard yourself Grigor? You have spent nearly half your life in the company of this man. How can you speak so glibly of what we have done?’

'Because I know that he would want us to protect Mother Tongue at whatever the cost.'

'But sometimes Grigor, the cost is too high,' said Doctor Mitrov, hanging up.

***

Jakov had lost a lot of weight, so moving him was just like lifting a helium filled balloon. Grigor and Doctor Mitrov waited until the early hours to take him home and were certain that no one had seen them.

Grigor welcomed the Pastor and showed him to Jakov's bedroom. A number of Jakov's neighbours had noticed the Pastor arriving. The word soon spread that given the presence of the Pastor, Jakov probably didn't have long left.

Jakov lay in the middle of his bed, motionless. The bedspread covered his shrunken body up to his chin. His face was pale. His hair was as white as the snow that lay on the mountains in the skiing season. In contrast, his eyebrows were black and full, like lazy slugs squatting above his eyelashes. His lips, like his complexion, were pale. They were only noticeable because they were painfully cracked which gave them a flesh-pink tint. On his bedside table was a cloudy glass of water and a damp flannel that Grigor and Doctor Mitrov were using to try to keep his lips moist and his body watered.

As they entered the room Doctor Mitrov raised his eyebrows to Grigor to show that Jakov was sedated. They both knew that it couldn't be any other way. They couldn't risk the Pastor hear him speak Global.

The Pastor sat at Jakov's bedside and opened his Mother Tongue Bible. Grigor was reminded of Apollos and how in church he would open his Bible to the reading and give it to him and Nastan to share.

The Pastor began to pray and Doctor Mitrov and Grigor looked on in silence. The Pastor was nearing the end of his prayer, when, without warning, Jakov sat bolt upright in bed.

Doctor Mitrov looked horrified wondering how he could have woken so soon after his injection. Jakov looked around the room as Grigor made his way hesitantly over to him.

'It's okay my friend, I am here,' he said to him while he waited anxiously to see in which language he would respond or if he would drift back to sleep.

'Grigor,' he said in Mother Tongue. 'Grigor, my trusted friend, you must protect our land from the terror that is about to take it over. You must protect our language from the evil that is lurking, the evil that wants to take over your soul.'

Grigor, saddened by the confused look on Jakov's face said, 'I promise you that I will be the keeper for as long as it takes, until we have a lifelong agreement from the MLWA.'

'I will read from the Scriptures now,' said the Pastor and he began. 'At Calvary, Jesus was hung on a cross between two thieves; two thieves who were guilty of their crime. One of the thieves turned to Jesus and said to him, "Lord, remember me when you enter your kingdom." 'Jesus said to him, "Today you will be with me in paradise." 'The thief, like the Roman guard who witnessed the conversation, knew that Jesus was indeed the Son of God. He knew that acknowledging this was the only way his soul would be saved. Jakov, my dear Jakov, even now as death is knocking at the door, Jesus extends the same invitation to you.'

Grigor thought again to Apollos' death at the museum and how he had looked so alive in death. How he had looked so contented, like he had just fallen asleep. The words of the Pastor reminded him that this was the reason why; it was because Apollos truly believed that he was going to be with Jesus forever and ever. Grigor suddenly remembered a word that Apollos often used, "mercy" and how he always prayed for God to have mercy. Grigor knew in his heart and soul that it was God's mercy that had allowed his dear Jakov to hear these words of eternal life in Mother Tongue, before he too fell asleep.

17

Stephen sat at his desk in his building. The transparent glass that surrounded him ensured his view of the city below. He opened his bottom desk drawer and retrieved the death notice concerning Jakov, the retired Mayor of his hometown. He sat and stared blankly at the words, wondering who from his hometown would have placed the article in the *Global Times*. 'Not Grigor,' he surmised, wondering if Grigor still detested Global as much as he did when they were teenagers.

He walked over to his filing cabinet, reached deep inside and lifted out Apollos' treasure chest. He unlocked it and placed the obituary alongside the Global newspaper cuttings of the missing person notices that Jakov had placed concerning Nastan Popov. Stephen had read the heartfelt pleas that Jakov had placed a number of years ago, but had chosen to ignore them. He'd ignored his requests to get in touch, to come home, to let him know that he was okay, that he was prospering.

Stephen had been tempted; he had been intrigued to know why the Mayor had swallowed his pride and placed the notices in a Global language newspaper. Stephen knew this went against everything he had stood for. He felt bemused by the irony that the *Global Times* seemed to be the oracle of news from his hometown. 'Perhaps his view had changed in later years?' he thought, wondering if maybe the Mayor had opened his mind to Global. The Mayor hadn't, of course, opened his mind to Global or named himself as the enquirer in the missing person notices; that would have been too dangerous, too liberal. But Stephen had known it was him. He looked once more at Jakov's obituary, realising that it was now too late to have regrets about any reconciliation that may have taken place.

Stephen stepped out onto the balcony of his building and stood by the balustrades. They were situated on a higher raised platform, which enabled him to gaze below from the top-most vantage point. Before he had acquired this building he hadn't considered heights; or whether he feared them or not. But living in the tallest building in the city had taught him something new about himself. He had learnt that he loved heights. He had learnt that he loved the woozy feeling he had each time he stepped out onto his balcony. He loved the dizziness he felt when he stepped up even higher and stood by the balustrades, peering down to observe the people below.

He revelled that the people below did not know they were being watched by him. They looked minute, unreal; whilst he felt so big, so alive. He felt that if he jumped, he would be able to swoop down, like a condor and scoop up a group of people, place them on his huge wings and fly them back up to his balcony. He would set them down safely and they would be in awe of him. They would be in admiration of his greatness. They would be amazed and wonder how he was able to accomplish such a thing. He would invite them to watch the people down below and then he would return them to their everyday lives. He would transport them back, on his huge wings and they would stand and stare in wonder as he soared above them and then disappeared out of sight.

Stephen had accomplished a great deal since leaving his hometown at just fourteen years of age to study at the Global International School. One of his biggest accomplishments was the acquisition of his listed building. When he'd first moved to Global City, as he liked to call it, just over three years ago, he had seen the building soaring above the other structures. He had ignored the demolition signs outside and wandered in, like an excited child, imagining how it used to look. Imagining how magnificent it could look, once more. Imagining how amazing it would be to live on the top floor.

'There will need to be a lift of course,' he had thought daydreaming, 'a lift on the outside of the building, with transparent glass. But it won't operate like a normal lift that hurries speedily from floor to floor. This lift will be more of an observational tool. It will function slowly and it will stop when I want it to stop so I can observe the city and the people for as long as I want. It will have to be a private lift of course, accessible only by me. It will have state of the art technology, like the rest of the building. It will be the most secure building in the city and have the most trustworthy employees, as my plans for Global domination in Global City will need to remain covert until the time is ready to unveil my new legislation concerning Global Standard to the world,' he had thought methodically.

'I will rename this city "Global City" because it will be the epicentre of Global Standard. This is where my plans for Global Standard domination will begin.'

He had carried on with his imaginary power trip, 'I will rename this country, "Global Motherland". The other countries where Global is an official first language will adopt Global Standard, which will supersede the corrupt version of the language they have been speaking for so long. Those countries will also be renamed as Global Sub Motherland 1, 2, 3 and 4. Each country will have a Sub City which, in line with Global City, will be epicentres for Global Standard.'

Stephen had travelled extensively throughout Global Motherland and the Sub Motherlands, as he called them. He was appalled by the standard of Global in countries in which it was a first language. Spelling variations, incoherent accents and so forth; Global City wasn't without its own language issues either. The standard of Global in all these regions was cause for concern. In Global City, which should set the precedent for all official Global speaking countries, the standard was inexcusable. But Stephen's future plans for a one world language, namely Global Standard, would resolve all current and future language problems in all these areas and eventually on a world-wide scale. He would be the one to standardise Global, which meant, one version, one spelling system and one standard pronunciation. There would be a Global Standard Language Test, which would have to be sat by anyone wishing to have Global citizen status. Once people passed, they would be tested monthly to ensure they were not slipping back into colloquial laziness. Some of the Global dialects he had heard on his travels had left him speechless. He couldn't bear the sloppiness of the current use of Global. He would ensure that it would be uniform across the globe according to HIS law – Stephen's LAW.

In the past his vision for standardising Global had seemed like such an unattainable dream. 'I will never afford such a building,' he had thought, 'even with Apollos' money. How will I ever move my ideas forward? How will I revive my father's plans for Global replacing Mother Tongue? How will I ensure Global Standard becomes the law and eventually replaces all Mother Tongue languages, from the most widely spoken to the most indigenous?' he had thought despondently.

When he had moved to the city, he was so full of zeal, so full of self-determination. But the city was a big, lonely place. Stephen hadn't anticipated how his self-confidence would be zapped from his very being in such a short time. But, he wanted to stay in this city – in Global City.

He needed to stay. But the harsh reality was that he was nobody in a city of somebodies. Even the money that Apollos had left him didn't seem so much now. He had used a substantial amount of his inheritance to fund his travelling. Moreover, when he had exchanged it into unfamiliar currencies it had seemed worthless, like confetti, blown aimlessly away by the wind.

The money he had left, he had used wisely. If he had stayed in his own country, if he had stayed in his hometown he would be rich by local standards. But out of his zone, he was just a mediocre person with dreams and ambitions, the same as everyone else living in the city. For the first time in a long time, Stephen had felt a sense of despair about his plans. He had stood in awe of this magnificent building, in this magnificent city, feeling frustrated that his father's vision would never come to fruition.

But his situation had changed, quite unexpectedly.

'Great panoramic view,' a stranger's voice had said behind him. Stephen had been startled and had turned around to see who it was speaking. He felt for sure he was in trouble because he had ignored the demolition signs.

'Don't turn around,' the stranger had continued, 'just admire the view. Best view in the city. You have good taste.'

Curiously, though, Stephen had turned around but couldn't see anyone. He had wondered if he was dreaming.

'Grand ambitions can sometimes be our downfall,' the voice carried on from a different direction.

'I shouldn't he here,' Stephen apologised, 'I'll leave.'

'Why leave? No one but me knows you are here. Stay and admire the view, Stephen.'

Stephen had been unnerved. He had only been in the city a few weeks. How could anyone know his name?

'Who are you?' Stephen asked, quizzically. 'Did you follow me in here? Is this your building?'

'No Stephen. I did not need to follow you. I know all about you and your plans for Global Standard domination. I know all about your father, Stephen, and how his life was tragically cut short before he had a chance to make a name for himself; before he had a chance to create his legacy for you. I know how eager you are to revive his work. I know how eager you are to take Global Standard to the ends of the earth and create a common language that can be used by everyone. I agree with you. Languages are so over rated. Languages are so yesterday. The world has moved on since Babel. The world hasn't got time to communicate in thousands of different tongues anymore. What it needs is *one* common language. I agree with your plans. I think they make perfect sense.'

'But how do you know all this about me? Are you from my hometown? Has Grigor sent you?'

'Grigor, no,' sniggered the stranger. 'He doesn't agree with you or Global. While you've been busy moving on with your future, Grigor has been busy staying in the past. Grigor is a hindrance. There are many Grigor's who will get in the way of your work, but with my help we can ensure Global becomes just that. I believe in your vision. I believe that Global Standard is the future. I believe it has immeasurable benefits for world peace, for empowering the impoverished, for drawing a close to the world's debt problems, for ending world poverty and for uniting the whole world, like one enormous, happy family. But most of all, I believe in you. I believe you can do it. It could start right here, in this building. Just think "Global Standard to the World Headquarters" could be where we are standing right now.'

'Global Standard to the World Headquarters,' Stephen repeated, transfixed.

'You are still young. You haven't acquired enough wealth to purchase a building like this. I know Apollos left you a trust, but that's not even pocket money for what you need to achieve your set purpose. Plus, you've already spent a lot travelling. But that's okay. You had to travel. You had to research the current status of Global in the world. How else could you move forward? Knowledge is the key to everything Stephen.'

'Look around and below you,' the stranger continued in a soothing, placating voice. 'All of this could be yours. I am able to give all of this to you.'

Stephen became uneasy again. He felt as if he'd already had this conversation before. Somehow the whole scene was familiar to him, but, paradoxically, it wasn't himself in the scene. It was someone else.

Someone that he couldn't recall. He didn't know whether he had dreamt this moment before.

Stephen laughed nervously. How could this be happening? How could someone he had never even met before know anything about his plans for Global Standard when he had never shared them? How could a complete stranger be offering him such an opportunity?

'You are nearly ready Stephen. A few more years research into the technology you are creating. A few more years to perfect your plans; just think how credible your name, Stephen Law, will be in this city, in "Global City" as you *would* like to call it. Just think how much status and power acquiring a building like this would afford you.'

Status and power; Stephen loved those two words. He knew he should have felt uncomfortable that this stranger knew about his nickname for the city and about the technology on which he had been secretly working. But there was something very alluring about this invisible presence. Even though Stephen could not see, only hear him, there was an exciting, powerful aura to which he felt inexplicably drawn.

'I have the deeds in my hands. All you have to say is "yes" and the building can be yours. It can be yours this very day.'

Stephen had burbled enthusiastically, 'Could we meet first; face to face, I'd love to tell you more about my plans for Global Standard.'

The enticing aura Stephen felt quickly turned to a cold, prickly sensation. He stood, as if glued to the spot. He felt a chill, as if someone was brushing past him, but nobody was there. He looked around and for a split second thought he could see someone's reflection in a section of broken glass on an outer wall. The reflection was a whole body reflection of someone dressed in a black suit. He couldn't see his face but he thought he saw the person holding a walking stick in his left hand.

'Papa, is that you?' Stephen ventured.

'Papa,' he shouted again. He had begun to shake uncontrollably, unable to move. The strong sunlight that had engulfed the derelict edifice turned to pitch black. Stephen forced his body into life. He wanted to get out of the building. He was only able to move slowly, his limbs felt so weak he thought he would collapse.

He made his way to the stairwell. At the top of the concrete steps was an old crate. He saw a plastic wallet glistening on top of it. He picked it up and couldn't believe his eyes. It was the deeds of ownership to the building. The deeds were in his name, in his new name, Stephen Law. He ran desperately back to his pitiful bedsit unsure what had just happened. He felt, an awful eeriness had engulfed his whole body.

But this unwelcome sensation soon dissipated as Stephen realised that if his plans for Global Standard were to succeed then he would be a fool not to accept this stranger's offer. For he had made his own sacrifices over the years. Yes, he had travelled but as the invisible stranger had already pointed out, that was a research trip; that was a necessity. Since he had moved to Global City he had lived like a pauper, ensuring that he would use what was left of Apollos' money wisely. If he had stayed at home he could have lived well, but his plans were not for material gain. His plans were to make a name for himself, to revive his father's legacy in the name of Global; to gain status and power in the name of Global. He had used his inheritance to advance his knowledge of both Global and technology. After all, it was these two areas in which his father had been involved. It was these two areas which his father saw as key to the success of replacing Mother Tongue.

The following day, Stephen returned to the site not knowing if the stranger would be there – unaware of what the stranger expected from him in return for the gift of the building. Stephen had indeed returned, but had not anticipated the scene before him.

The building was a hive of activity. Builders, carpenters, plumbers – every tradesman Stephen had ever seen was there. There were a few men in suits too, walking around with plans in their hands, giving orders to the workmen, one of whom noticed Stephen standing gaping.

'Can I help you? Are you here to work? What trade are you?' the man bellowed dismissively. Stephen had not answered. 'Do you speak Global?' he had asked Stephen slowly, as if he was addressing an uneducated person. 'Quickly, what is your name so I can tick you off my list,' he reiterated, losing patience. 'The new owner will be along soon and we have been told that Mr Law is a hard taskmaster. He will want to know everything, down to the tiniest detail. Stop gaping man. What is your name man so I can tick you off my list?'

'Do I speak Global?' Stephen mused, seeing the irony.

'What is my name?' he responded, softly.

'Global, that's good,' the suit responded in a colloquial Global dialect. 'Yes, your name man?'

'My name is …' Stephen replied, his voice becoming stronger.

'Yes? Stop dithering man … what is your name …?'

'My name ... you want to know my name,' said Stephen, infuriated by the attitude of this man and his equally awful version of Global.

Stephen said authoritatively, 'My name is Stephen Law, the taskmaster as you so rightly referred to me. I am the owner of this building and for the time being, until this job is finished, your employer.'

'Mr Law, sir. My apologies. I wasn't expecting you ...'

'*You* can start by getting me up to speed. I want lists. I want to know the names of everyone working for me; from the labourers to the architects. I want to see the blueprints. I want to see it all.'

'Yes sir. My apologies once again.' The change from colloquial Global to business Global was quite startling.

'Right away Mr Law,' said the suit, briskly.

Stephen looked up, admiring his building.

He had looked up to the highest point and saw the balcony and balustrades which looked like they would fall on someone's head at any moment.'

'See that balcony and those balustrades,' he motioned.

'Yes sir.'

'Do what you need to secure them.'

'Yes sir. Immediately, sir.'

Stephen looked up to the balcony once more. The sun was glinting in his eyes.

He blocked out the sun by placing his right hand over his right eye. He noticed someone standing on the balcony. A man wearing a black suit and a red paisley tie, the same tie that Apollos wore to church every Sunday. Stephen noticed that he had a walking stick in his left hand. The invisible stranger looked down, towards Stephen, but Stephen was still unable to see his face.

'Papa,' Stephen thought emotionally. 'I knew you'd be back to watch over me. I knew you'd change your mind about Babel.'

18

The cooing of two mourning doves perched on those very same balustrades broke into Stephen's reverie. He looked once more at the obituary and missing person notices. There was something odd about them. A few words, even though they were written in Global, didn't seem to fit with the rest of the Global words. They seemed like an anomaly on the page.

Then quite suddenly, he thought he saw the letters on the obituary and missing person notices, floating away. He blinked a few times to moisten his eyes. He peered down again and the documents were completely blank; all the words had disappeared. He rubbed his eyes then looked once more. As he sat dumbfounded, letters appeared in mid-air from nowhere. The letters floated down calmly, found their rightful position and imprinted themselves boldly on the sheets. Then, the letters and words started to change shape; to change order. As Stephen looked on in disbelief, the letters on the notices stopped moving. Then, again out of nowhere, symbols appeared. These symbols were familiar to him, even though he couldn't remember where he had seen them before. The symbols deposited themselves above certain letters.

Little by little, the notices began to fill up with new letters, words and signs. Stephen's mind went back to his first day at the International School when he had imagined the boys from the lake were morphing into

Apollos and Grigor. Of course, he'd put that episode down to losing Apollos. But this seemed supernatural in comparison. Stephen watched transfixed. He picked up the notices and shook them hoping the words would float away once more, but nothing happened. In desperation he crumpled them until the words were illegible. But before his very eyes, the notices became smooth again and were still being filled with new letters, words and symbols.

One symbol imprinted itself above the second and fifth letters of a word – it looked like a squiggle. The same symbol appeared above the second letter of another word. It was then that Stephen realised what he was looking at. It was then his memory of his home town came flooding back. It was then he realised he was looking at his old name, Nastan Popov in his *own* Mother Tongue. It was then he realised he was looking at Jakov's name. He hadn't read or spoken his Mother Tongue for over ten years. He'd had no need to speak or read it. He had eradicated all traces of it from his name, accent, mind, tongue and soul. He didn't want to see it now. He didn't want his Mother Tongue forced upon him. He didn't need any language reminders from the past.

He picked up the notices and fed them through the shredder. He watched as the words disintegrated before his eyes. He watched, relieved that he hadn't allowed his brain to fully activate its Mother Tongue area. Mother Tongue played no part in his life because, just like Jakov, his language was dead. Stephen decided that he would make a new law concerning nomenclature. He decided that all Mother Tongue names would adopt a Global Standard version. There would be no trace of a person's culture or heritage identifiable by their name.

He had changed his name. He was impossible to trace. He couldn't believe how he hadn't thought of it sooner. But of course, what Stephen failed to realise is that you can change your name but unless you change your eyes, mouth, skin colour and memories, no amount of denouncing your Mother Tongue will alter the essence of your being.

In addition to using his power and status within Global City to persuade the government about the benefits of a "standardised" Global language throughout the districts and eventually the world, Stephen decided he would also introduce them to the benefits of standardised names. There would be no room for dialects not in speech, written form or names. He would be the one to convince the World's Leaders.

19

Three years later …

“Global Protocol Committee (GPC) Headquarters, Global City, Global Motherland”

‘The version that will become compulsory in all official Global speaking countries is the original variety of language, as spoken here in Global Motherland. The type spoken in the Sub Motherlands will become as obsolete as the ark itself,’ said Stephen commandingly.

Rod, the Sub Leader of the Global Protocol Committee (GPC) Sub Motherland 1, rolled his eyes at the other Sub Leaders sat around the conference table at the GPC Headquarters. He wouldn’t dare roll his eyes at Mr Law in person, but he was certain that even Mr Law couldn’t see through the conference phone. ‘Who is this Stephen Law anyway?’ Rod pondered, wondering how he had attained so much power, status and influence over the GPC Directors in such a short time. Rod didn’t understand why Mr Law would go to the trouble and expense of flying the Sub Leaders from their regions to meet at the GPC Headquarters in Global City and yet not meet them in person. He couldn’t comprehend why he would conduct a meeting via a conference call when he could have sat in the same room.

Out of the Sub Leaders, Rod was the newest recruit to the GPC, though the others had worked there for some time in menial roles. But now it would seem that out of nowhere they were being ordered to sign their names to a legislation that had the GPC's full support. Rod wondered why they were needed at all when Stephen Law seemed like the type of man who would not be told "no". Rod pondered what the other Sub Leaders really thought about the situation. He had heard about corporate corruption and people signing their name to a policy for a "returned favour". Rod looked around the room once again wondering why these ordinary people, him included, had received promotion to Sub Leaders just days before this treaty was to be signed. Something felt very wrong.

Stephen continued, 'To clear up any misunderstandings about spelling variations, the omission of letters from words, etc. the GPC are devising a dossier which will outline the linguistic rules of Global Standard. This will ensure that all Global citizens have clear guidelines and are able to follow the new language protocol. Global will be renamed Global Standard. The colloquial vernacular that is currently spoken in the Sub Motherlands will be replaced with Global Standard as of the twenty first of August. All resources that are currently produced in Global, that is, educational, civil, legal and so on will be sent to Global Standard to the World Headquarters for archiving in a vault that I have already prepared. The GPC, in conjunction with my company, GSW will be offering free Global Standard language lessons to all citizens in the Sub Motherlands in preparation for the launch date.' Rod rolled his eyes again as Mr Law couldn't make it any clearer which was the superior country. 'Of course, citizens within Motherland do not need language lessons because their Global is already faultless,' thought Rod, miffed.

'The decision has been made. The GPC's and GSW's mission statement will be "ONE LANGUAGE, ONE VERSION, ONE VISION".' Stephen continued, 'Leaders of the Sub Motherlands, you have twenty-four hours to sign the treaty or be left behind. There are many ambitious people within the GPC who are more than willing to sign and are ready to take your place if you refuse. I have a call waiting, goodbye,' finished Stephen, abruptly, looking at his watch. He did not like talking into the telephone for more than a few minutes.

'There you have it,' said Rod, flippantly. 'Sign or be left behind. You heard the man; Mr Stephen Law is now THE law on all things Global. Or should I say Global Standard.' Rod looked down at the GSW treaty that was endorsed by the GPC. He picked up his pen and hovered hesitantly over the blank space where his signature should reside.

'I'll sign first if it will make you feel better,' said Leo, Sub Leader 4.

'Be my guest,' said Rod, sarcastically, handing him the relevant treaty, knowing that Leo's country stood to gain the most. It had the largest indigenous population out of all the countries involved with GSW and the GPC. His government had been trying to phase out regional dialects for centuries so it was no wonder that he wanted to be the first to sign. Rod concluded that Leo had been paid handsomely to sign and not ask any questions about the implications of Global Standard.

Rod watched as Leo hastily signed the treaty. Sub Leaders 2 and 3 pulled out pens from their pockets as if they were preparing for a duel.

'Who's next?' asked Rod, as he handed out the other treaties, one for each country. Sub Leaders 2 and 3 signed as hastily as Leo had done leaving all but Rod, pen in hand, hovering again. Leo made a weird sound with his throat, which Rod took as his cue to hurry up. Rod put his pen down on the signature line, pressed down on the nib and very slowly began to write the first letter of his name, wondering why signing it felt so wrong. He wondered whether, when his reward came, signing the treaty would still feel so wrong.

'I'll phone Mr Law to let him know it's done,' said Leo, smiling like an excited child on Christmas morning.

'Mr Law, sir, I have Sub Leader 4 on the line for you,' said Joan, waiting on his instruction.

'Connect him,' said Stephen.

'Mr Law, sir,' began Leo, 'I am very pleased to tell you that all the leaders have signed their treaties in favour of Global Standard. The electronic copies will be with you within the hour. I would like to thank you for this opportunity, sir, and would like to reassure you …'

'Thank you,' responded Stephen brusquely, 'I have a call waiting, goodbye.' Stephen sat back and allowed silent tears to flow. He hadn't felt emotion like this since his first night at the International School; the night he had cried enough tears to fill his town lake, the very night he had found out about his father's vision for Global. He composed himself, glad of the privacy he had from the one-way glass. No one could ever see him display emotion.

He looked through the glass to see Joan, his secretary, sitting at her desk, waiting on his command as usual; knowing that she wouldn't leave until he had given her permission. Joan had been his secretary for three years now; a single woman in her mid-twenties, who was more than happy to wait upon Stephen's instructions, day after day. She had been involved with GSW since its inception. Stephen had methodically vetted hundreds of job applications. He had personally hand-picked Joan. There had been no interview, no discussion, just a job offer with an excellent salary. In return, she was expected to work long hours, which ordinarily meant twelve-hour days.

At first, Joan found his impersonal manner a little odd but, as money talks and she was having difficulty securing a permanent job in a city where there was a surplus of secretaries, it really did seem too good to be true.

Three years on and Mr Law had proved to be a trustworthy employer. He had only asked of Joan what her contract stated. She felt privileged that she had seen the rise of Mr Law's company, GSW, from just three employees to over three hundred. Yet, during its rise, Mr Law had never taken a back seat and was still the head of every section of his company. He knew the names of all his employees. He knew where they lived, all about their families and how much he was paying them. He knew how many days they'd had off sick and the reason why. Mr Law was a fair employer who expected excellence in every detail. If an employee didn't like Mr Law's business practices, then they should leave. People knew that Mr Law expected a great deal, but he also rewarded handsomely, paying superb salaries, private healthcare (so he was the first to know about all his workers' possible sicknesses) and many benefits for employees in his "top 10". The "top 10" didn't have anything to do with position in the company. The "top 10" were rewarded for attributes, such as attitude, commitment to work, loyalty to GSW. One of the cleaners, Eva, couldn't believe it when she was awarded a brand new car.

Mr Law was idiosyncratic, there was no question about that, but he was also fair. Joan had concluded some time ago that despite his quirks Mr Law's, offhanded demeanour was always consistent and that, in a weird way, made her feel comfortable. She had worked enough temporary jobs to know that there was nowhere else she would rather be.

There were a number of employees that outwardly hated Mr Law and criticised his methods. But criticising him was not acceptable behaviour from a GSW employee. If someone didn't turn up for work, if someone just arbitrarily left, then the situation and employee was said to have been "handled". It always induced an odd mixture of trepidation and loyalty amongst the employees. People knew that whatever they were feeling, it was not wise to voice their opinion within the building.

One employee, after being "handled" turned up at GSW with a banner insisting that GSW employees are Microchipped; that their thoughts, comments and actions are illegally being tapped. Sadly, that employee was sent away to the GSW's hospital, on the advice of the "company" doctor. Nobody mentions that day or the employee anymore.

But Joan couldn't hate Mr Law. She couldn't work for someone she hated. Neither did she believe she had been microchipped. She didn't take it personally when Mr Law never returned a 'good morning' or 'thank you' or 'you have a good evening too'. The distant, professional relationship they had, suited her needs perfectly. She knew nothing about her employer. She didn't even know how he liked his coffee; or even if he liked coffee *or* tea. She had no idea what he ate for lunch or even if he ate lunch. He never asked her to run errands, collect his laundry or buy a present for his wife or children because he had forgotten or hadn't had time. It really was quite an exceptional employer-employee relationship, one that her friends couldn't figure out. They were secretaries too and were forever picking up dry cleaning and buying forgotten presents and paying for and booking this and that with the company credit card. They couldn't understand how she could be his secretary and not know a single detail about his life, professionally or personally. But Joan didn't know and she didn't care that she didn't know. It made her job a lot easier.

Like all GSW employees, she had signed a confidentiality agreement, which meant that she could not discuss any aspect of her job or the projects in which GSW was involved. She knew that Mr Law only allowed her to see things that he deemed suitable for her eyes. She knew there was a lot more that went on without her knowledge. But, she did not ask any questions. If Mr Law thought she needed to know, then she would. In Joan's eyes she had the perfect job.

Moreover, Joan was enthralled by the mystery that surrounded her employer. She was fascinated by his appearance. His eyes, which one day looked blue and the next day green; that he never was tired or ill; that his suits seemed new every day and that he never needed a haircut. She was in awe of his decisiveness and the fact that people literally quaked in their boots when he had reason to question them. She was bemused that they would rather quake than work for someone else. Joan's only ambition was to have a look inside the briefcase that never left his side. It was more like a small suitcase that he pulled behind him everywhere he went. Even if he just left his desk to go to his private lift, the briefcase trailed behind him. But, the thought of peering into his "Pandora's Box" actually made Joan tremble. She couldn't foresee the day that Mr Law would willingly say to her, 'Go on Joan. It's okay; you can have a look inside.'

She was intrigued that even though he was the epitome of Global, sometimes, though not very often, there seemed to be a hint of another nationality hidden within his flawless demeanour. She had noticed it a lot more over the last few weeks, especially since he'd had a privacy communication device built into her headset. This was an intimate method of communication that he had chosen, to ensure that only she could hear his instructions. It was this intimacy that had enabled Joan to detect the anomaly in his accent. His Global, perfect as it was, at times, seemed to stop mid-sentence, as if he was making sure that his words were perfectly formed before he carried on speaking.

At times, Stephen's off-guard accent reminded Joan of how her grandmother, Aphia Joan (after whom Joan was named) had sounded when she tried to learn Global in the years before she died. For someone of her generation, Joan's grandmother's openness to Global had been remarkable. Her grandmother had not seen it as a threat to their culture or family life. Quite the contrary. She had seen it as progress, as a means to an end until the next world language came along, as they so often did. She hadn't wanted to be like the other grandparents of her generation who could and would not communicate with their grandchildren in Global because they were too stubborn to learn a new language. Joan took solace in the thought that Mr Law would have approved of her grandmother.

Joan thought fondly back to her home and the parents she left behind. She owed her place in Global City to her grandmother. She had left Joan all she had to ensure she had every opportunity to make a name for herself in the new Global world. Joan knew that her grandmother would have been ecstatic that she was working for a man like Mr Law, whose vision for Global was limitless.

Aphia's view of Global in her town had sparked controversy, as she had stood up against the Mayor in a public meeting in favour of Global replacing their Mother Tongue. That had been a sad day for their town because one of the oldest men in their community had had a heart attack and died in that very meeting. Joan couldn't remember his name. It seemed like such a long time ago. She wiped a tear that had formed on her cheek. It didn't want to trickle away. Thinking of her home town transported Joan back to another world: memories of childhood; swimming in the lake; picking oranges from the trees, the closeness of the community, the security of being known by everyone in the town, cherished memories of her parents, grandparents and sisters. She had known she was dissimilar to the rest of her family. She had always wanted to leave. She had always had a different plan for her life. How grateful she was that her parents were supportive and encouraging and that they didn't see her desire to leave as a curse on their family ties. It had made all the difference knowing that she had their blessing.

Three years later and Joan felt that she had achieved her goal to make her family proud. She sent regular updates and money, which her parents returned to her each time. But, as proud as Joan's parents were of her achievements, each time they spoke to her, or "virtual timed" they could see how "Globalised" she had become. She still had traces of her childhood face, but her accent, her aura, her ability to communicate with them in their Mother Tongue was slowly diminishing. Joan's mother tried to hide her emotions, but she knew deep down that her own daughter belonged to the Global Wave generation. When Joan had left, not many children were doing so. But lately, within the last few months, there was a Global outpouring sweeping across their land and other countries across the globe. What they hadn't anticipated was that their own daughter would be playing an instrumental role in the spread of Global. What Joan didn't know was that since she had left, things had dramatically changed in her hometown. But, her family spared her from the details. All they cared about was that she was okay, that she was prospering and that she was fulfilling her Global ambitions. Everything else was out of their control.

'You may leave,' Stephen instructed Joan through her headpiece, catching her unaware for the first time ever.

'Thank you, Mr Law. Have a good evening sir,' she replied dutifully, hoping he hadn't spotted her moment of sadness, but knowing that he noticed everything. The one-way glass, looking out from Mr Law's office, usually kept her completely focused, as she never knew when he was watching. In three years, she had never allowed herself to lose that edge and she had to make sure she never let it happen again.

Stephen watched Joan as she collected her belongings, in the same methodical manner that she did every night. He sat staring at her through his one-way glass as she walked effortlessly away, her coat draped over her left arm and her handbag dangling over her right wrist. 'Joan,' he said out loud, not realising he had done so. 'Joan,' he said again with a question in his voice. He wondered why she had such an old name. She hadn't recorded any others on her job application but he couldn't help thinking that Joan was not her christian name. It just seemed so out of place for someone so… someone so … well it just didn't suit her at all.

Joan smiled warmly at Frank, the security guard. He had been riding the lifts within the building for the same time that she had been sitting at her desk. She stood front facing, like a mannequin as the lift doors closed and her and Frank chatted away oblivious to Stephen's observations of them. Like her, Frank was part of the furniture; even though he had probably seen less of Mr Law over the last two years. Since Stephen's penthouse had been completed, which was on the top floor of the building; he had installed another lift to which only he had access. The lift was situated in his office which made it possible for him to visit any part of the building without being detected. If he needed to leave the building, the lift also took him to the lower ground floor where his car was parked. He could come and go unnoticed without the assistance of Frank. Frank was security guard for the building, not for Stephen. Not that there was a remote chance of anyone who didn't have appropriate access getting into GSW headquarters. It had the most advanced biometric entry system in the world. It was more difficult to get into GSW headquarters than to gain entry into some of the most exclusive diamond vaults in the world.

Stephen scanned his right index finger facing upwards across the biometric device, which was hidden under his desk. This enabled him to "lock down" the building at the end of each day. To unlock the building, phone lines, computers, internet connections and filing cabinets, he had to repeat the process with his left index finger.

He stared unblinkingly into the biometric machine that worked the lift. The doors opened, inviting him in. He never tired of the journey home. As he'd envisaged, his private lift was on the outside of the building, with clear glass, so he could admire the view of Global City. It wasn't officially "Global City" just yet, even though it was already referred to as this by his employees. But with the imminent signing of the treaties by the leaders of the Sub Motherlands, the official launch of Global Standard would precede forthwith – ushering in the name change to "Global City".

As Stephen stood in his lift, which was slowly creeping upwards, surveying the view of his city, he clutched the treaties proudly to his chest. Phase 1 of his plan was nearly complete. Over the next two years, within Global Motherland and the Sub Motherlands, Global in its colloquial form, would be phased-out within all spheres of education, technology, business administration, printed materials, government and the law courts. Global Standard would take its place. Once this had been achieved, then it would be time for Phase 2 – the termination of all Mother Tongue languages, everywhere across the world.

Stephen's technology that the invisible stranger had known about, the technology that was being pioneered within the confines of a "secret room" at GSW, would then be unveiled to the planet. A hand-held, solar powered, translation device, that will be capable of translating every Mother Tongue spoken throughout the world into Global Standard would be freely and easily available. This device would ensure that all people would be able to communicate in one common language – Global Standard. As for the non-conformists within Global and the Sub Motherlands, as for the language traitors who dared to question his vision, it was only a matter of time before they would be forcibly removed back to their Mother Tongue countries. Eventually, Global Standard would become the official language in all countries, all over the world.

Stephen smiled to himself at the thought of there being no prospects for people unless they became Global citizens and renounced their Mother Tongue in favour of Global Standard.

20

Stephen woke to the familiar cooing noise of the two mourning doves that had made his balcony their home. He stood perfectly still, with his left arm outstretched. The seeds for the mourning doves formed a small pile in the palm of his left hand. He started to whistle his usual call, knowing that within minutes they would succumb, unable to resist the ready-made breakfast for which they didn't have to forage.

As the doves fed from his hand, Stephen thought contentedly about the signed treaties that he was planning to courier to the GPC that morning. These papers endorsed his blueprint for moving Global Standard forward. The joy he felt knowing he was emulating his father's original plan for Global replacing Mother Tongue. This was the culmination of the work that he had spent nearly the last twenty years of his life building towards. Stephen closed his eyes and heard his father's voice speaking to him in praise of his accomplishments. 'I am so proud of you Stephen. You have taken my vision and turned it into reality. I am so proud of you.' Stephen opened his eyes not realising that the doves had finished feeding. They were nestling happily in the conifer tree that Stephen had had planted, by the balustrades.

Stephen looked at his wristwatch. The time was 6.30 am. He revelled at this time of year - that it was light early and did not get dark until late. It was these long summer days that gave him a sense of achievement for he literally worked from dawn to dusk.

Stephen picked up his cup and finished the last of his tea. He always ensured he left his penthouse before Eva the cleaner came to perform her daily duties. There were only so many platitudes of gratitude he could take. He picked up the treaties, enthused about the day ahead. As he entered his lift, he opened the treaty for Sub Motherland 1. The official GPC stamp visible on every page, endorsing his work, filled him with delight. As he turned to the last page he was confused as he did not recognise the named signatory. He felt puzzled, as he tried to decipher the name, which should have read Rod Jones. But instead the named signatory was Nimrod Nazareth. 'Nimrod Nazareth,' he said out loud, alone in his lift. 'Nimrod Nazareth,' he repeated again, even louder, hitting the speed button, causing the lift to almost fall to his office floor. 'Is this some kind of joke?' he mused. 'Is this some kind of trickery by a language traitor within the GPC?' he thought furiously, quizzically pondering why a GPC Sub Leader had a Mother Tongue Christian and surname. 'This is not acceptable. This is not acceptable!' he reiterated, hurrying out of his lift.

'Get me Sub Motherland Leader 1 on the phone immediately,' he bellowed at Joan, causing her ears to ache. He did not even realise or appreciate that she was an hour early for work.

'Yes sir,' she responded, unquestioningly.

'Connecting you,' said Joan to Rod whose hands were clammy with anxiety. Rod knew it was barely dawn in Global Motherland. He knew Mr Law was an early starter but wasn't aware that Joan kept the same hours as her employer. He had never been summoned by

Mr Law before. He wondered if it was the rolling of his eyes in the telephone conference. Or the comments he had made about Mr Law being THE LAW. 'He CAN see through the phone line,' Rod thought, anxiously. 'He DOES have the offices bugged, or, worst, we ARE all microchipped!'

'Mr Jones,' began Stephen.

'Yes sir, good morning sir, you're bright and early. It's early afternoon here already in …' said Rod babbling.

'Mr Nimrod Nazareth,' said Stephen.

'Sorry?' responded Rod.

'I have in front of me the signed treaty for your country. However I am a little confused because at no point do I ever recall the GPC informing me they had employed someone with the name Nimrod Nazareth. I am sure I would have remembered someone with such a non-Global name.'

Rod's throat seized up. He was unable to respond.

'Do you know who Nimrod Nazareth is?' queried Stephen again.

Rod couldn't believe he had been so careless. He couldn't believe he had signed the treaty using his birth name. He had been so careful since being employed by the GPC, to ensure that he was the essence of a true Global citizen. His family history, his education, had all geared towards securing employment. When he had been promoted to Sub Motherland Leader 1 after just six months, his family had been so proud of him.

'What have I done?' Rod asked himself, wondering how he would explain to his family why he had been "handled". He looked at the picture of himself with his family that he had as a screensaver on his mini pc. He hadn't been able to delete the photographs even though he knew they posed a risk to his true identity. After all, he was the Sub Leader, so no one ever had access to his mini pc. He forbade it. It was password protected. No one could ever log into it.

Rod's mother's words echoed in his ears, 'You must go to the land of opportunity. You must make a name for yourself. You must do whatever it takes,' her words were forceful as if she wished she were going herself. 'There is nothing here for any of us. Global is the future. You must go to the land of prosperity. You must, for the honour of your relatives. An unmarried man of your age still living at home brings shame upon the family.' So he had gained illegal entry into Sub Motherland 1. His judgement was proved right, for he had prospered and gained the status of Sub Leader to the country, second in line to Global Motherland.

Hundreds of families, who believed that Global was the future (despite legislation to stop its citizens learning the language, because of fear that the younger generation would leave and never return) were spending their life's savings on "closet Global lessons" for their children. Once that child's knowledge of Global was of the relevant standard, families were sending their eldest child, albeit covertly (to ensure their government was unware), to Global and the Sub Motherlands. They were arranging new identities, fake passports and fake Global citizenship. Some children wanted to go, some, like Rod, had no desire for foreign lands, status or opportunity and just wanted to stay at home. Rod had written to his parents. He had lied, telling them he was working at GSW Headquarters within Global Motherland itself. He had reassured them that their life's savings had been well spent. But now it seemed that his carelessness could cost him his job and his family's honour. 'If only they had sent my sister; she would have been a better choice. If only they had had the foresight to send her instead,' thought Rod, wearily.

'Are you Nimrod Nazareth?' Stephen barked at him down the telephone.

'Yes sir,' he responded compliantly.

'Then we need to talk, face to face. I'll send the GSW helicopter for you immediately.'

Stephen hung up the phone. He was infuriated with himself. He was irate with the GPC. He was in disbelief that the GPC had given a Mother Tongue nobody a position of authority. 'The only people who will gain employment within my company or the GPC are people with a pure Global heritage; people whose first and only language is Global. People who have a passion and vision for Global Standard being the *only* spoken language throughout the world. Nimrod Nazareth and his type have no place in GSW or the GPC. When he arrives here he will renounce his Mother Tongue in favour of Global Standard or bear the consequences,' thought Stephen, callously.

Stephen watched on the monitor as Joan exited the building at the end of her working day. She was unaware that Stephen had sat in the same position since arriving in his office, tracking the GSW helicopter on which the language traitor, Nimrod Nazareth was travelling. He scanned his right index finger across the biometric machine and "locked down" the whole building. He waited, unwilling to move until Nimrod Nazareth sat facing him, ready to give an explanation as to how he had gained illegal employment within his company. He wanted to know: how many more "illegals", how many more "language traitors" were there in GSW and the

GPC? Once he knew, he would decide how to resolve the situation.

21

Joan arrived at work to find her desk overflowing with personnel files. She opened her internal email on her computer and discovered an urgent message from Mr Law, which explained her task. She noticed that he had also copied the Director of the GPC into the email, asking him to ensure that the same task was carried out at the GPC. She looked over to his office but the one-way glass made it impossible to know if he was there. She assumed he was, so began "the task of utmost urgency" as he had put it. Oddly, there were two dirty cups on her desk which she took to the kitchen and placed in the sink. She picked up the cups and smelt the residue that had formed a circular stain at the bottom of each cup. One smelt of coffee and the other of tea. She was extremely puzzled about who could possibly have been drinking out of the cups. She was also vexed as to who would have had the audacity to place them on her desk. Everyone knew about the "no liquids policy" which forbade drinks of any kind in the building because of the damage spillage could cause to the technology. Joan left the cups in the sink assuming that they had been used by two males, because there were no lipstick stains anywhere in sight.

As she was about to leave the kitchen she heard a bell "ding", which signalled that someone was about to exit the lift. She couldn't believe who she saw. Mr Law stepped out of the employee's lift, with a very flustered expression indeed. His complexion looked like he had stood in front of a blow torch and his suit had an odd substance on it, which, if she wasn't mistaken, looked rather similar to ash. In fact, he looked as if he had been trapped in a fire but had just about managed to get out alive. It reminded her of the fire fighter hero films that she had watched when the people who are caught in a fire look dishevelled, suntanned and grubby all at the same time. Joan hid behind the kitchen door, not wanting Mr Law to see her. She really did not know what to say in such a situation. She observed something else that was odd too. He didn't have his briefcase with him. He always had it. 'Why didn't he have it now? Had he lost it? Was it in his office?' she quizzed herself, extremely bothered by its absence. Joan watched as Mr Law approached her desk, knowing that he would notice her bag and her switched on computer. But, in the most unpredictable manner, he walked straight passed her desk to his office, opened his door, went in and closed the door behind him. Joan didn't know what to do. Her heart was racing with uncertainty. After a few seconds, she came out from her hiding place and walked casually back to her desk. She sat down in disbelief at what she had just witnessed. She put on her headphones in case Mr Law was trying to communicate with her but there was silence. She looked at the telecom device on her desk, which indicated that Mr Law was on a call. About thirty minutes passed and he was still on the phone, which Joan thought extremely peculiar. Mr Law didn't like lengthy telephone conversations. If he had to communicate with someone for more than a few minutes then he preferred to use "virtual time". This way, he kept people alert as they never knew when he would contact them.

Joan left her desk, trembling at the thought of knocking on his door. This was not how they did things. If she didn't understand an instruction then she sent him an internal email. In trepidation, she approached his office. She scrunched her fingers and thumb together and then straightened out her index figure to use as the door tapper. But before she had a chance to use it, she noticed that the door was slightly ajar. She stood motionless, not knowing whether to tap, to ease it open a little more or just go back to her desk. She turned her body to the side, closed her left eye and moved her head slowly back and fore trying to get Mr Law's desk in her line of sight. If she could see his desk then she would know if he was there or not. She moved her head slowly to the left and then she saw it – the briefcase, all alone in the middle of the floor. 'Is this my chance?' she thought, in trepidation. 'Is this my opportunity to look in Pandora's Box?' But she still didn't know if Mr Law was in his office. She pushed the door ever so slightly and his desk was now in her sight line. He wasn't sitting there. She felt so relieved. But she still didn't know what to do. 'If he catches me in here without his permission that will be enough to get me dismissed. If he catches me in here looking in his briefcase, I can't imagine what he would do,' she thought slinking back from the door.

As she stood there for what seemed like an age, she heard the familiar sound of the lift bell dinging. But, it wasn't the employee's lift; it was Mr Law's private lift. It was about to open and let him out into his office. Joan couldn't move; she knew she should rush back to her seat but she just couldn't move. She watched as Mr Law came out of his lift, head held high, the personification of perfection. She watched as he retrieved his briefcase and positioned it by his side. She watched as he placed the signed treaties from the Sub Country leaders into a packet that she knew he would ask her to courier to the GPC. She crept slowly backwards away from the door and sat down, relieved that she was back at the safety of her desk. Something about Mr Law's demeanour seemed more odd than usual. He seemed transfixed, robotic even. Something had happened and she wished she knew what.

Joan set about her task, trying to distance herself from the morning's events. She arranged for a courier to collect the treaties and tried to act normally. Nevertheless she had an uneasy feeling that Mr Law had seen her peering through his office door and for some reason chose not to question her. If she was right, that in itself was not right. She returned her attention to the personnel files on her desk. This task was going to be laborious but she would undertake it, without question, as was her duty. She didn't know what had brought about the housekeeping of all these papers, but she suspected it had something to do with Rod Jones, Sub Leader 1.

Joan picked up personnel file number one, perplexed as to why Mr Law wanted the information manually duplicated in such an outdated way. All this information about his employees was already held on computer. She looked at the photograph of the employee, remembering the day that Louise had started working at GSW. She trawled through Louise's personnel file and manually recorded on an A3 sheet of paper (as given to her by Mr Law, with the columns already prepared and enough blank copies to keep her going for months) details pertaining to her: date of birth; place of birth; parents' names; siblings (if applicable); nationality; educational history; employment history; passport number; current residence; previous addresses; eye colour; skin colour; height; weight; marital status; dependants; employee number; first spoken language; any other spoken languages; Global citizenship identity number; date of citizenship; province of citizenship; GLT score; driving licence number and GSW hospital number.

Joan was extremely puzzled and slightly annoyed that she had to hand write duplicate information onto a sheet of paper. Recording data manually was something Mr Law had never previously asked her to do.

There were currently 359 employees at the GSW epicentre in Global City. In addition, there were the linguists working on the translation technology within a secret room that was situated on the Executive Floor. The "secret room" employees were virtually ghosts with whom only Mr Law had any dealings. They had a separate kitchen and toilet area that was only accessible via biometric scanning, as was the secret room itself. Joan saw the linguists from time to time entering and leaving the building. Sometimes, if Joan walked passed the secret room door, as someone was leaving, the babbling of all the different languages in the room was mind-blowing. The secret room was something of an anomaly. It was the strangest of contrasts – no other language except Global was allowed to be spoken throughout the whole of the GSW building, yet in the secret room every Mother Tongue known to man was conversed in and discussed, day after day. Of course, Joan and Stephen were the only people who knew what was going on in the secret room. The other GSW employees referred to it as the "technology room" or the "geek room". It was ironic that the busiest and nosiest room in the whole of the building was the most overlooked by the other GSW employees.

'File number two hundred and sixty-four,' muttered Joan to herself, wondering what exactly it was that Mr Law was looking for. His instruction was to meticulously scrutinise each file and record the information he had requested – a lengthy, but simple, process that could certainly have been delegated to an administration clerk. So far, all the employees she had audited were Global citizens whose native language was Global and who had been resident in Global City for over three years. Plus, they had all acquired the maximum Global Language Test Score, which was extremely difficult but this is what gave GSW employees the "Global edge" over other potential recruits. His request was the pinnacle of a curiously odd day.

'Three hundred and fifty-nine,' murmured Joan, relieved to be opening the last file. 'Phoebe Burnham,' she read out loud tirelessly, looking at the photograph of a very pretty young woman. Joan recorded Miss Burnham's date of employment, realising that she had only been working at GSW for a few weeks. 'The newest recruit,' thought Joan, feeling like an old lady in comparison to this young woman who was just starting on her GSW journey. Joan turned a few pages to the residence section. As she recorded Phoebe's address, something about "Straight Street" seemed very familiar. Joan looked at all the pages of information she had compiled and flicked back through a few. 'There it is,' she said to herself, 'I knew I'd already come across Straight Street.' She looked again and noted that Phoebe lived at 22; George Bishop resided at 21. Even though the city was a metropolis, it was plausible that it could just be coincidental. It was possible that two GSW employees could be neighbours. Joan completed recording the information for Phoebe, feeling puzzled about the duplicate address. She placed all the completed sheets in a neat pile on her desk and decided to take a look at the residency data for every employee, just to settle her curiosity.

She was steadily working through the information when she saw the same address once more, but a different number, this time number twenty. Three employees living at consecutive addresses in the same street seemed more than a mere coincidence. 'It must be in a suburb of the city because the city itself is home to vast tower blocks of apartments,' mused Joan, knowing that the addresses within the city followed a pattern like her own address - Apartment 368, Neon Block, Zone A. 'Jodi's address is Apartment 299, Bridge Block, Zone C,' she pondered, further examining the information. 'This "Straight Street" just doesn't make sense,' she thought, curiously typing the name into the satellite device on her computer, which would usually find an address and zoom in on it within seconds. But, as she thought, there was no location for Straight Street within the city limits. She extended the search to include the suburbs of Global City, but still nothing. Joan carried on with her hunt, extending her search to a thirty-mile zone around the GSW building, but to no avail. She made a separate note of the employees who claimed to live in Straight Street.

Joan did not know what had alerted Mr Law to these anomalies, but something was amiss. Something had sparked this wave of mistrust and Joan was unsure what to do with the information she had uncovered. For now, she would keep it to herself. For now, she would inform Mr Law that she had completed her task and everything was in order. She just hoped she was doing the right thing and that keeping this knowledge a secret from Mr Law didn't have a detrimental effect on GSW – Mr Law and herself for that matter, had worked too hard over the years for something amiss to happen now. Joan hoped that she wasn't being foolish. The official launch of Global Standard was just a week away. Over the next few days she would observe the residents of Straight Street. If she uncovered anything further then she would bring it to Mr Law's attention. For now, she would handle things her way.

22

The Global Wave

"Sunday morning at six o'clock
Quietly closing her bedroom door
Tiptoeing outside, she is free
She is leaving home

Why would she treat us so badly?
Why has she gone
Without saying goodbye?"

Georgia placed her Global language learning cards in her bag along with the rest of her possessions. The learning cards that she had used to act out different life situations. They were supposed to be used with a partner but since her eldest sister Phoebe had left she'd had to use them alone. For months Georgia had imagined what it would be like to be the "she who is free". She had tried to empathise with her parents who she was about to "treat so badly". But now, just like Phoebe; Georgia *was* the "she" leaving home. Months of secretly learning Global, months of covert meetings with other closet Global speakers had brought her to this moment – the time to leave. Her parents had been distraught when Phoebe left. Georgia was concerned for their wellbeing. How would they cope, losing another child to Global? But just like the song, whose tune she had never heard, but whose words she had learnt, she was leaving at six o'clock - before her family woke, before the sunrise; before she changed her mind. She would follow in Phoebe's footsteps and many others would follow after her, once she got word to them that she was safe.

She, like her sister, belonged to the Global Wave, to a new generation, who dreamt of life in the land of opportunity. They had worked relentlessly, learning Global covertly. They did not want to draw attention to themselves. They would leave one by one. Georgia had written a note to her parents, explaining that she was going to be with Phoebe; instructing them what they should do; reassuring them that when they had made a name for themselves they would send enough money back home so they, too, could leave; so they could all have a better life in the new Global world. The letter would tell her parents what to say to the authorities to ensure they did not bear the wrath of her actions. The letter reassured her parents that she was following a straight path that would lead her directly to her sister. They did not need to worry. They would all be together, very soon.

***

Joan looked at Phoebe's photograph once more questioning the age she had recorded on her job application. Her documents certainly proved that she was twenty-four years old, but Joan, who was the same age, felt like she had lost the zest that was so evident in Phoebe. Phoebe still had a "teenage glow". Her complexion was flawless, her hair lustrous and her eyes sparkled in expectation of something wonderful. Her mouth was loose and relaxed as if she wanted to beam a smile but had held it back for the purpose of her identity photograph. Phoebe's photograph reminded Joan of how she herself had felt leaving home to live in the new Global World. Joan pulled up her own personnel file on her computer. Just as she thought, the glow, the anticipation, the excitement – it was all there, as in Phoebe's photograph. The only difference was the contrast in their hair and skin colour. Phoebe had black hair and Joan's was light brown. Phoebe's hair was straight and Joan's naturally curly. Their hair was about the same shoulder length and, oddly, they both had the same aqua blue eyes. Joan's skin was fair, she didn't like to sunbathe, whilst Phoebe's was olive, which suggested that she didn't have to, enviably it was her natural pigmentation.

Joan didn't need to know Phoebe's workstation number, she would recognise her instantly. Although Joan had no official jurisdiction over any GSW employees, as Mr Law's secretary, people assumed that she was, kind of, second in command. It was this notion that caused tongues to stop wagging wherever she went in the building. Not that she wandered around very often. Stephen liked her to be at her desk at all times, except during her official lunch break – he did allow her to take lunch. So it was during her lunch hour that Joan decided to pay a visit to Phoebe. She would use her "bogus" authority to ensure that Phoebe stayed as late in the building as she herself so that Joan could follow her home to Straight Street. Joan had decided that keeping Phoebe in her sights was the easiest way to discover if anything untoward was going on.

Joan approached Phoebe's desk. She hadn't yet come up with a valid reason why Phoebe should work late. Joan looked around, feeling sets of eyes peering at her through transparent workstation partitions. The desks were laid out in sets of four, ensuring that each person had a clear view of the city. Stephen thought it was a much healthier way to work. After all, who wanted to look at the same face hour after hour? Or who wanted to have a wall as their daily view? Each floor in the building had the same layout, except for Stephen's and Joan's. They were on the Executive Floor. Stephen, of course, had the biggest office, which had a conference table and two large leather settees. His office door opened directly into Joan's. Beyond Joan's office was access to the lift, a small kitchen which was solely for Joan's use, and another kitchen used by the secret room employees. Joan never had any random visitors to their floor. If anyone wanted to see Mr Law, it was on an appointment only basis. Of course, no one ever willingly wanted to see him. It was only if they were summoned to his office, which didn't usually end well.

Joan actually liked Phoebe's floor better. She liked the presence of people. She liked the business of the room. She glanced around observing a kitchen area, toilets, the lift and a room, which was full of stationery items. A man was coming out of the stationery room, weighed down by reams of paper. 'That's it,' thought Joan, 'stock take.'

'Miss Burnham,' said Joan, in an official manner.

'Yes,' replied Phoebe, quizzically, seemingly not realising who Joan was.

'Good morning Miss Marsh,' interjected another employee. 'How is Mr Law today?' he asked, hoping Phoebe would realise she was talking to Mr Law's secretary.

'Very well, thank you,' she replied dismissively, thinking what an odd question. No one ever enquired about the wellbeing of Mr Law.

'Please, forgive me Miss Marsh,' said Phoebe, catching on. 'How can I assist you?'

Joan continued, 'As a new employee there is one task you have yet to complete.'

'My apologies, I thought I had completed all the compulsory tasks,' replied Phoebe politely.

'I'm afraid not. You will need to remain behind after you have finished for the day and complete a stock take of all the stationery that falls within your floor's remit. You will remain at your desk until you have handed over the inventory which I will collect from you personally.'

'Very well,' said Phoebe, unperturbed.

'That will be all,' said Joan, relieved that she had thought of a plausible reason.

As Joan walked away, Phoebe's colleague said to her teasingly, 'Not the stock take. The last person that was asked to do the stock take… well let's just say "stocks" are the appropriate word.'

Phoebe laughed nervously, pretending that she knew what he meant, but not having a clue.

'I was never asked to do a stock take,' she heard another colleague comment.

'Neither was I,' someone else reiterated.

'Should I be concerned?' Phoebe wondered. 'Is it a genuine request or should I be concerned?' Phoebe couldn't wait until her own lunchtime, until she saw George and Eddie. She needed to tell them about the stock take and to let them know that she would be home very late.

***

Joan sat fidgeting, waiting for Stephen to dismiss her for the evening. The time was eight thirty pm; Joan was concerned that given the lateness of the hour, Phoebe might have decided to leave.

'That will be all,' Stephen instructed Joan.

'At last,' thought Joan whilst simultaneously replying, 'Goodnight sir.'

'Eight forty-five pm,' mumbled Joan annoyed that her evenings were being determined by her employer. She couldn't remember the last time she had seen her friends, or been out for a meal. 'What is the point of living in a city if I never get to do anything?' she thought, agitatedly.

Joan grabbed her coat and bag and hurried towards the lift, which arrived without Frank. 'Even Frank gets to go home,' she moaned. She angrily pressed the lift button for the second floor.

Stephen watched as Joan hurried away, thinking that her behaviour seemed out of character. She usually took at least three minutes to glide to the lift in an elegant manner. But tonight, for some reason, her coat wasn't draped over her arm; neither was her handbag dangling on her wrist. For some reason, Joan was clutching them both in her right hand in the most dishevelled way. Stephen watched the CCTV monitor as he usually did, waiting for Joan to appear outside the building. Once she was outside he would proceed to "lockdown". Seven minutes passed, which was the usual time it took and she hadn't appeared. He waited a few more minutes but she still wasn't there. He rewound the CCTV thinking that he had missed Joan but knowing that he hadn't. He looked to the other monitors. He was surprised to see Joan on the second floor, talking to another employee. They exchanged a few words, the employee handed Joan a piece of paper, collected her belongings and left. Joan followed instantly, but instead of taking the lift with the other employee, she took the fire exit stairs. Stephen was intrigued. He shifted the focus on the CCTV cameras to the stairwell and saw Joan hurrying down as if she was in a race. On a different monitor he saw the other employee exiting the building. Then, a few seconds later, Joan appeared. She had calmed her pace to a slow walk as if purposely lingering behind her colleague. They both turned the corner, disappearing off the CCTV monitor. Stephen, locked down the building.

Stephen sat for a moment, pondering Joan's behaviour. He looked to the blank CCTV images. The building was peaceful. Everyone had left. He looked at the CCTV monitor that showed the GSW entrance and the reception desk. The CCTV cameras had built in motion sensors, which picked up any movement anywhere in the building. Stephen replayed Joan's movements in his head. He saw her grabbing her bag and coat and rushing away. She seemed disgruntled, angry even. Stephen broke her actions down into fragmented scenes. He heard himself telling Joan she could leave. He heard her usual reply. He paused her words in his mind, rewound them and regurgitated them over and over.

'Goodnight sir,' Joan had said to him, as she had done so hundreds of times before. But there was something different about this "Goodnight sir". Her voice didn't carry its usual sentiment. Her voice didn't hold its usual genuine overtones. Her voice was distant, as if she didn't want to be there. This worried Stephen. Joan was his constant. Joan was his one source of security. Her loyalty, her consistency, her unquestioning demeanour; Stephen needed Joan in his life. He needed her unwavering commitment. He needed her sat at her desk, each and every day. That she believed in him, that she believed in his vision; that she shared in his vision. Of course, they'd never physically sat down and discussed anything. He'd never asked her opinion on Global issues. Her support was silent. She didn't need to voice her opinion. Her loyalty was complete. Her admiration for Stephen's plans to standardise Global was genuine. He would not allow one out of character action to cause him to doubt who she was. But, in fact, Stephen knew very little about Joan. He only knew what was in her personnel file. He knew nothing of her private life, what she did outside of work; who were her friends– did she have friends or a family? She worked such long hours, as did he, was it possible for her to have a life outside of GSW? Stephen had personally chosen her to be his secretary. She had been his first recruit and then Frank. Just the three of them, for all those years but he did not know either of them.

Out of all Stephen's employees, he never had cause to "spy" on Joan. He randomly listened and watched the comments and actions of his staff as they sat oblivious, getting on with their day. He didn't feel guilt about his secret intrusion. After all, while they were in his building, their only discussions with each other should be GSW business. But Joan, he had never listened in on Joan, he had never had any need. But now he felt as if he had need. Joan rushing off to talk with a new employee, Phoebe Burnham required clarification.

Stephen pressed play on the CCTV recording.

'I have completed the task as you requested,' he heard Miss Burnham say to Joan.

'Thank you, you may leave. Goodnight,' said Joan.

‘Thank you. Goodnight Miss Marsh,’ said Miss Burnham.

He replayed the words over and over. He slowed the recording down ensuring that he hadn’t missed anything. As he listened over and over he noticed something in Joan’s voice that he had never spotted before. Her Global was perfect, as anticipated from a GSW employee and Global citizen - as expected from the secretary to the future leader of the free Global world. But there was a slight anomaly in her voice that Stephen could only detect when the recording was played back in slow mode. She had the trace of an accent. It gave him a familiar feeling, but he couldn’t decide whether this was good or not. He wanted to know what the “task” was. He wanted to know why Joan had taken it upon herself to allocate a “task” to a new employee. He would ask her about it tomorrow. But more importantly, he needed to remember of whom Joan’s voice reminded him.

23

Stephen woke abruptly. His mouth was dry and his throat ached like when he'd had tonsillitis as a child. He went to the kitchen and poured a glass of water. As he drank he looked at his image in the windowpane. He filled a second cup, put it to his lips and was drawn to his reflection. He saw himself as a teenager. The day he'd run all the way home because he had been late as usual for tea with Apollos.

As he stared at his teenage face he thought he saw a figure shadowing his. But this shadow was not a comforting one. It was a dark, unnerving figure. Stephen accidentally dropped his glass onto the floor. He looked down at the shattered pieces, scattered around his toes, which had miraculously missed them by millimetres. He carefully stepped away from the broken tumbler and picked up as much of it as he could. He scooped up the rest with a dustpan and brush and deposited it in the bin. He looked up hesitantly at the windowpane, relieved that the only face he saw was his own.

He went back to bed, closed his eyes and fell into a tortured sleep. Fragments of that day, all those years ago, flooded his dream. He was running up the hill. Then he was standing at the kitchen sink, drinking water hastily. He felt so thirsty in his dream. The grandfather clock was chiming reluctantly; Apollos' head was cast down, looking at his wristwatch. Apollos was looking up at him, giving him the same scolding look, over and over.

Stephen opened his eyes, yet felt as if he was still in his dream. He thought he could see a neon sign reflecting in the glass of his building. “Global Standard – One Language, One Version, One Vision”. The bright colours began to hurt his eyes. He tried to close them, but somehow they were already closed. He could hear a tapping sound. A distinct tapping that had a regular beat. Then an insistent dripping noise that fell in between the taps to make a continuous beat. It mirrored his heartbeat; tap, tap, tap, drip, drip, drip, were the only sounds he could hear.

Then above these sounds, he heard a faint, familiar voice, in anguish pleading, ‘Nastan, Nastan. Why are you against me? Why do you persecute me? What about Babel, Nastan? What about the killer language?’

‘Papa is that you?’ Stephen cried out in his dream state. ‘Papa?’ he moaned again and again.

‘Yes Nastan, it is I, Papa,’ said a tender voice that he recognised and loved.

‘Why are you persecuting me Nastan?’ the voice asked once more.

‘I’m not persecuting you. I’m making a name for myself. I’m reviving my father’s name. It’s what he would have wanted,’ replied Stephen, still in his dream state.

Stephen felt a surreal calmness at the sound of Apollos’ voice. Tears started flowing from his eyes.

‘I’m sorry Papa. I’m sorry if I have disappointed you. Please forgive me,’ said Stephen, despairingly.

Then, another voice shattered his dream.

‘Listen to you,’ accused an angry voice Stephen didn’t recognise. ‘I’m sorry, I’m sorry,’ it mimicked, taunting Stephen. ‘Sorry for what? Having a vision? I told you Stephen, all of this can be yours. I told you I am able to give you the world. Global Standard world domination will be yours Stephen.'

It was then, Stephen recognised this intrusive voice. It was the invisible stranger who had made it possible for him to acquire his building; the invisible stranger who had made it possible for him to proceed with his Global dreams.

'Who are you?' the voice demanded angrily of Stephen.

'Stephen Law,' responded an uncharacteristically hesitant Stephen, as fragments of his earlier dream of Apollos poured through his mind.

'Who are you?' the voice asked him again, compellingly.

'Stephen Law,' he responded more firmly, as Apollos' voice drifted away.

'And Nastan Popov, who is he?'

'Nastan Popov has ceased to exist. I am Stephen Law. I am the LAW. I am THE LAW …' he was still repeating powerfully when he awoke fully from his dream.

24

'*Live on air in three, two, one …*'

'Good morning and welcome to Global Daily Update. This morning I am pleased to welcome Mr Rod Jones, who is the Operations Director of Global Standard to the World, whose headquarters are in our very own city. Mr Jones has agreed to join us this morning to clarify what the launch of Global Standard in all official Global speaking countries will mean for Global citizens. Mr Jones, good morning and thank you for agreeing to be with us today.'

'It is my pleasure, Penelope.'

'I'm sure many of our viewers are, as am I, eager to know more about the impact Global Standard will have on our current society.'

'Well Penelope, GSW's vision concerning Global Standard is "One Language, One Version, One Vision". For a number of years, many of the leading world nations have been talking about "globalisation". It is a term that is being used more and more and has significant meaning. That is, we, as human beings, should view ourselves as global citizens – in other words, we are all of planet earth and therefore we should all have the same rights and be able to access the same resources as our neighbours. Be it food, education, water, I could go on. But of course, for the world to be united, we need to be able to communicate as one and this, Penelope, is where GSW's vision for a uniform version of Global – namely Global Standard, plays an integral role.'

'So why standardise Global? Why not choose another prominent language?'

'Global has been selected by the GPC, that's the Global Protocol Committee, as they believe – and this research has been endorsed by language linguistics – that Global, as spoken here in our wonderful country, is a vernacular that can be easily learnt by all world citizens. The statistics for Global as an official, second and foreign language taught in schools, is currently at the highest it has ever been. Linguists believe, given the popularity Global already has across the planet, it makes complete sense to standardise the language, firstly, in countries where it is already an officially spoken tongue and eventually to make it the one common language of the world.'

'So, Rod, am I rightly informed that you have had to relearn Global and adopt Global Standard for your role within the GSW?'

'Yes Penelope, you have been rightly informed. I am a Global citizen of Sub Motherland 1 and as such, have been, since childhood, speaking a corrupted version of Global. As you and the people watching at home are aware, centuries ago, when Global spread from this country to the Sub Motherlands, the receiving countries altered its form. The Sub Motherlands are in full agreement about reverting to Global Standard, which for them is an easy exercise as it simply means changing a few spelling variations.'

'So to recap, Global Standard is simply the version of Global that we have here in our country. All other Global official speaking countries will adopt this version which will be renamed Global Standard.'

'Yes Penelope, that's right. The GPC and GSW have been working on new dictionaries that will replace the existing Sub Motherland ones. These will be issued free of charge and will be available to collect from bookstores, libraries, designated collection points and online.'

'What is the actual date for the transition to Global Standard?'

'It is just two days away, Penelope. August the twenty-first.'

'How exciting! So there you have it viewers, the launch of Global Standard is just two days away. Be sure to visit your local bookstore, library, designated collection point or online at gsdict.un for your free Global Standard dictionary.'

'Fade out, one, two, three ... '

'Are we off air?' Rod asked, relieved that the interview was over.

'Yes, you did well considering you've never been on a live set before.'

'I have a good teacher,' replied Rod smiling.

'Do you really believe Global Standard and globalisation are for the good of the world?' Penelope asked Rod, quizzically.

'Yes, wholeheartedly,' responded Rod, trying to hide the deceit in his voice.

'Why? Don't you?' he asked, curiously.

'Global is my taught language. I studied it for my degree to get a job in the media. I cannot ever imagine not speaking my Mother Tongue with my family. Family meals, reunions; just the very essence of communication would not be the same in Global. Besides, none of my family speak the language. There is no need where they live.'

'Have they ever visited you here?'

'No. They have satellite TV and can pick up the Global channel but they have no idea what my programme is about!' laughed Penelope. 'My mother writes to me and tells me that she is happy that she can see my face. But, it makes me sad to think that when I open my mouth, she knows it's me, but it's not really me. It's my Global façade,' Penelope stopped talking, remembering to whom she was speaking. 'I shouldn't be saying any of this to you, forgive me …'

'It's okay. You are entitled to your opinion. After all, we are the free Global world,' reassured Rod.

Penelope stood up. 'It was a pleasure to meet you Mr Jones,' she said, holding out her right hand.

'Likewise,' replied Rod taking hold of her hand, realising how long it had been since someone had shown him kindness.

'I've asked a security guard to escort you out of the building – the secret route. I don't know how people got wind of your interview this morning, but it's probably not a good idea to leave through the main exit,' said Penelope.

'Sorry? What people?'

'Mother Tongue protestors,' answered Penelope. 'I'm sure this is just the beginning of the protests. I hope you have a good security team at GSW.'

Rod exited the Global TV building under the cover of a security guard. His car was already waiting. He drove past the Mother Tongue protestors who were waving their banners in various languages in indignation at the imposition of Global Standard. These protestors, who had lived in Global Motherland for many years, some since birth, were rightly concerned for their future. Rod looked on in empathy. He looked on knowing that a high percentage of them would fail the Global Standard Language Test and would not gain Global citizenship status. He looked on in compassion, realising that the future for these people would be dire.

'Anything?' prompted Penelope's producer.

'Nothing. Loyal to the core. Too much so in fact,' she responded.

'What do you mean?' her producer asked hoping this was the beginning of a story.

'When I told him how I felt about speaking in my own Mother Tongue, which was a genuine emotion by the way, when I told him about my mother's letters; he seemed genuinely moved, it was as if he could relate to it in some way.'

'That's good, that's very good. Do you think he has a hidden nationality?'

'No. You heard his Global. Replay the tape if you like. His Global is perfect. Only a native Global speaker could sound like that. Unless?'

'Unless what?'

'There was something else he implied. When I complimented him about his performance, he said he had a good teacher. I wonder to whom he was referring. Maybe we are going after the wrong source? Maybe we need to find out who the teacher is?'

'If that's your hunch then go with it. I'll leave it with you.'

'Yes, you do that,' affirmed Penelope, planning how she could meet the Operations Director of GSW again without drawing suspicion. Wondering how she could persuade him to introduce her to the teacher.

Stephen sat at home, watching Rod's early morning interview with Penelope that was being broadcast to all official Global speaking countries. Stephen was pleased with Rod's performance. Rod had come a long way since Stephen had summoned him to GSW headquarters. Stephen turned off the TV, knowing that Rod would be the most loyal employee a master could ever wish for. Stephen stepped into his lift, remembering the terrified look Rod had worn the night he had shown him that it was his way or no way. That it was be Global or be nobody.

When Stephen had first uncovered that Rod Jones was in fact Nimrod Nazareth, he had been seething that not only had Rod infiltrated his way into the GPC but he had gained a position of authority. Rod had sparked a wave of paranoia in Stephen. But, as Stephen had sat, waiting for Rod to be delivered to him by his security team, contemplating how he would interrogate him, he had had a genius thought about how he could use the situation to his advantage.

It had only been because of his Mother Tongue name, Nimrod that Stephen had decided to show him leniency. If Rod had had any other name, then his Global dream would have been in ruins. But his name played a key role in proceeding with the situation.

As a child Stephen had been fascinated by Nimrod, "the mighty warrior". Apollos, his grandfather, had told him how Nimrod had been instrumental in setting the people against God. How Nimrod had gone about from place to place building mighty cities. How Nimrod had incited the people to build Babel. So from one Nimrod to another, Stephen would make his language traitor instrumental in ensuring that no Mother Tongue upholders ever infiltrated GSW. Nimrod would be Stephen's mighty "language warrior". He would be responsible for ensuring that GSW employees within

Global Motherland and the Sub Motherlands were "pure" Global citizens.

Rod emerged from the GSW helicopter, not realising that he would be landing directly on top of the GSW building. He didn't like heights and the fact that he was stepping out onto the tallest structure in Global City filled him with as much trepidation as his meeting with Mr Law.

He was accompanied by Stephen's security detail, who, after not speaking to him on an eight hour flight, thought it necessary to grab him by his arms and lead the way. He wasn't sure whether this was for his own safety or because they thought he might try to run. He was happy enough to assume it was for his own protection, which enabled him to close his eyes until he was safely inside the building.

They led him to Joan's office where he sat and waited. The security men, who themselves seemed to have no fear of Mr Law, made themselves tea and coffee and stood either side of Rod, whilst drinking silently.

Mr Law's office door swung open, which caused the men to put their beverages on Joan's desk. They lifted Rod out of Joan's chair and set him down outside Mr Law's office and left.

'Mr Nazareth,' Stephen said, 'this way.'

Rod entered Stephen's office and to his surprise Stephen was already waiting for him in his lift. Rod didn't speak; he had just walked shakingly and joined Stephen in the lift. Rod had heard all about Mr Law's lift and how he was able to slow it down so he could get a panoramic view of the city. So when Mr Law hit an unnamed button and they plummeted as if they had dropped to hell, Rod was in shock. As the lift doors opened, Rod smelt burning sulphur. There was a bright orange glow engulfing the whole area. As Rod had stepped out of the lift, his ears were attacked by a number of intrusive hissing, banging and crackling noises. The smell was actually very pleasant and it transported Rod back to Bonfire night. He loved the smell of burning wood and paper and that's what he could smell. He realised they were in the bowels of GSW. He wasn't sure what exactly went on here but it was obvious that whatever was brought to the dungeon probably ended up being burnt to cinders. There were huge furnaces strategically placed in each corner. Each furnace had a glass door. Rod looked around, perplexed as to where the smoke escaped. The GSW building was in the heart of the city. These furnaces would generate a lot of smoke, which would need to be let out somewhere. As Rod stood gaping at the furnaces, he felt his face get hotter and hotter. He was anxious as to why Mr Law would think it necessary to bring him down here. 'What had happened to their "talk"?' he wondered. 'We need to talk,' Mr Law announced before he sent the GSW helicopter to collect me. Okay, so let's talk,' thought Rod, nervously, as he watched Stephen open one of the furnace doors.

'Hand it over,' Stephen commanded.

'Sorry, sir, hand what over?' Rod asked confused.

'The device, which nobody who is part of the free Global world can live without.'

Rod knew he was referring to his mini personal computer. He put his hand in his pocket and wrapped his fingers round it. It contained his life. Mr Law was right. He couldn't live without it.

'Hand it over,' Stephen ordered again.

Rod held onto it even tighter, knowing that if he let go he would truly be abandoning Nimrod Nazareth. If he relinquished it then Rod Jones would be his only persona.

'I'm confused,' Stephen began. He didn't seem bothered by the unbearable heat generated by the furnaces. 'You have gone to a lot of trouble to be Rod Jones. You have gone to a lot of effort to become a Global citizen, fake or real. You have worked hard to leave your Mother Tongue life behind, yet here we are. The final hurdle to become second in command at GSW and you can't do one simple task.'

'Second in command at GSW,' thought Rod, 'what does he mean?'

'Nimrod. Nimrod. Nimrod,' said Stephen patronisingly. 'Do you even know the origins of your name?'

'No, sir,' replied Rod, burning from the heat.

'Well let me enlighten you. Many, many years ago, there lived a mighty warrior named Nimrod. He went around the place creating havoc. But most importantly, he went from place to place trying to make a name for himself. He upset a lot of people along the way, but guess who he upset the most?' asked Stephen.

'I don't know,' uttered Rod.

'You don't know,' repeated Stephen, 'well let me enlighten you. He upset God by building a mighty city and a mighty tower because from there he planned to rule the whole world. One place, one people, one language; are you beginning to see a familiar picture?'

Now Rod was puzzled. He hadn't set out to achieve anything like Mr Law was delineating. He just wanted to better himself by becoming a Global citizen and working for the GPC. In fact, the person that Mr Law was describing sounded more like himself.

‘Nimrod did make a name for himself, because here we are, thousands of years later, discussing him. Quite a legacy,’ finished Stephen.

‘But I’m nothing like the man you are detailing,’ said Rod in trepidation.

‘No, it’s quite ironic that the man I am describing sounds more like me,’ Stephen, sniggered. ‘But I wasn’t named Nimrod, you were. So this is what we will do. You will live up to your counter-part. You will have the chance to make a name for yourself. You will have the opportunity to renounce your Mother Tongue and I will exalt you to a position of authority within GSW, just as, I’m sure, you have dreamt. In return, you will pledge your unquestionable fidelity to my vision. You will declare your loyalty to my new law concerning Global Standard. You will sign the treaty for your country in your real name – Rod Jones. Nimrod Nazareth will cease to exist. In return, I will name you as Operations Director for GSW. You will be my second in command. You will make sure that no one ever infiltrates GSW. You will ensure that the only people who work within GSW are of pure Global heritage.’

Rod didn’t understand why, after his deceit, would Mr Law trust him?

‘Don’t get me wrong. I’ll be watching you. I’ll be your voice, but you will be the face of GSW. You will get to be as famous as the mighty warrior Nimrod was in his day.’

Rod felt his fingers lose their grip on his mini pc. He would be a fool not to accept this offer. How proud his parents and family would be of him; the face of GSW. His mother had told him often, what a handsome face he had. She had also commented that one day he would be noticed – it seemed as if this was the day.

Rod pulled out his mini pc from his pocket and handed it to Stephen.

'My family,' he began, 'I would like my family to live here with me in Global City.'

'As long as they are prepared to renounce their Mother Tongue, bring as many as you want.'

Rod had stood and watched as Stephen threw his life into the furnace. But it didn't matter because very soon, his life would be complete again. Once his family were safe and in Global City, his new life could commence.

'You may depart,' Stephen said. 'I have left a new mini pc for you on my secretary's desk. It contains everything you need to know about your new role as the face of GSW.'

Rod left Stephen alone in the dungeon. He collected his mini pc and settled himself into his new office at GSW. His new address, vehicle details and instructions from Stephen were ready and waiting for his attention. He looked at the cups that were on Joan's desk, thinking how different things had seemed just a few hours ago. He couldn't wait to send word to his family to make their way to Global City where there was a fresh start waiting for them in the free Global world.

Meanwhile, Stephen stood staring at the flames. He opened the furnace door and a pile of ash flew out at him, covering his hair and face. He brushed off as much as he could. He loved the heat from the furnace. Even though it was August, the city was so cold and damp. The furnaces in a surreal way reminded him of the heat of his hometown at the peak of the summer. The old people did nothing but moan about how the heat would be the death of them. All people did in this city was moan about the rain. Sunshine was rare here. Stephen opened his hand and looked gleefully at Rod's mini pc which he had pretended to throw into the furnace. He would hand it over to the "secret room" and they would retrieve any Mother Tongue data. He wanted to know from what part of the world Nimrod Nazareth originated.

***

Joan sat transfixed watching the live interview that Rod was conducting. Joan was bewildered as to how in just a few days Rod Jones had gained a substantial position as Operations Director at GSW. In less than thirty-six hours, Rod had left his job as Sub Leader at the GPC, relocated to Global City, and, as it would seem, was now "the face" of GSW.

Joan knew Mr Law was a very private man and that he didn't like attention. Apart from the meetings he went to, he lived as a recluse. But with GSW about to become world news, he needed someone who would be the "front man". Judging by Rod's TV debut and how at ease he seemed to be in front of a live audience, it would appear that Mr Law had made an exceptional choice.

Joan was impressed by Rod's confidence and demeanour. He most certainly did have a TV face. He seemed to know when to look serious, when to smile, when to talk softly and when to project his voice. His appearance was immaculate. His black hair was slicked back off his face, which accentuated his engaging brown eyes. His navy suit was complemented by a champagne coloured tie. In his breast pocket nestled a navy and cream polka dot handkerchief. Joan was certain that Rod had been dressed by the same outfitter as Mr Law. In fact, if Rod's hair was light brown and his eyes green or blue, then he could easily have passed for Mr Law. He was most certainly a product of the same school as Mr

Law, which showed in his expedient transition to Global Standard. But as impressed as Joan was that Rod had eradicated all traces of his Sub Motherland accent, she felt saddened that his voice seemed to echo a past version of himself. Before Rod's "globalisation", his voice had swooned in a comforting manner. Joan had always looked forward to their communications as Rod's persona, which was characterised by his voice, truly lifted Joan's spirits. The singing tone of his words, the happiness, the positivity; the silence while he listened to what Joan had to say, all made for an extremely pleasant experience. But while Joan listened to this new version of Rod, as impressive as he was from a GSW perspective, she couldn't help but feel saddened that his new voice expressed a fabricated personality; a steady, well pronounced, flat, dull, monotonic, autocue opinion. If Rod represented the stereotypical Global Standard citizen, it made Joan feel quite depressed. Standardising Global for the common benefits of trade, education and the legal system was one thing, but to standardise a human being, to what Rod represented, that was something else.

Joan heard her toilet flush and remembered that she had company. It was odd to share her home with someone. Phoebe emerged looking less stressed than she had the night before, when Joan had followed her. Just as Joan had suspected, Straight Street didn't exist. Phoebe, George and Eddie were living a meagre existence in an unused building, that, even though it was dry and offered safe shelter, had no electricity or running water.

When Phoebe had exited the GSW building, Joan had discreetly followed her as she had walked hurriedly through the city. Joan had felt an instant empathy towards Phoebe as she obviously felt vulnerable, walking through the urban jungle, which showed in the way her head was cast down. Her bag was clutched safely under her left arm and her pace was more of a mild jog than a walk. Joan found it quite difficult to keep up with her. Joan knew the city well, but when Phoebe had disappeared down a side street and then in and out of back alleys, Joan found herself almost running to keep up with her. It was only because Phoebe was so intent on reaching her destination and did not look behind, that Joan was able to remain covert.

Joan stopped and watched as Phoebe twisted her body between a corrugated sheet and a small gap in an unused building which Joan concluded was Straight Street. Joan looked around for street signs, some indication as to how Phoebe would have come up with the name but there was nothing around that gave any clues. With Phoebe inside her makeshift home, Joan stood by the corrugated sheet, trying to figure out which part of her body she should put through first without snagging her expensive coat. She turned her body to the right, tucked both arms by her side and very slowly eased forward. Joan suddenly found herself, unannounced, in Phoebe's home. Joan looked around and waited for her eyes to adjust to the darkness that surrounded her. She gently edged forward, not knowing if the floor was clear or if she was about to stumble on objects that could hurt her. She gained a few inches and thought that she could smell an orange aroma. She breathed in deeply and the most wonderful, comforting smell engulfed her senses. Joan was instantly transported back to the Christmas Eve Christingle services at her family church. Memories of her family came emotionally back, as she recalled them each holding an orange. In the middle of the orange was a candle that they would light as they entered the church. As the hot wax from the candle dripped down onto the orange it infused the most wonderful aroma. As a child, Joan had always had an orange in her Christmas stocking; a tradition she had forgotten about until now, a smell she had forgotten about until now. Orange trees in her hometown were abundant; unlike in this city. The only oranges she ever saw were the ones for sale in the market. But they didn't smell like this. They didn't send her into a reverie like this. Feeling more confident about moving forward, Joan followed the aroma until she could see a faint light in the distance. As she approached the light, the aroma became stronger and stronger. Joan stopped suddenly, as she saw Phoebe resting on a chair that had most definitely seen better days. As she watched Phoebe sitting in silence staring at the candle flame, Joan felt very conscious that even though this was no place for a young woman to be living, she was intruding on Phoebe's personal, private, space. Phoebe moved suddenly, sensing she was not alone. She turned to see Joan standing there. Phoebe looked at Joan, aghast, wondering how she was going to explain herself. But Phoebe didn't need to explain herself. Joan, who was overcome with pity, simply told Phoebe to pack up her belongings as she was coming to stay with her.

Joan had been horrified that this young, intelligent woman was living in a squat just to be in the "land of opportunity" as Phoebe called it. Worst of all, that she had fled her home and her family, believing that being in Global City was worth risking her life.

'Sleep well?' asked Joan, caringly.

‘You cannot begin to imagine how good a real bed felt. I’d forgotten the luxury of sleeping on a mattress,’ said Phoebe.

‘There’s fresh coffee or tea if you prefer. Would you like breakfast? You must be hungry,’ stated Joan, fussing.

‘Tea will be great. I can make it. You’ve done enough already. I cannot thank you for …’

‘There’s no need. I’m just sorry I couldn’t offer George and Eddie a place to stay. You do understand don’t you? The city is very strict on the residential tax. They’ve even been known to carry out spot checks on properties to ensure the residents are legal. You are welcome to stay of course you are, but I will have to declare you are living here. If Mr Law was to find out that I was evading the residential tax, it would bring GSW into disrepute. In a few days we will go to the Resident’s Tax Office and make your living arrangements official. I will update your personnel file in work today so that you are no longer linked to Straight Street. I’m not sure what to do about George and Eddie though. If Mr Law finds out that I have deliberately deceived him then I could lose my job and then we’ll both be living on Straight Street,’ mused Joan, realising that even though she was doing the right thing, she had landed herself in the middle of a difficult situation.

‘Couldn’t you have afforded a place between you? Mr Law pays well. Even with the residential tax, I’m sure you could find something decent to share,’ said Joan, suddenly wondering why they hadn’t considered this an option.

‘I suppose we did things the wrong way around. When we arrived in Global City and secured jobs at GSW we were so thrilled. The employment process was so difficult. I never thought it possible that I would pass the GSW Language Test as Global is not my first language. But all those years of learning Global secretly had benefited me greatly. The other tests were stringent too but we passed everything. It was such a relief not to have a face-to-face interview. The three of us were offered employment and that's all we cared about,' said Phoebe, her eyes filling with tears. 'We promised our parents that we would make a name for ourselves in the land of opportunity. We each wrote the same letter asking for forgiveness for leaving without their permission but promising them that as soon as we had made enough money, we would send for them; so they too would have a future in the free Global world. We thought that it would be better to save our money so we could send for our families sooner. I miss them so much,' said Phoebe, breaking down. Composing herself she continued, 'Then of course we realised that even though the building is dry and warm, it has no electricity or running water. So the only way we could look presentable each morning was to join the fitness centre so at least we could shower and dress. Then our clothes needed dry cleaning because we had nowhere to wash them. Before we knew it the money we should have been saving was being spent on merely surviving.'

Joan sat next to her and said reassuringly, 'Don't worry, you are safe now. We'll figure something out for George and Eddie. But the first thing I need to do is change your addresses on your personnel files. If Mr Law decides to complete an audit himself then he will most certainly be curious about the residents of Straight Street. It doesn't exist anywhere in Motherland. How did you come up with such an address?' asked Joan, curiously.

'Because when I was younger, my mother would pray, "Lord, keep my children on a straight path that leads directly to you,"' said Phoebe, welling up again.

'Well, I don't know if I figured in your mother's prayers, but it led you to me here,' said Joan, forgetting what it was like to be around someone with faith.

'My mother would say that the Lord intended it and that you are an angel,' said Phoebe, smiling and wiping her tears away.

'My mother used to call me her little angel,' said Joan, poignantly.

'How long have you been in Global City?' asked Phoebe.

'Over three years. Along with Frank the security guard, I was Mr Law's first employee,' started Joan, omitting that even then Mr Law did not conduct face to face interviews.

'Things have changed so much since you … I mean since …' said Phoebe, unable to carry on.

'Changed? In what way?' asked Joan, enquiringly, glad Phoebe had opened up this line of communication. Joan didn't want to overwhelm her with questions but there were a few things she had said that were alarming. Secret Global lessons, leaving home without permission, asking for forgiveness; it all seemed so underhanded. When Joan had left home it had been with her family's blessing. Despite the divisions Global had caused in their community, her parents had been proud that she had such gumption. Phoebe's situation seemed completely different, very worrying.

'I've bored you enough with my life story,' said Phoebe, hoping Joan would desist. 'We should get ready for work,' she said, stalling.

'We have time,' said Joan, in a serious tone. 'What has changed? Where are you from exactly?' Joan asked, sensing the change Phoebe was referring to was somehow personal to them both.

'From Mother Tongue Country Orange,' said Phoebe, 'as we are referred to on the GSW world map; the same country as you.'

'We? What do you mean we?' asked Joan feeling perplexed, wondering if she had been deceived by Phoebe.

'Do you know me?' asked Joan, 'do you know me from our town?'

'No, I do not know you. But I know of you through your grandmother's stories of your life in the new Global World. My grandmother lived in the same mountain village as your grandmother, Aphia. They would sit and chat about you. Aphia was so proud of you. When I first heard about you through my grandmother and the stories of your glamorous life in the big city, I was so enthralled. You know what our town is like. The Mayor is still fighting to keep our Mother Tongue alive. It is a protected language and Global is forbidden. It is not even accepted as a taught tongue any longer. Most of the younger generation want to migrate but they feel guilty about leaving their families behind. The Mayor only tolerates the use of Global amongst tourists. It is like taking a step back into a forgotten time. During the tourist months, the Mayor employs people to dress up in traditional costumes and parade around the town. It is to attract more tourists. It is a strange thing because even though Global is forbidden, it is Global speakers who holiday in our country in droves. In peak season, everywhere you go you can hear it spoken. It seems so hypocritical that we are forbidden to learn Global but are expected to share our town with Global tourists. It is so hard not to respond to someone in Global. You wouldn't believe the urge I have when a tourist asks me for directions or where they can eat breakfast or even what time it is. It is illegal to respond in any other language than our own. The Mayor seems to have lost all reason. Even the old Mayor realised that Global played a small role and used it for marketing and trading with other countries. But, apart from the tourists, he seems to have cut us off from the outside world completely. He stresses that we are to strive to be self-governing and self-sufficient and that we will accept Global-speaking tourists so we can earn a much-needed income. But we will not revert back to allowing Global to form part of our education, as it plays no part in who we are as a nation. There are rumours that this new rule concerning Global is in memory of the man who died trying to protect our Mother Tongue? There is a statue of him outside the museum. Is it true that your …?' said Phoebe, but then thought it not right to continue with her question.

'Is it true that my what?' asked Joan, feeling as if she was being interrogated in her own home.

'Well, the tale that has been told, which is still being told, is that the people's desire for Global caused the death of one of the most respected men in the community. That your grandmother stood up against the, then Mayor in a public meeting in favour of Global replacing our Mother Tongue and that the man, statue man, dropped dead because of the shock that someone of his own generation would stand against our language. Then, because the whole town blamed your grandmother for this man's death, they shunned her and that is why she went to live up the mountain.'

Joan couldn't believe that she was having a history lesson and that the source was her own family! Joan thought vaguely back to that day in the museum. She could remember standing next to her grandmother and looking up at her, as she spoke passionately about something. But Joan couldn't recall exactly what was said, just a lot of angry voices. Then, an old man collapsed to the floor and a teenage boy was pleading with him not to die. Then everyone left the meeting and that was that. Her grandmother did then move to the mountain. She had told Joan that she needed the mountain air because of her asthma. The doctor had recommended it. Joan recalled her father and mother loading their car with her belongings. She remembered waving goodbye and that her grandmother looked sad. The part about her grandmother being shunned by the whole town did not form any part of Joan's memories of her wonderful grandmother.

'Was it Global replacing Mother Tongue?' Joan wondered. 'In the museum that day when my grandmother was raising her voice? Could it have been she was making a stand for Global? That would explain her support. That would explain why she gave me my inheritance whilst she was still alive. That would explain why she was so supportive when I told her I was leaving. Most parents and grandparents will do anything to keep their children close but my grandmother; she blessed me and sent me on my way no questions asked.'

Joan was confounded and annoyed that she was hearing such a tale of shame about her grandmother. 'So you based your future plans on the ramblings of an old woman? On the tales of a grandmother, who doted on her grand-daughter. You are telling me that you have shunned your own family for Global?'

Phoebe felt scolded. She did not expect that Joan would react in this way to her confession. She thought that Joan would be flattered. Joan was secretly revered amongst the younger generation in their hometown as someone who had started the Global Wave.

'You silly, silly girl; your careless actions have put us both in danger. I have to defend myself. I have to protect my own interests. You have left me no choice but to tell Mr Law that there are indeed illegals working at GSW. I will not jeopardise my own future.'

Phoebe started crying uncontrollably. 'Please, please, let me stay. I cannot go home. I cannot go back without making a name for myself. The shame it would bring on my family would be unbearable. I have to stay. I have to be here for when my sister arrives.'

'Your sister? Please tell me she is not following you here.'

'Yes, as soon as I get word to her she too will make the journey. Many more are planning to follow.' Joan sank despondently into her chair.

'What have I done? What have I got myself involved in?' she wondered, despairingly. Joan looked at the clock, knowing that if she didn't leave for work within the next twenty minutes she would be late. She rushed to get ready, omitting her usual immaculate hairstyle that would stay in place all day, to leaving her hair hang loose. She hurriedly put on a blouse, not realising that she had fastened the last button in the wrong hole, which made the shirt sit unevenly on her skirt. She looked out of the window realising that it was quite sunny, which was as it should be for an August day, so decided against putting on tights. She put on her usual shoes, collected her usual bag and hurriedly grabbed her light raincoat from her coat rack, just in case it did rain.

Phoebe got ready for work, relieved that she didn't have to be in as early as Joan. She stayed in her bedroom until she heard the front door slam, signalling that Joan had left. Joan had told Phoebe that until she decided what to do, that if by any chance they did bump into each other at work, they should act as if they did not know each other. Phoebe had agreed, hoping that Joan would not say anything to Mr Law; knowing that her fate was in Joan's hands.

Phoebe hadn't expected Joan to react in this way. When Joan had approached her unexpectedly that day at work; when she had told her that she needed to complete the stock take, Phoebe had so wanted to tell her about their hometown connection. But she had decided not to say anything because of the rumours that the building was bugged and that Mr Law listened to all conversations. Phoebe thought she had done an excellent job of pretending not to know who Joan was. But Phoebe had not anticipated that Joan would follow her back to the squat. She had not expected to be living with the Global legend, Aphia Joan, within twenty-four hours of their initial meeting. Phoebe was incredibly annoyed that she had handled the situation so terribly. All she could do was wait and pray that Joan would see the situation from her perspective and not tell Mr Law. Phoebe knew that today would be the longest day of her life.

25

Joan arrived at work for the first time in three years with just minutes to spare. She switched on her computer expecting to see a communication from Mr Law, but her internal mailbox did not contain any new messages. Joan was relieved. She carried on as usual, even though her head was whirling with the morning's revelations. Joan had been so flummoxed by Phoebe's announcement that they were from the same town that she had omitted to ask Phoebe if she knew her family. If she knew whether they were well? Joan had gone into survival mode. She had put up a barrier as tall as the GSW building, which she would not allow Phoebe to penetrate. Joan felt invaded. She felt torn between the life she had happily left behind, to being caught up in something that should not be her concern. Joan accessed Phoebe's personnel file on the computer. She stared at her photograph wondering what to do. Should she omit Straight Street from the residency section? If so, what address should she put instead? Thinking logically, how could she record her own address for Phoebe? How would she explain to Mr Law, if he decided to check the records himself that she was in the habit of inviting strangers into her home? Joan heard her internal mail notification, which confirmed that Mr Law was at his desk.

'I should go to him. I should go and tell him what I have discovered. Phoebe is not my responsibility. I will go and tell him face to face. I will go now,' she thought studiously, about to leave her chair.

But, she didn't need to do that. Stephen was one step ahead, questioning if Joan had found any untoward information amongst the personnel files. Joan stared at the message, knowing that Mr Law, who was just the other side of the glass, would expect an answer forthwith. He would wonder why she hesitated before responding. It was either yes or no. Yes, she had found something untoward, or, no, everything was in order. Joan looked once more to Phoebe's photograph that was static in the corner of her computer screen. She started to type her reply in the body of the email, 'After going through each file meticulously, as per your instruction, I can confirm that all GSW employee files are in order and have the appropriate documentation.' She hesitated, before clicking send. She hated lying to Mr Law. She valued his opinion of her and her employment but she could not be held responsible for sealing the fate of Phoebe, George and Eddie. She clicked send and set about changing the address information for the three of them. For Phoebe, she used her friend's address and for George and Eddie she used random addresses from the city directory. After all, it was only for the purpose of their internal employee records. No one would ever request private address information for a GSW employee. If someone ever did, then the information would have to come from Joan anyway. She felt sure that their secret was safe and that she had protected herself from any discrepancy. She would help Phoebe, George and Eddie secure a place to live and then everything would be okay. It was the right thing to do. Joan felt relieved when she saw the 'read notification' from Mr Law and that he had not quizzed her further.

She hoped that whatever had sparked his curiosity had now been laid to rest.

Phoebe sat at her desk in trepidation that at any moment she would be summonsed to Mr Law's office. She racked her brain for answers should she be questioned about her status within Global City. She hadn't told Joan about the fake passport, the falsified Global citizenship, the fake documentation that had allowed her to make the journey with ease. She hadn't told Joan that papers come at a high price yet are readily available if you have the right connections. She hadn't confessed to Joan that she had, ashamedly, stolen the money from her grandmother. What Phoebe hadn't realised was that all she had needed to do was ask her grandmother for the money and she would have given it to her gladly. Aphia wasn't the only grandmother who had aspirations for her grandchildren. Aphia wasn't the only one of her generation who believed in the benefits afforded by Global. The only difference was that Aphia was the only one who had the courage to speak her opinion in public.

Phoebe's grandmother had praised the day that Aphia came to live next to her in their quiet mountain village and mourned the day she had fallen asleep. The forgotten generation who resided in the mountain were shunned by most of the middle and younger generations despite not having done anything wrong. Their families just didn't have time for them. The forgotten generation loved their quiet mountain life. Yes, they cherished their Mother Tongue but not all of them objected to Global. Some of them believed that their Mother Tongue and Global could cohabit peacefully and that future generations would benefit from the knowledge that both languages could impart. They were convinced that God gave languages to people at Babel, yes to show his power and authority, but most crucially to show his grace and patience.

Aphia Joan and Phoebe's grandmother had enjoyed being neighbours. Their small mountain community was like the days of old when people would sit around discussing, debating, agreeing and disagreeing. They loved how, in their twilight years, they were using their last ounce of intelligence. There was plenty of life being lived in the quiet mountain village. If only the younger generation would take the time to visit their elderly relatives they would have known. But Phoebe had decided to visit her grandmother in the dead of night, when no conversation had taken place.

Joan looked in the direction of Mr Law's office annoyed that, as usual, there was no indication if he was sitting at his desk. She caught a faint glimpse of her reflection and paid no attention to her somewhat dishevelled appearance. Joan concluded that as it was the day before the official launch of Global Standard, Mr Law must be working studiously and she would assume he was there. The one-way glass had never bothered her before but for some reason, over the last few weeks, not knowing whether she was being watched or not was really beginning to niggle at her. In fact, she felt like walking over to the glass and making a silly face or doing something that was totally out of character. But what Joan didn't realise was that her less than perfect appearance had already attracted the attention of Mr Law, who had been in his office since Rod's early morning appearance. Her near lateness, her casual look, her bare legs which exhibited her silky white skin and her abstracted manner were drawing more attention than pulling a silly face. Stephen watched Joan at work, puzzling over her. But he really had too much to concentrate on today to concern himself with Joan's dress code. As long as her work was as faultless as always, the rest he would ignore – for now.

26

Global Standard Launch Day

“Happy birthday to you,
Happy birthday to you,
Happy birthday dear Nastan,
Happy birthday to you …”

Stephen woke in a sweat, remembering that today was his birthday. Every few years he had to remind himself how old he was. He hadn’t shared his birthday with anyone since he left the International School at eighteen years old. He shuddered as memories of younger birthdays with Apollos, Grigor and Grigor’s family came flooding back to him, with vengeance. How he hated that today of all days - the most significant day of his life – the launch of Global Standard, would be shared with past demons. When Norman, the Director of the GPC had named the twenty-first of August as the official launch date for Global Standard, Stephen had been floored. Nobody knew his past. Nobody knew it was his birth date. Nobody knew that the day he should be celebrating life, was the day he shared with death. Nobody knew about the graves that he had visited this day, each year, with Apollos. Nobody knew about the monastery bombing – nobody knew.

The repetitive, annoying, unimaginative birthday tune played over and over in his head. He could hear

Apollos singing strongly and joyfully. Each year, Apollos had put on a public display for his grandson's sake. But as each passing year made Apollos weaker and sadder, the toll of having to celebrate his grandson's birthday and commemorate his wife, son and daughter-in-law's deaths showed more painfully in his face. Stephen had no memories of his mother, father or grandmother singing this tune to him. They had died on the day of his first birthday. What he did have was a surreal memory of a huge birthday cake with layers and layers that looked like a ziggurat. Grigor's mother had been responsible for creating this masterpiece. It was her signature birthday cake. She baked the same style for her family, Nastan and Apollos year after year. In fact, she always seemed to be baking birthday cakes for someone in town. It was how she made her living.

Stephen was alerted to a message on his mini pc. He picked it up in anticipation of a communication from Norman, the Director of the GPC – it was Global Standard launch day after all, he was expecting a number of correspondences. But instead, when he clicked on the message, a woman with an awful Global accent that was a mixture of Sub Motherland 1, 2, 3 and 4 began singing the *Happy Birthday* tune quite heartily. Stephen swiped his mini pc, trying to stop the awful disturbance but for some reason the tune wouldn't stop until it had played all the way through. Stephen was enraged that he had forgotten to turn off the personal data application on his new device. He looked at the screen and was further peeved that he could choose to replay the tune. He accessed the personal data application and took out his birth date. He didn't need it now the device was fully functional. "*Happy 31st B'day Stephen*", the application couldn't resist displaying once more, before Stephen deemed it redundant. ‘B’day,’ said Stephen vexed. ‘B’day, what kind of word is that?’ he demanded irately, vowing that after today’s launch he would contact the company responsible for this device’s sub-standard version of Global and ensure that they reprogrammed it in Global Standard. ‘In fact, I will ask Joan to give me a list of every technology company within Global and the Sub Motherlands to ensure that all their products have Global Standard installed. Words like ‘B’day’ and other urban colloquialisms will soon be a thing of the past,’ thought Stephen, petulantly.

As the message disappeared from his screen Stephen retorted, ‘Happy thirty first birthday,’ emphasising the word ‘birthday’ in its purest form.

‘Thirty first,’ he mused despondently, as he acknowledged that his Global programme was running one year late. His original plan had been to launch Global Standard by the time he was thirty. ‘But it’s okay,’ he thought to himself, choosing his red paisley tie, ‘what I have achieved by my thirty first birthday, most people never achieve in their lifetime.’ He looked at himself in the mirror as he fixed his tie. Memories of his first day at the International School, when he had found the photograph of his father as a teenage boy amongst Apollos’ belongings and other photographs of his parents at various ages, came flooding back.

He took the photograph of his teenage father out of his wallet and secured it in the corner of his wardrobe mirror next to the one of his parents at eighteen. His parents had shared the same birth year. Stephen had placed another photograph of his parents in the top right corner of the mirror – they were both twenty-four years old in this picture. Stephen looked at the images; a younger and older version of his father smiled approvingly at him. His mother smiled also, like a ghost he had never known.

Now at thirty-one years old, Stephen studied himself in the mirror wondering if he still resembled his father or had time reflected in him his mother's face. Stephen opened his dressing table drawer and looked intently at two sealed envelopes. He recognised his own smudged handwriting. He remembered how his tears cascaded as he had painstakingly written "*30 years old and 31 years old*" on each one.

The few photographs Stephen had of his parents, he'd placed in sealed envelopes many years ago. He had arranged the photos chronologically. It had been easy to work out the age of his parents because Apollos had a consistent habit of recording the year on the back of each picture. Stephen only remembered his birthday for each year he had a sealed envelope. For each year he could see his parents at the same age. The trail stopped at thirty-one. That was how old his parents were, when they died.

'The last of the envelopes,' thought Stephen, as he looked at the photographs he had already opened over the years. 'Then that's it. No more left. No more birthdays.'

He pensively broke the seal on the envelope that was labelled "*30 years old*". Like his plans for the launch of Global, he was a year late opening this one. He had deliberately postponed it because he wanted to do so in sync with the Global Standard launch.

As his right finger and thumb delicately grasped the photo, Stephen's heart pumped with anticipation at the images he was about to see. He inhaled deeply, closed his eyes and eased the image out from its hiding place. He lingered, his eyes still closed then, after counting to five in his mind, he opened his eyes to see his parents beaming an exuberant smile. Lydia, Stephen's mother, was standing side on, proudly showing off her pregnant stomach. Stephen's father was standing beside her with his left arm engulfed around his wife's back. Lydia's long, dark brown hair was brushed back off her face. Whoever had taken the picture had captured her as she was about to say something, which meant that she was full faced. Her dark brown eyes were wide and sparkling. Her mouth was in mid-sentence and was accompanied by a humorous smile.

Stephen's father was beaming and he was front-facing, enabling Stephen to peruse every feature of his appearance. Stephen was bemused that his dark black hair had been replaced with grey. Stephen had always known Apollos with grey hair but had thought that was because of old age. He had never considered that he may have been grey since his thirties, as was his father. Stephen moved closer to his mirror, inspecting his own hair, looking for silver traces, but not finding any. He wondered how his father had felt about having grey hair at such a young age.

'Maybe this is *my* last year with brown hair,' deliberated Stephen, hoping that he *would* follow in his father's footsteps. Stephen's father's hair colour didn't match the vitality that was strewn across his face. Again, whoever was taking the photograph had managed to encapsulate the joy that he had obviously felt within his soul, which Stephen believed was due to his mother, Lydia, and their baby to be.

Feeling overwhelmed, Stephen opened the second envelope reflectively. He couldn't recall the photograph, but if it had been taken a year later, then logic suggested he would soon be looking at his baby self. Just as he thought, the last picture in Stephen's possession showed a happy family scene with him as the centre of attention. The poignant family photograph this time contained not just his mother and father but his grandmother, Damaris and his grandfather, Apollos. His grandparents were clothed in their "Sunday Best" and Apollos wore his red paisley tie.

As Stephen put his tie clip in place, ensuring that it was perfectly straight, a dark shadow brushed passed his bedroom window. He turned around quickly, wondering what it was. As Stephen looked out, he saw the hazy silhouette making his way to the balcony. Stephen rushed out of his bedroom through the hallway that led to the kitchen and open-plan living area. He opened the double doors that lead to the balcony but there was nobody there. However, what Stephen saw happening in the distance completely distracted him from his immediate quest. It couldn't have been a more appropriate birthday present. On the top of the GPC building, there were men at work putting the finishing touches to neon signs that could be seen from every vantage point in the city. The neon signs were an endorsement of Stephen's life's work. "GLOBAL STANDARD – ONE LANGUAGE, ONE VERSION, ONE VISION" stood out prominently with the GPC and GSW company logos embedded on each corner. As Stephen watched the workmen complete the installation, the lights were turned on. The morning sun hadn't quite risen and the red neon signs glowed spectacularly in the distance.

'Maybe this year I should celebrate my birthday. Maybe this year should be the start of many birthday celebrations,' thought Stephen, feeling his spirit soaring to the sky. Stephen recalled his dream of a few nights ago. In his dream the sign was already in place.

He put on his watch and shoes, picked up his mini pc and headed to his lift. He put the sighting of the brooding presence to the back of his mind. He pressed the lower ground floor button that would take him to his private car park, looking forward to driving through the city as the founder of the free Global world. He couldn't wait to get the day started. The GPC and his company, with the faithful assistance of Joan, had planned this day scrupulously. Stephen had complete confidence that nothing would go wrong. Rod had been briefed and was raring to be the face of GSW. The GPC had arranged a number of media interviews with Rod and Norman. There would be a live broadcast from the GPC building, which would show people queuing in anticipation of collecting a free copy of the new Global Standard Dictionary.

As Stephen had expected, people started queuing as early as seven am to ensure they obtained a free GS Dictionary before starting their working day. Most employers in the city had sent designated staff to collect as many copies as they could to ensure they were able to adhere to the new Global Standard rules as soon as possible. There weren't that many changes for Global citizens in the Motherland but employers wanted to be sure that all their workforce, especially those originally from the Sub Motherlands, made the transition forthwith. The broadcast would also stream live from the Sub Motherlands when their days began, showing the Sub Leaders at the GPC epicentres paving the way for Global Standard. Like Motherland, the queues shown on the evening news at the different time zones, for the new Global Standard Dictionary were out of sight.

From the wings, Stephen watched the day unfold. He had told Norman that he did not want any media attention. He was more than happy for Rod to be the company spokesman. After all, Rod was "the face of GSW". As far as Stephen was concerned, he would take a back seat at the GPC HQ and watch with joy as his life's work came to fruition.

***

As the queues subsided, city workers went about their business, armed with their dictionaries stored in GSW carrier bags. Stephen had thought that the whole idea of a GSW carrier bag was a cheap gimmick. After all, they weren't retailers; but Rod, who had come up with the idea, had proved him wrong. The city was overtaken with its people proudly carrying the bright yellow carrier bag, imprinted with the GSW and GPC motto "ONE LANGUAGE, ONE VERSION, ONE VISION" in neon red. Rod, who had been amazed when Stephen had relented and agreed to the manufacture of GSW carrier bags, looked on in glee as citizens left the GPC building weighed down by the most sought after book of words, in the modern era.

While the world watched the launch of Global Standard, the phone lines at GSW headquarters were ringing non-stop. The leaders of those countries in which Global wasn't an official language, were keen to negotiate with GSW as to how they could join the free Global world. Stephen's plans to advance Global Standard across the planet were closer than he could ever have envisaged.

The printers hurriedly delivered more copies of the dictionary in the expectation of a lunchtime rush. The

GPC building was to extend its opening time to seven pm, to enable citizens to collect their free copy after work, if they hadn't done so already. At eight pm there was a Global Standard launch party arranged. The GPC had insisted that they deserved to celebrate and Stephen had no choice but to attend. Joan, under the direction of Stephen, had sent an open invitation to every GSW employee in the epicentre (excluding those in the "secret room"), thinking tactically that if the party was overflowing with people then he would be able to leave unnoticed. But, it didn't quite work out that way.

As exhilarating as the day had been, Rod was looking forward to the launch party. It was good to see Penelope again, but the constant media attention that came with being the face of GSW was arduous. Rod had found out very swiftly that the persona needed as the GSW frontrunner was relentless – little wonder that Mr Law had no desire to be "front of house".

'Six forty-five pm,' thought Rod, looking at his watch longingly. The constant flow of people since seven am had been lessening for the last half hour. There were just a few stragglers who rushed in, grabbed their free dictionary and rushed home. The GPC clock that took centre stage next to the others that showed the different time zones in the Sub Motherlands, ticked slowly. "6:55, 6:56," watched Rod, wishing a speedy advance to seven pm. His feet ached, his voice was hoarse and he hadn't eaten since breakfast. As the security guard was about to close the main doors, a distinguished looking man, in his late eighties entered the building.

'Good evening, sir,' said Rod cheerfully, in auto pilot, handing the old stranger a dictionary. 'You have made it with one minute to spare.' Rod was bemused by the old man, who seemed oblivious to time. Old people didn't usually venture into the city. They were usually content to stay in the suburbs. Most of them feared the city; the noise, the business, the buses, the trams. If you weren't looking, bicycles would mow you down in a second. But this man, even though he obviously belonged to the third generation, seemed to have a vitality that Rod hadn't witnessed before in someone of his age.

'Thank you, young man,' replied the elderly stranger, gratefully taking the dictionary, 'but I am also here to see my grandson.'

'Your grandson,' replied Rod quizzically, wondering if the poor fellow had dementia and was lost. When Rod was a boy, he had witnessed the frustration of dementia. His grandmother, who had lived with them, had taken to wandering around their town, thinking it was time for school, believing herself to be a young girl again.

'Yes, my grandson. It's a very important day for him. I'm so proud of him. I'm so proud of his achievements. Is he still here?' he asked.

'What is his name?' asked Rod, trying to recall how he had dealt with his grandmother when she was having an episode.

'His name … I can't quite remember,' replied the old stranger. 'But he is the founder of something or other … I wanted to surprise him with a visit to tell him how proud I am of him.'

Rod was speechless. This man who had a slight Mother Tongue accent, this gentleman who had bags of personality and vitality, despite his memory loss; this old stranger was Mr Law's grandfather! This must be some kind of joke! Some kind of public relations test set by Mr Law to see how he handles the situation. Rod looked around but there were just the two of them standing in the foyer. As Rod continued scanning the building, waiting for someone to own up to the prank, the man said suddenly, 'It's okay, I can see him. Thank you for your patience young man.'

Rod tilted his head upwards and saw Stephen and Norman walking hurriedly up the stairs to the second floor. They had their backs to the old man and Rod and were oblivious to Rod's conversation with this curious fellow. Rod watched as the man scurried away, aided by his walking stick.

Rod was flabbergasted that Mr Law did, after all, have a family. He was amazed that he had such a character for a grandfather – he reminded him of his own grandfather – the same grey hair, the same walk, the same paisley tie and, a true emblem of that generation, the trustworthy companion – a walking stick. Rod was slightly peeved yet intrigued that Mr Law's grandfather had a Mother Tongue accent. He had expected any relative of his to have an infallible Global pronunciation. It almost seemed contradictory, given what Mr Law had put Rod through and what he was setting out to achieve in the name of Global Standard.

'Maybe I should take Mr Law to the dungeon and have him renounce his grandfather. I wonder how he would like that?' thought Rod, suddenly feeling remorseful and ashamed that he had allowed Stephen to "handle" him.

'I wonder how much Penelope would pay for an inside scoop on this?' he pondered, enraged as he thought back to that night.

Rod looked over to his sister chatting happily away. When he had invited her to the launch party, she protested at first, telling him that he would be too busy to bother with her. But Rod reassured her that the party was not work, it was a time for celebrating and eating and maybe some dancing. He wanted to introduce her to people so she could start living her Global life. But most importantly Rod wanted to introduce her to Mr Law. Even though he would probably be dismissive and think it rather odd, Rod didn't care. He wanted Mr Law to see for himself why he had sold out to Global. Why he had renounced his Mother Tongue. He wanted him to know that he had done it for his family and he would ensure that he would have Mr Law's attention, even if it was just for a few seconds. He needed him to know that family comes first, no matter what.

'If only my parents had wanted to come,' bemoaned Rod, not understanding the irony of life. They had pushed him into leaving and when he had made a name for himself, just as they had always wanted, they decided that they were happy in their hometown, speaking their Mother Tongue until the day they went home to be with their Lord.

'Everybody needs somebody,' mused Rod, 'even the infallible Mr Law. But if I need to, in the future, I will play the Mother Tongue grandfather card!' assuming he had one over on his employer.

***

Joan sat at her desk. It felt odd that for the first time ever, she knew for certain that Mr Law was not at his desk and wouldn't be there all day. She wondered where he had put Pandora's Box.

'Probably in a high security vault for the day,' she quibbled, knowing she had missed her only opportunity of looking inside. Joan switched on the TV so she could follow the live coverage of the launch from GPC. Stephen had had TV's installed on every floor of the building so the employees felt involved in the day's events, even though they weren't physically there. Joan had a TV all to herself. It was only 6:45 am and she was flabbergasted as she watched people from all over the city flocking to the GPC building. Stephen had paid Global Daily Update handsomely to report live from the air, showing the activity of its citizens, which was centred on the GPC building. As Joan listened to Penelope's reports from the helicopter, she couldn't help but feel jealous that she hadn't been invited to the launch. She knew every minute detail. She knew what Rod was supposed to say and when to say it. She knew what Stephen was doing (which in itself felt completely alien as nobody ever knew what he did all day long). Joan had, after all, been instrumental in planning the event and its timings were down to her diligence. Liaising with the printers and carrier bag manufacturers, hiring extra security – all these were down to Joan. Yet, here she sat, watching in the same manner as all the other GSW employees.

'Well, I'm just going to take it easy today,' thought Joan, haughtily. 'I'm going to sit back and watch my hard work unfold.' Joan marched to the kitchen, made herself a cup of tea, sat back at her desk and did nothing. She just sat and watched the live broadcast, consulting her watch to see if everyone involved was keeping to her timings.

Noticing that her nails were looking a little shabby, she pulled out her nail file from her bag and proceeded to manicure them. She sank slovenly into her chair; rather enjoying not being watched, wishing that Mr Law spent more time out of the office. She didn't know why, but lately, being the perfect secretary was beginning to take its toll.

'I could really do with a holiday,' she thought, as a "*Nice Jet*" holiday advertisement promoted a glamorous location. 'I wonder how much these companies have paid for their advertisements today,' Joan wondered, knowing the media channels would exploit the launch for their own gain.

As Joan thought of distant lands, sand, sea and lazy days, she began to feel overwhelmingly nostalgic for her own homeland. 'Mama,' she said aloud, feeling tears well up inside. Joan pulled out her mobile telephone from her handbag and without thinking dialled her home telephone number. It rang a few times and then the most wonderful, warm, loving, familiar Mother Tongue voice answered in a soft 'hello'.

'Mama,' said Joan in her own Mother Tongue.

'Aphia, is that you?' Joan's mother gasped.

'Yes Mama, it is me. I cannot speak long as I am in work but I wanted you to know that I love you and I miss you and as soon as I can I will come home Mama, I will come home to see you and Papa and …'

'Oh Aphia, my angel,' uttered Joan's mother, unable to hide her joy at the prospect of seeing her daughter. It was close to four years since she had left home, since she had seen her daughter's face or held her close.

'I cannot believe it. That will be wonderful. I will tell the family what you have planned. I am so excited my angel. When do you think you will come?' she asked.

'I'm not sure Mama, but soon I hope. I will come, I promise.'

'Who is on the phone?' Joan could hear her father asking in the background.

'It's Aphia; she wants to come home to visit. Quickly say hello, but hurry she is in work.'

'Hello Papa,' said Joan, unable to hold back her tears. 'I will come home as soon as I can. But Papa, make sure Mama doesn't tell the whole town. I know what the situation there is with Global and I don't want to cause trouble for you. It will just be a quiet homecoming so I can see you all. Do you understand?'

'Yes of course, we will keep it a secret; we know it is difficult for you. Do not worry. I love you,' said her father, wholeheartedly.

'I love you also,' said Joan, nearly sobbing. 'Let me say goodbye to Mama.'

'I'm here my angel,' said Joan's mother.

'I have to go but just expect me when you see me. If I cannot get word to you do not worry. Just expect me soon,' said Joan, longingly, reluctantly ending the phone call.

Joan felt elevated that she had spoken with her parents but also deflated at the realisation of her loss. Hearing about her hometown from Phoebe had ignited a homesickness in her that she never thought possible. Her longing to go home for a holiday was the easy part. Asking Mr Law for time off, that was the hard bit. But asking him for time off to visit a Mother Tongue country totally opposed to Global; that was most certainly asking to lose her job. But Joan, for some reason, felt at the end of her tether. The only way she would be able to continue living in Global City and working for Mr Law was if she had some time out, time away from both. He didn't need to know her holiday plans. He could never know her intended destination.

27

Living life as a recluse suited Stephen's plans perfectly. The isolated lifestyle he had chosen was a sacrificial requirement to achieve his dreams. He didn't want anyone or anything hindering his plans. Plus, he didn't want anybody to recognise him as Nastan Popov. He had to ensure that the transition from teenager to man fully protected his identity. Thus far, all his plans had worked out very nicely.

But Stephen wasn't oblivious to the fact that, at some point, as founder of GSW and of the free Global world it was only a matter of time before people would want to know and see the "real face" of Global Standard. Rod was only a diversion until the time was right for Stephen to present himself to the world.

Stephen had decided that his first public appearance would be at the launch party. Apart from Norman and the Sub Leaders, he didn't need to communicate with any other GPC staff members. It was the same at GSW. Apart from Joan, his communication with his workforce was minimal. His presence in the building was enough to keep them productive. So Stephen had decided that an internal get together, free of media attention, would be the perfect opportunity for his employees and GPC employees to witness the "actual face" of GSW.

The staff started to arrive promptly at eight o'clock. The foyer was decorated with GSW and GPC paraphernalia. Balloons, banners, pens, pencils, rubbers and mannequins exhibiting Global Standard t-shirts – it truly was a marketing circus. In the foyer, behind the reception desk, there was a covering on the wall, which was hiding a new engraving. Only the GPC Director (and the engraver) knew what it contained. It was to be unveiled at nine pm precisely.

Stephen watched from a distance as his employees arrived in their evening finery. He was looking out for Joan but couldn't see her. People chatted, drank and ate the food that had been freshly delivered by a catering company. A string quartet played soothingly in the background, which gave for a very relaxing atmosphere.

'There you are,' said Norman to Stephen, who was still waiting for Joan to arrive. 'Ready to face your public,' Norman asked, jokingly.

'Yes,' responded Stephen, steadfastly.

As Stephen descended the stairs to the foyer, his attention was drawn to an old gentleman who was wearing a black suit, red paisley tie and in his left hand a walking stick. His hair was cloud grey, the same colour as his father's and grandfather's.

As Stephen smiled, greeted and thanked his employees for all their hard work and for attending the party, his mind was preoccupied with finding the old man.

'Good evening sir,' said Joan, distracting him.

'Joan. Good evening. I was waiting for you to arrive. I never got a chance to thank you for all your hard work. The launch was a great success and I couldn't have done it without you.'

Joan looked dumbfounded at Mr Law. In nearly four years this was the longest conversation they had ever had and it was the first time he had ever acknowledged or thanked her for anything.

'You are welcome sir. It has been my pleasure to be part of the launch. I don't suppose now is a good time to ask for a few weeks off?' she blurted out, not meaning to ask the question out loud.

'Go on Stephen, give the girl a break. She deserves it,' chipped in Norman.

Stephen felt his heart sink. 'A holiday: Joan is asking for time off work. No, no, no. How will I manage? Why would she need a holiday? She has the weekends and national holidays off. Why now? Why does she want to leave?' he puzzled, feeling his spirit plummet.

'Cat got your tongue,' said Norman, annoyingly. Stephen hated that he talked in phrases. It was so … so … non-Global.

'Of course you can Joan,' said Norman, answering for Stephen. 'Take as long as you like. I'll lend him a GPC secretary. Don't you worry; just go and have a nice time. We all need to refresh our batteries from time to time.'

Stephen looked on in disbelief as Norman spoke for him.

'Sir, is it okay? It will just be a few weeks. I will leave on Friday. I will ensure everything is up to date before I go and …'

'Permission granted,' said Stephen formally, feeling let down that she would even consider leaving at such an important time.

'There you have it,' said Norman. 'Oh, is that the time?' he continued, looking at his watch. 'Stephen, if you would kindly follow me. I have a surprise for you.'

Stephen followed him to the foyer. Norman motioned for Stephen to stand behind the reception desk with him. Stephen looked at the covering on the wall not knowing what Norman had planned. Norman banged on the desk loudly to draw people's attention. Stephen stood looking out at everyone looking at him. Joan looked at Stephen, knowing that she had hurt his feelings. But for once she was considering her own feelings. Rod stood next to Joan and introduced her to his sister. The next introduction Rod wanted to make was to Mr Law.

'Ladies and gentlemen,' Norman began. 'Thank you all for being here to celebrate this monumental day. Today, GSW and the GPC have made world history. Today, we have witnessed the vision of one man, Mr Stephen Law, come to fruition. Today we have seen the success of Global Standard within our own Motherland and the Sub Motherlands. From tomorrow, we will see the spread of Global Standard to the ends of the earth. It is with this in mind and in recognition of Mr Law's vision to unite the whole world in one common language that the GPC have decided that a rebranding is in order. From today, the Global Protocol Committee is pleased and proud to be called the Global *Standard* Protocol Committee,' finished Norman, cheerfully.

'Mr Law if you would be so kind,' he continued, indicating that Stephen should pull on a red cord by the side of the covering. As the curtain effortlessly parted, the plaque revealed the new GSPC logo – the old wording Global Protocol Committee had been replaced by Global Standard Protocol Committee with a strap line "official overseers of Global Standard". Stephen was elevated as everyone applauded him. He was extremely proud that the GPC – the GSPC believed in him and his vision for Global Standard. He held up his hand to thank people for their kindness, genuinely choked by his emotion.

'Mr Law speechless,' joked Norman, 'will wonders never cease. Ladies and gentlemen, please enjoy the rest of your evening.' The staff dispersed and continued celebrating.

As Stephen walked away from the engraving, drinking in his success, he felt a tap on his shoulder. He turned around to see Rod, beaming him a mushy smile. Before Stephen could speak Rod began, 'Mr Law, I would like to introduce to you my beloved sister ...'

'Angelina,' said Stephen mesmerised, before Rod had finished.

'Yes, Angelina,' uttered Rod taken aback, not recalling telling Mr Law that he had a sister; let alone telling him her name. Angelina held out her hand to accept Stephen's that felt warm and sweaty.

'I am very pleased to meet you Mr Law. I want to thank you for arranging my move to Global City. I have been speaking Global for many years and this opportunity will enable me to make the transition to Global Standard and become a true Global citizen,' she said gratefully.

Stephen was unable to respond. 'Is this my Angelina? Is this my Angelina who took care of me for all those months after my grandfather died?' he wondered, transfixed.

Rod began muttering gratitude. His babbling seemed to go on and on but Stephen was glad that he didn't have to speak for a while. He couldn't find any words. As he looked at Angelina, he recalled her kind face, her blue eyes, her smile, her expression. But most of all, it was her accent he recognised. That was the first thing he had noticed about her all those years ago. All those years ago when he'd sat on the stairs in Grigor's house listening to strangers refer to him as a bereaved child; then he had heard Angelina speak - it was her accent that set her apart. When she had been able to respond to him in

Global, he had been filled with joy. 'At last,' he had thought, 'someone who understands my Global dream.' Angelina had supported him through those months until he had moved to the International School. She had understood his desire to learn Global and had not judged him. She had cared for him but then she had left him; gone, without an explanation, just disappeared out of his life, without a trace.

'You must be very proud of what you have achieved Mr Law. I know that Rod feels truly honoured to be working for the leader of the free Global world. I know …' Stephen just listened to her talk.

'Please, call me Stephen,' he said, daydreaming as she spoke.

Rod looked at Stephen as if he had suddenly grown two horns. 'Call me Stephen,' he repeated silently to himself, 'call me Stephen.' Rod had been excited to introduce Angelina to Mr Law but had never imagined that she would have this effect on him. It was as if Mr Law had gone back to being a child. He was obliging and sheepish and his tone was soft. He looked like he was listening to every syllable that came out of her mouth. He didn't know if Angelina had noticed how odd Mr Law was acting – then, realising that she had never met him before, she wouldn't know that this was a version of Mr Law unknown to him.

As Angelina continued talking, Rod interrupted and said, 'I wanted you to meet Angelina so you could see how important my family is to me.' Feeling bold he continued, 'By the way, did you manage to catch up with your grandfather? It must have been such a nice surprise that he came to support you on the biggest day of your life. Is he still here? I suppose he was probably tired after travelling for hours. Has he gone home? Does he live in the city? I knew he was your grandfather from the moment I saw him,' babbled Rod, on and on. Stephen put up his hand authoritatively to stop his chatter.

'Papa, here, today,' thought Stephen feeling a little odd.

Stephen relaxed his hand so Rod continued, 'He cut it a bit fine though. We were nearly closing the door. He sauntered in, looking very dapper indeed. We had a fine chat and then he spotted you on the stairs and rushed after you. Although rush is probably not the best description. He went as fast as he could with the aid of his walking stick.'

Stephen was overcome. 'Papa,' he mused, comforted that Apollos was watching over him. Comforted that he wasn't annoyed with him after all; comforted that he had changed his mind about Global being a killer language.

'Interesting Mother Tongue accent,' whispered Rod in Stephen's ear. 'Is he still here? I'd love to converse with him again.'

'Sorry, what?' replied Stephen, absentmindedly.

Stephen was unaware that Norman had called the crowd to hush once more. He was wheeling a huge trolley and whatever was on it, was hidden by yet another covering.

Without warning, Norman started singing:

'Happy Birthday to you,

'Happy Birthday to you,

'Happy Birthday dear Global Standard,

'Happy Birthday to you.'

As the people joined in the singing, Norman threw off the cover to reveal an enormous birthday cake that looked like a ziggurat. There were layers and layers of the most delicious looking sponge and on the top sat a first birthday candle that was sparkling jubilantly. As

Stephen looked on, his body and mind took a step backwards. The room started spinning and people's actions slowed to a halt. The scene felt freeze framed as flashbacks of his hometown came flooding back; birthday after birthday with Apollos, Grigor and Grigor's family. Stephen looked at the detail of the cake. The only thing that was missing was a sign confirming it had been made by Grigor's mother. It was identical to the birthday cakes she had baked year after year. The ziggurat style that Apollos claimed reminded him of the biblical description of the Tower of Babel.

'Where did this cake come from?' asked Stephen, flummoxed.

'I know you didn't want a fuss. It was my wife's idea and I couldn't resist. To tell you the truth I just wanted to taste the cake again.'

'Where did it come from?' he repeated.

'That's quite a story,' Norman began, 'a while ago when my wife and I were on holiday in … well on your map Stephen, the country is labelled Mother Tongue area orange. Anyway, while we were there, in the most beautiful town, with the most striking lake and orange trees and the people, what a friendly, welcoming lot … anyway, while we were there we had the pleasure of witnessing the Mayor's birthday celebration. The whole town came together, it was so wonderful, so homely and the sense of community was overwhelming. It really brought home how lonely our city can be sometimes … sorry, I'm digressing. While we were celebrating with the townsfolk, it's quite amazing how the art of dancing can replace verbal communication – well we couldn't join in the conversation much because Global speakers were few and far between – that's something you will look forward to addressing with that country's leader, eh

Stephen,' joked Norman. 'The whole town joined in singing Happy Birthday in their Mother Tongue as the Mayor stood on a platform next to a statue of a man who is revered for something or other, but we never found out what. This massive birthday cake was wheeled in on a trolley. I had never seen anything like it. I was so impressed with the cake; I could taste it for weeks after. My wife came up with the idea.

'"Cake," she said. "Every celebration needs a cake." I don't think she thought I would order one from another country though. It was very tricky with the language barrier, but we got there in the end. I won't tell you how much it cost. I've sent you the bill,' laughed Norman.

The more Norman spoke, the more agitated Stephen became. Not only had the GSPC Director holidayed in a Mother Tongue country, he had, it seemed, holidayed in Stephen's hometown and celebrated Grigor's birthday. Stephen assumed it was Grigor he was referring to as the town Mayor. And how did the Director of the GSPC communicate with a non-Global speaking country to order a birthday cake? Stephen was so irate he just wanted the whole conversation to be over. Stephen had seen many flaws in the Director during the day and he would make it his goal to see that he was replaced with someone who took his vision seriously. Stephen did not expect the Director of the "overseer of Global Standard" to fraternise with the enemy. 'Is my vision not clear enough to the Director – Global Standard to the WORLD is my company's name and Global Standard to the WORLD is my aim.'

Before Stephen could object, the Director had taken out his mini pc, accessed the photographs of his holiday and thrust the device in Stephen's face. Stephen mechanically took hold of it and swiped his way through each image. He was not prepared for what he saw; the lake, the ski lift that stretched from the town centre up to the mountains, the churches; Stephen's church that he had attended with Apollos and then the ultimate shock; the statue that had been erected in memory of his beloved grandfather. Stephen continued swiping, unaware that everyone was watching. They were waiting for him to blow out the candle. But Stephen carried on, only stopping when faced with the photographs of the Mayor's birthday celebration. Stephen looked, as he remembered his teenage friend, now a grown man, who obviously loved his life as Mayor, beaming a smile, addressing the crowd and blowing out his candles. Stephen felt the colour drain from his face. He felt quite ill. He felt as if his complexion would match the grey colour of his father's hair. Stephen couldn't believe that today of all days he had come face to face with tangible reminders of his home town. He couldn't believe that Angelina, his rescuer, was standing next to him, unaware who he was. He couldn't believe that for all these years he had lived with no connections or reminders of his hometown and now, on his day, on the day that he had been waiting for all his life, his world was closing in, crushing him. He felt an intense pressure on his chest.

The crowd followed the Director's lead and once more started to sing Happy Birthday. Stephen looked on as face after face smiled and clapped. The candle, which seemed to have been burning forever, was sizzling away until quite suddenly it made a loud bang, mimicking an explosion and then fizzled out. This caused Norman and the guests to start laughing. The laughter seemed never ending. Stephen wanted to run. He wanted to scream. He wanted to pick up the cake and throw it at the crowd. He wanted to tell them to leave him alone. As the laughter dissipated, Norman began to cut the cake and handed a piece to each guest. He was oblivious to the distress he had caused Stephen. He was oblivious that Stephen had just had a painful trip down memory lane in the strangest of circumstances. Stephen undid the top button of his shirt. He smiled politely and whilst everyone was busy eating cake, he made his exit, hoping no one would notice.

But Angelina had noticed. She had been watching Stephen. She realised that something was wrong, but did not know him well enough to ask if he was feeling okay. She watched as Stephen slinked away, wondering why she felt as if she knew him. Wondering why she had wanted to reach out and reassure him.

'Cake?' asked Norman, handing her a piece. As Angelina prepared to take a bite, her nostrils started twitching as she smelt vanilla and orange. As she ate, the infusion of different tastes hit her senses like a catapult. Her mind was alerted to a time she had sung Happy Birthday a long time ago. She remembered the scene. The people in the room were singing the tune in Mother Tongue, not in Global. She closed her eyes as the taste from the past brought to her memory, a child's face – a teenage boy. 'Nastan,' she recalled instantly, 'Nastan Popov.' She remembered him vividly. He was sat in a corner of the room mouthing the tune but his lips weren't in sync with everyone else. It seemed as if he was speaking another language. The image of Nastan evoked memory after memory in an overflowing wave. Angelina pictured Nastan's sadness and his lost expression. Then she recalled his bereavement. He had lost his grandfather, Apollos Popov, the most revered man in Nastan's town.

‘May I have a look at your holiday photographs Director?’ asked Angelina politely.

Norman was only too happy to hand over his mini pc. As Angelina swiped her way through the same photographs that Stephen had been looking at a few minutes ago, the realisation of why she felt she knew him came flooding back.

‘Nastan,’ she mused. ‘Stephen Law is Nastan Popov,’ she concluded, handing back the Director’s mini pc, feeling sure that Nastan had recognised her too.

***

Joan sat on the plane homeward bound. She had left the party early. When Norman unveiled the celebration cake and everyone was preoccupied, including Mr Law, she thought it the perfect time to slip quietly away. Sitting on a plane felt good. Joan had forgotten the thrill of taking off. The rush of the acceleration and the swift rise made her feel as free as a bird; a migrating bird released from its cage. Joan felt exhilarated to be out of the city. To take a taxi ride, a train journey and now to be on a plane heading home. She couldn’t believe that she had asked Mr Law for time off. She chuckled as she thought about the audacity of Norman speaking on his behalf. She felt sad that Mr Law had been so dismissive of her when he had realised that she had wanted to leave.

Joan relaxed into her seat and put in her earphones. She had left her mini pc in her desk drawer. This had been quite a liberal move, as she was certain Mr Law was not expecting to be cut off from her completely. She knew he would be irate when he realised that she was uncontactable for he did not have her personal mobile number.

She had travelled using her own country's passport. It was still valid and as far as she knew, it was still acceptable to travel as a regular person and not just a Global citizen. She had left her Global citizen identity card and travel card at home. She wanted to be sure that Mr Law could not trace her location. She wouldn't know where to start with an explanation of her true heritage. If he knew that she was holidaying anywhere other than a Global speaking country, he would be outraged. He knew nothing of her true identity. She had wanted to tell him so many times but his opposition toward Mother Tongue citizens was unnatural. Plus, until recently she didn't view herself any longer as a Mother Tongue citizen. She was a Global citizen through and through. After all, how many people get to say that they played an instrumental role in the launch of Global Standard? As far as Joan was concerned she had proved her Global citizenship to Mr Law time and time again. To him, she was Joan Marsh, his loyal secretary, whom he had no reason to question.

Joan knew it would be odd not seeing Mr Law or sitting at her desk every day. She couldn't believe that in nearly four years she had never taken a proper break from GSW; neither had Mr Law for that matter. He worked seven days a week. Joan felt annoyed that she had allowed herself, be it inadvertently, to become so "globalised". Mr Law and GSW had become her life. A person that she didn't even know properly consumed her very being. Mr Law's dreams and vision for Global Standard had become her dreams and vision too. But something had changed in Joan. Phoebe's misconception that turning your back on family, heritage, language, everything you have ever known can be replaced by acquiring status and opportunity of becoming a Global citizen. That people like Phoebe, George and Eddie were risking their lives to gain what exactly? - an unknown existence in Global City. This is what had changed her view and opinion of Mr Law and what GSW really stood for. Phoebe's naïve confession of closet Global lessons, leaving home like a fugitive, the upset and stress that she had so obviously caused her parents – that her sister Georgia was planning to do the same. But what bothered Joan more than anything was that Phoebe had talked of a Global Wave generation. A generation, it would seem, who believe that all Global speaking countries are filled with immeasurable wealth – that the streets are literally paved with gold. But what was this fixation that Phoebe and the Global Wave generation seemed to have with her? Joan had become an icon, some kind of figurehead or role model to whom the young aspired. What they didn't realise was that Joan hadn't left home because she wanted status or riches or power. Joan left because that was who she was. As a person, she wanted to leave and that was that. Her parents had never stifled their children into making them stay. They had encouraged them to travel, to see the world with the hope that once they were satisfied and had seen what else the world had to offer, they would return home.

'If you tell your children no, or that they can't, or shouldn't, then your children will most certainly say yes and try to succeed at the things you have stopped them doing or seeing. You have to use wisdom and keep them from danger. When you have your own children, Aphia, let them experience who they are. Listen to their hopes and dreams, encourage them and pray. Pray without ceasing,' she remembered her mother telling her, the day she left home.

Joan closed her eyes and listened to a track on her playlist. As the words penetrated her mind, she felt silent, warm tears trickle down her cheeks:

"Big dreams, big city, big life
Big hopes, ambitions, lonely life
The years have passed by, too many to count
And here I am going back
Back to where my dreams first came to me
For big hopes, big city, big life
Back to where I once felt safe and loved
Back to my little life ..."

Joan pressed stop on her phone; the lyrics from the song proving too much for her to bear. It was as if she had written them herself. Joan felt so tired. But it wasn't a yawning tiredness because she had gone to bed too late. It was a tiredness that made every inch of her body and soul ache. She drifted off to sleep and woke to the pilot's announcement that the plane was beginning its descent. Joan looked sleepily out of the window to a completely different view – there was not one skyscraper in sight; just blue sky and masses of green land below. Her eyes welled up again at the sight of her homeland. But this time they were tears of true joy.

28

Meanwhile, back at GSW epicentre, it was business as usual for Stephen. After his near public meltdown, he had left the party worried that he was losing control over his destiny. He had not planned for so many variants; he had not anticipated ever coming face to face with anyone or any reminders of his life as Nastan Popov. He had perfected his persona as Stephen Law. He had eradicated every trace of his former self.

'How dare these people interfere with the progression of my vision by unconsciously catching me off-guard?' thought Stephen angrily.

'Grigor my old friend; I see you are prospering as Mayor,' he thought, recalling Norman's photographs. 'I see that your childhood ambition has come true. Well, it seems as if both our childhood dreams have come true,' he thought to himself. He picked up his magnifying glass and placed it in front of the images of his father.

'Papa,' he said out loud, 'I will not let you down. I have succeeded in phase one of my Global plan. Phase two is about to begin. I have to ensure that I am never surprised again. I have to make certain that no one ever realises my true identity,' he finished, not knowing that Angelina had already deduced he was Nastan Popov. Unaware that the memory of him as a teenage boy had conjured in her so many emotions of guilt because she felt that she had abandoned him to a lonely existence in the International School. Nastan had viewed Angelina as the only person in the world who understood him and his desire for Global.

However, Angelina's experience had been quite different to Stephen's as it was Angelina's father who had insisted that she and Rod learnt Global. Her father, after returning from a conference abroad, had felt totally inadequate that he had been unable to participate fully as he had been the only non-Global speaker. The delegates, who were from different countries, had this one common denominator. Angelina's father had returned with a new goal for his family – they would all learn Global.

'It is the language of opportunity and status,' he had announced on his return. Whilst away, he had bought as many Global language books as his luggage limit would allow. He set a new rule in his home. All his family were to learn Global; even Angelina's mother. But they would learn it secretly. Her father did not want to upset the Minority Language Council whose job was to protect their Mother Tongue from becoming obsolete. He did not want to be seen as a language traitor. Angelina and Rod had learnt Global since their teenage years. Angelina loved learning it and had loved the excitement that it was a secret. She thrived at it, developing stronger language skills month by month. But Rod, he had been opposed to it. Not because he had anything against the language itself or because he saw it as a threat to his Mother Tongue; simply because Rod did not have a desire to ever leave his country. He could not foresee a time when he would ever need to be able to speak Global – if only he had known!

Then, just before Angelina left home for University, her dog, which she had had since six years old as a present when her tonsils were removed, died. It was this experience that made Angelina reflect that if losing a pet could cause so much pain, then how much more hurt and suffering would a child experience at the loss of a parent, grandparent or friend. The day that she had gone to Grigor's house, was Angelina's first day as a Bereavement Counsellor. Therefore, it had also been the first time she had had the opportunity to use her Global language skills to gain a child's trust. The months she spent with Nastan truly gave her the opportunity to use a language to build a relationship with a child that she was certain would have clammed up and would probably still be in some kind of counselling today.

Her involvement with Nastan in Global had enabled him to refocus and move on. But Angelina couldn't hold Global responsible for whom Nastan had become. Stephen had a different agenda to the teenage boy who simply wanted to learn a language. Something else must have triggered this Global obsession. Something or someone else must have caused this fixation with taking Global Standard to the ends of the earth.

Although Angelina could speak Global, she didn't know if she fully believed in Stephen's ultimate plan for Global Standard to be the one common language of the world. Despite her father's rule, in his later years, when he had retired and didn't need to leave home for business trips, he had reverted to speaking only in his language. Her mother had been glad, saying that speaking a language that did not come naturally to her had been hard work. But her mother insisted that Global had benefited her children – Angelina especially. Angelina had always been a self-sufficient, motivated person but Rod; well Rod had needed a push, a big push to leave home for the land of opportunity and to make his parents proud of him.

‘You owe it to your father,’ urged his mother, ‘he has sacrificed so much for you. He has sacrificed his health for you to have opportunities that he never had. You must go to the land of prosperity. You must make your father proud. Now go and make a name for yourself.’

Angelina remembered how her mother had pushed Rod away, thinking it was for his good. She was amazed that the actions of her mother all those years ago had unintentionally enabled her to be reunited with Nastan Popov. Her mother had forced Rod along a path, for which he had no yearning. Angelina knew she couldn’t tell Rod the truth about Stephen. For now, she would keep his true identity hidden. She would allow him to carry on with his plans but if at any point she believed Stephen was overstepping the mark, then she would confront him – she owed that much to his grandfather. Angelina recalled Grigor’s mother telling her that Apollos had detested Global. Angelina was certain that he would not be pleased with whom Stephen had become. As long as the launch of Global Standard remained the focus of Global speaking countries only, and did not cause tribulation to other nations or her brother as the front-runner, then she would not speak up. For now, she would watch and wait. Little did she know that Stephen’s plans for Global Standard did not consider the feelings of Mother Tongue citizens as Rod could testify. Neither did Angelina know that what Stephen had envisaged, no one – even someone he had cared about a long time ago –would get in the way of his plan.

***

Stephen could not concentrate. He looked out at Joan's empty desk; the blank space was bothering him. He was so used to seeing Joan that her absence was upsetting the equilibrium.

'If Joan would rather be on holiday then I will find myself a new constant,' he thought, pettily.

He accessed the personnel files of his employees, intent on finding someone suitably skilled who could replace her. He started his search, alphabetically, by surname. He reached the end of those surnames beginning with A but there was no one with the appropriate skills. He moved to surnames beginning with 'B'.

'Phoebe Burnham,' he said out loud, recognising her name and remembering Joan's conversation with her and subsequent odd behaviour.

'How did I forget to question Joan?' he deliberated, annoyed, remembering that he had wanted to ask Joan about the nature of their conversation and why Joan was tracking her.

Stephen looked at Phoebe's information. Her residence and Global citizen identity number both seemed to be in order.

'Excellent Global Testing Score,' he thought, impressed. 'My latest recruit,' realising that Phoebe had been a GSW employee for less than two months. After his shock discovery about Rod's background, he was considering changing from an online process to a face to face, old-fashioned style interview.

'Who has the time for interviews these days?' he wondered, implicitly answering his own question within seconds of asking. He had decided that as Rod had alerted him to a flaw in the interview process, he would be extra vigilant. No one would ever gain illegal employment in his organisation. Besides, the recruitment tasks were so demanding that most people gave up before the most gruelling test of all – the language examination. All his employees had to achieve a minimum score of 999, even if they passed all the previous tasks.

'Miss Phoebe Burnham will do just fine,' he thought, looking at her score, which was the maximum.

He messaged her instantly. Even though the message was sent by Stephen, directly, it was doctored to make the employee believe that GSW had a personnel department. The message read:

"GSW Internal Application Process – GSW Human Resources Department
To: Miss Phoebe Burnham
Global citizenship Number: PB07135
Message:

Miss Burnham,
GSW is pleased to inform you that you have received an internal promotion. Your new, temporary position is: 'SECRETARY TO MR S LAW – DIRECTOR OF GSW AND LEADER OF THE FREE GLOBAL WORLD'.
Your new position is situated in the office of 'JOAN MARSH', which is accessible via the Executive Lift. Lift code is '666999'. Instructions concerning your secondment employment are available upon log on. Your access code for log on is '210801'.
GSW wishes you every success in your new role. If you have any questions then please access the virtual help desk, which is available via the staff area. We will aim to respond to your query within 24 hours."

***

Phoebe sat at her desk not expecting that her life was about to change forever. An urgent internal mail notification flashed up on her screen. She froze, wondering if Joan had told Mr Law the truth before she went on holiday. She tried to ignore the message, frightened about its content but she couldn't access anything on which she had been working. Then, without even opening the message, it appeared on her screen.

Phoebe read the notification in disbelief, "Internal promotion. Joan Marsh's office. Secretary to Mr Law" - Is this some kind of joke?' she pondered. Phoebe read the message in its entirety over and over. She was aware that Joan was on holiday but, of course, she couldn't let on she knew. As far as anyone else was concerned her relationship with Joan was the same as every other GSW employee - non-existent.

'If this is a George and Eddie prank then I won't get further than the Executive Lift,' she considered, gathering her belongings.

She pressed the lift button and waited patiently for it to arrive. She looked once more at the code that had been recorded in her email. The lift arrived and Phoebe entered "666999" wondering if anything would happen. The doors opened instantly and she stepped inside. As the doors opened on the executive floor, Phoebe's heart began fluttering.

'I've done it!' she exclaimed to herself proudly. 'I've already made a name for myself! Mr Law knows me. I will write to Georgia instantly and tell her to come to Global City because I have already paved the way.'

But sadly, what Phoebe didn't know was that Georgia had left already. She hadn't had the patience to wait. Phoebe's letter arrived at her parents' home, but because it was written in Global they had no way of reading it. They had no means of knowing what Phoebe was saying. They had no way of responding to let Phoebe know that Georgia had already left – just like her elder sister – she had left under the cover of darkness and taken with her all the money her parents had in the world.

***

Stephen sat in Norman's office feeling irritated by the very sound of his voice. Norman's colloquial behaviour on launch day had affirmed to Stephen that to Norman, being Director of the GSPC was just a job. Norman was on countdown to retirement. The Director's job had landed on his lap. A favour someone thought they owed him; a big salary to bank in readiness for his later years. Norman hadn't even heard of the GPC before being approached by his long-standing government friend, David. At first, Norman had been somewhat confused over the role of the GPC. He had questioned who had sanctioned it and had asked if it was an officially backed government programme.

'Norman, you ask too many questions my friend. Didn't someone once say that convention is practically the same as law? Look, it's simple. The world has gone Global crazy. Outside of the Motherlands it is a primary language in over sixty self-governing countries. GSW, that is Stephen Law, has a phenomenal vision to make Global Standard, GS, the one common language of the world. I believe it could work. I believe that if these other countries adopt GS as an official language with a view to phasing out their various Mother Tongues, the GPC will be more than just a convention my friend.

'The technology Mr Law has pioneered is mind blowing. He needs us and we need him. If you don't believe me then the next time you watch the world news look out for Global being spoken by the majority of world leaders. It's a travesty that they are not representing their country by speaking their own language but that's a good thing for us and Mr Law. Don't get me wrong, not every country will want GS as an official language, but let me tell you my friend, a lot will. Mr Law is so passionate about taking GS to the ends of the earth; as he stated in his blue print, I believe that he will stop at nothing to achieve his goal. In the meantime, the GPC gives GSW an endorsement that people will believe is the law and all we need to do is sit back and watch the money roll in. There's a big bonus at the end of your five years Norman. Mr Law has done all the headwork. We just have to be seen holding his hand, so to speak. Think of all those future holidays you can plan. You will be set up financially for life, as there's a clause that you will receive a percentage of all future profits for the duration of your life. Norman, it really is a no-brainer my friend,' finished David.

So, Norman, who hadn't been able to think of a reason for saying "no", had agreed to be Director of the GPC. But David was the *real* Director, a silent leader, who made decisions based on profit margins alone. Norman, as Stephen had deduced, was a "yes" man – in the nicest possible way; a "nine to five" man who faithfully turned up for work each day and then went home, happily giving no thought to Global issues until nine o'clock the following morning. Norman, who was a perfectly ordinary, nice man, with a somewhat complicated family life, had no ambition, no passion and no desire for Global Standard. Stephen was certain that Norman answered to a higher authority - someone who Stephen had never met. Someone that Stephen was determined to meet in due time.

'Great launch party,' said Norman, 'I can still taste that delicious …'

'Did you bring the figures?' Stephen asked dismissively, wondering when he had given Norman the impression that they were anything but colleagues.

'The figures, yes, I have the figures,' Norman answered, sensing that Stephen wanted to get down to business. Norman pressed a few digits on his mini pc and confirmed, 'Eighty-one per cent saturation in Motherland and one hundred per cent saturation in the Sub Motherlands. We have a number of leaders in Mother Tongue areas here and here,' he said, pointing to the GSW map on the wall, 'who have expressed allegiance to Global Standard. We are drawing up contracts for the purchase of your translation technology. I need to confirm a shipping date to them. Have your technical team programmed the technology with these particular languages? Is the technology good to go?' asked Norman.

Stephen held up his arm to stop Norman continuing.

'Let's backtrack shall we Director. I thought I heard you say that the saturation for Motherland is eighty-one per cent. Motherland is this country – the epicentre for Global Standard; our figures should be one hundred and one percent. They must be wrong,' said Stephen, disturbed.

Norman looked worried. He thought he had begun building a rapport with Stephen. But today, Stephen's demeanour was fierce. Norman left his seat and unpinned the GSW world map from the wall and placed it on the desk in front of Stephen.

'There's your problem,' he said to Stephen, pointing at an area on the map within Motherland, colour coded blue. 'There's your pocket of resistance,' he continued, trying to shift the blame. 'Even though they are in Motherland itself, their language is protected. It is spoken and used daily by about nineteen per cent of the population within the region. There is a decline year on year as the younger generation leave, but, amongst the late-middle to older generation, their native tongue is revered and cherished. They will not give up their language without a fight. They would probably die for their right to speak it,' said Norman, knowing that what he was telling Mr Law was correct.

Stephen was furious. Here he was, a week after the launch and it was only now that Norman, "the overseer of Global Standard" had brought the blue problem area to his attention.

'Did I not alert you to this Mother Tongue locality myself? Did I not tell you that this region within Motherland had to be globalised? Did I not, months ago, sit around this very table with you, doing the same thing that you are doing now, that is, pointing at the GSW map of the world, whilst telling you that this region needed to be dealt with.'

'Yes you did and I did my best to "globalise" the region in question but you do not understand the complexities involved. There are new bills to be written and passed into law. Then there's the Education Committee. I cannot override an official first language, which has been a medium of instruction for centuries; I cannot do it. It is not within my power. The Global

Standard launch was a success because the countries involved are Global-speaking. We have successfully sparked an awakening amongst primary Globalists who want to adopt Global Standard as an official language, but, surely you realised that it would not be that easy? Baby steps, Stephen. Baby steps are needed. We cannot force a region or non-Global speaking country to adopt Global Standard if they do not want to. Global Standard is not the law. It's just an excellent vision of what the future could be for the countries who want to be involved. Global citizenship and speaking Global Standard is an option, not the law,' he reiterated. 'I'm sorry Stephen but you will have to bide your time until the language in this area phases out naturally. It will happen, probably over the next twenty years or so. But our hands are tied. You have to remember that you are the leader of the FREE Global world. You are not an autocrat or a king. You are simply an entrepreneur with a superb business plan that is drawing more attention than I ever dreamed possible. Our profits have excelled over the last few days alone and country leaders are buying into your vision. You have to be patient Stephen. Global Standard is not the law. People are still free to communicate in whatever language they desire and until the official world leaders state otherwise, you are going to have to be grateful for what you have achieved so far,' finished Norman, rationally.

'An autocrat,' he thought, pleased that Norman had bestowed him such a title. 'But not the law,' thought Stephen, angrily, 'not the law; I am the law, I am Stephen Law and there will be a new law concerning Global Standard that will eradicate all other languages. My Law, in memory of my father, will be the only law in place concerning languages. People will bow down to my law. People will become Global citizens and renounce their Mother Tongue in favour of Global Standard or their lives won't be worth living,' choked Stephen, irrationally.

'But you are right,' he said calmly to a very relieved Norman. 'Rome wasn't built in a day,' he commented, knowing Norman would love that phrase.

'Yes, that's the spirit. Rome wasn't built in a day. Baby steps,' concluded Norman, picking up the map and pinning it back on the wall.

Stephen glared scornfully at Norman, thinking, 'If you haven't got the power to pass my new law concerning Global Standard then I will not stop until I find the person within the GSPC who can,' vowed Stephen.

29

Norman wasn't sure if he had handled the situation concerning Mother Tongue area blue, correctly. He regretted using the term 'baby steps' with a man who had no interest in a dawdling, long-term strategy. Norman sensed there was an urgency to Stephen's plans, which had nothing to do with profit margins. He felt certain that Stephen was ready to take those plans to the next level. There was a ferocity about Stephen's demeanour that Norman hadn't sensed before – it made him feel uneasy. Even though Norman was an excellent administrator, he was concerned that he was inadequately skilled to handle Stephen's ambition. Stephen was just beginning his career. Norman was coming to the end of his. Plus, he knew that he would not be able to stand in the wings if the time came to force Global Standard upon Mother Tongue citizens in area blue.

'How has he been today?' Norman asked his wife on his arrival home. He glanced at his father who was dozing in his favourite chair.

'He's not wandered into the city again, if that's what you mean,' she replied, jokingly.

'I see he's wearing the same clothes as yesterday and the day before,' said Norman.

'Yes, they could really do with a wash but I don't want to upset him. He's still calling them his city clothes. He still thinks you're his grandson. I'm not sure who he thinks I am today, but he seems to like me,' his wife responded, softly.

'That's something at least,' muttered Norman, feeling guilty that his wife, Linda, had to deal with his father whilst he was in work.

When Linda had phoned him on launch day to tell him that his father had left the house again, she had been frantic.

'What clothes is he wearing?' Norman asked.

'What do you mean? What is he wearing? Oh no, that's the first question the police will ask if he is deemed a missing person,' she continued, apologising, saying that she had only turned her back for a second and he had gone.

'That's not what I mean. Don't worry. Does he have his suit and tie on? Is his walking stick in the house?' Norman asked methodically.

'Yes, he is wearing his suit and paisley tie. His walking stick and wallet are gone too,' she carried on.

'That's good,' Norman admitted.

'How is it good?' she asked bewildered.

'Because I know where he's heading,' Norman had said.

Sure enough, just as Norman deduced from his father's attire, he had turned up at the GPC building. After a lovely chat with Rod, and spotting Norman, he followed Norman to his office.

Norman immediately phoned Linda. He knew she would be beside herself with worry. 'Father's here. Safe and sound.'

'I'll come and get him,' she blurted out, relieved. 'He'll only be in your way.'

'Okay. He's resting on the settee. Hopefully he'll fall asleep.'

'On my way,' she murmured, selflessly.

'Linda,' he said lovingly to his wife, 'I'm sorry that you've been lumbered with father-sitting. You should be here, by my side, celebrating our success.'

'Don't worry. There'll be plenty of time for celebrating when you've retired. We have the rest of our lives. Let's make sure your father has what he needs for the rest of his,' she said.

'Have you got your pass to my office, in case I'm summoned upstairs?' Norman asked.

'Yes. You won't even know I've been and gone,' she soothed, hanging up the phone. Norman watched his father as he slept, wondering, when he eventually awoke, would he know him as his son? Wondering if he would tell the story over and over again; the tale that they pretended they had never heard before, even though they had had to listen to it hundreds of times:

'It was a terrible time,' his father would begin in their own language, and they would know what was coming next.

'When was it a terrible time?' Norman would utter, inviting his father to tell him the old, old, story.

'Your great, great, great-grandfather's knuckles were red raw from the lashing – wood is a terrible object for inflicting pain. Right across his knuckles on both hands, day after day, all because he wouldn't conform.'

Then his father would stop until Norman encouraged him in a surprised tone, 'Conform? To whom?'

'To the language traitor; a disloyal man who betrayed his own people; who brought too much negative attention to our heritage, culture and language. He thought that speaking our native tongue made us stupid and uneducated. Even then Global was seen as the superior vernacular, which gave status and opportunity.

Our small nation soon became the focus amongst the educators within our country. It was decided that speaking our Mother Tongue had to stop. It was agreed that our region would conform and learn Global. Our nation would be culturally oppressed, denied from speaking our ancient language – that was the new law. The law, that stood by and watched as children were severely punished for speaking their own Mother Tongue. Of course, speaking your own language is the most natural thing in the world. So for doing what comes naturally, the children; your own great, great, great-grandfather included, were humiliated and beaten. The children tried their best to obey the new law but it was difficult. Most children weren't purposely ignoring Global but their own language was simply more spontaneous to them. They opened their mouths and their own language came out. However, the new act would not make allowances. Each time a child spoke their native tongue and not Global, the consequences were unbearable.

The language enforcer would tell them to sit at the front of the classroom causing maximum humiliation. They would be ordered to place both hands outstretched on the teacher's desk. Then, the enforcer would strike their knuckles with a wooden ruler, which was purposely thickened to inflict pain. Next, the enforcer, using an ink pen which had a very sharp nib, would tattoo the initials NN, which stood for *Native No*, on two knuckles. They would choose whichever knuckles looked most sore so that the ink would seep into the wound, sometimes causing infection. Some children, to ensure they would be spared punishment, would become elective mutes not wanting to speak either language for fear of getting it wrong.

But your great, great, great-grandfather, he was fearless. He had a different spirit to the other children. Not a bragging spirit, but one that gave the others a hope that one day their lives would return to normal. He refused to speak Global. He would not relinquish conversing in his language, no matter what the cost. His mother pleaded with him not to be a martyr, telling him that sometimes you just have to submit and obey. But he would not. Being denied the right to speak his ancient tongue was too much anguish. He would not bow down to an unjust authority. He did not agree with the new language law and word of his defiance soon spread throughout the nation until it reached the educators in parliament. Your great, great, great-grandfather had "NN" inked on his knuckles so many times that in the end it became indelible. But his tenacity was rewarded. His "stand" resulted in a new act that superseded the Global law. Our Mother Tongue was reinstated and became our country's official language in recognition of his stand. Global was introduced gradually into the schools but only as a second language. The rights for our Mother Tongue that are in place today, Norman, are due to his foresight to stand up for what he believed. He didn't have a problem with Global. He just didn't think it right that one language be forcefully imposed over another.

Norman, who had heard this story on countless occasions, for the first time since he had been Director of the GSPC, felt a deep burden of shame. This old, old, account of his ancestor's legacy weighed heavily on his soul. For the first time ever, he felt relieved that his father was not aware of his current job; a job that went against everything for which his great, great, great-grandfather had stood. Norman felt privileged that he had grown up fully aware of his heritage and that his father had taught him their own language.

'Global Standard to the World,' sighed Norman, 'one common world language that will unite all citizens regardless of ethnicity - that is so wrong.' Norman knew he couldn't work for the GSPC any longer. It simply was not ethical. 'Besides, when Stephen finds out I have a cultural tie to area blue and still converse in that vernacular, he'll probably figure out a way to have me "handled". So, I will resign. I will tell David that my father's dementia has worsened and that Linda needs my help,' thought Norman, determinedly.

30

Joan sat beside the town lake in awe of the sunrise. In the city, the tower blocks limited the aura of the early morning sun. But here, at home, Joan was able to witness the sun waking up, stretching its rays and the burnished glow of its full awakening. The sun's peachy tint turned to hazy yellow and sat peacefully on the lake, like a warm blanket, then moved slowly upwards signalling the passing of time. Living in the city had made Joan an early riser. For years her alarm had woken her at dawn. For years she had struggled out of bed, wondering why, in the winter months especially, she was getting up at what felt like the middle of the night. But all those years of training her body to rise early had paid off. Now, at home, she didn't need the alarm to wake her. Her natural body clock did that.

'Beautiful morning,' said someone in Mother Tongue, to Joan's surprise.

She looked up in the direction of the voice but the sun was blocking her view. She could see the outline of a man walking towards her, weighed down by fishing tackle but his face was not visible. The warm, yellow glow of the sun, for some reason, had turned his face a ghostly shade of white. The paint like, eyeless face of this stranger was very eerie, yet his walk was jolly and lively. Joan looked away, not allowing the unusual mask of the man to affect her good mood.

‘Yes, it is,’ she replied, quite naturally in her Mother Tongue.

Joan placed her left and right hands in front of her eyes, wondering if the sun would play a further trick. She wanted to see the face of the man to whom she was talking, but the sun wouldn’t allow it. The white mask had been replaced by a fuzzy orange glow.

‘If I get up to leave now,’ thought Joan, ‘I will appear very rude.’

She tried to relax back into the morning reverie but was intrigued as to whom the voice belonged.

‘Best time of the day to fish,’ the voice said. ‘The sun is just beginning to warm up the water which will wake the fish and hopefully they will come to the surface to say hello.’

Joan laughed.

‘It’s true,’ smirked the angler, ‘fish are very friendly creatures.’

‘Until they end up on your fishing rod,’ said Joan, sounding as if she disapproved.

‘Friendly and considerate,’ he replied, causing Joan to laugh again.

‘When I was a boy there were no fish this side of the lake. All the fish were on the other side waiting to be caught by the tourists. But one day, something amazing happened. One day, I was sitting in this very spot and a fish appeared. Then another one came, then hundreds upon hundreds of fish all at once were swimming around, excited to be free. They had escaped from the dull tourists; escaped from captivity.’

Joan knew exactly how those fish must have felt. She had escaped from the city. She had escaped and didn’t know how she could convince herself to return. The last two weeks had passed by in a whirl. She hadn’t told

Stephen how long she would be gone but she knew that three weeks was the absolute limit.

'So you have lived here all your life?' asked Joan.

'Yes, since birth. What about you? Your Mother Tongue is excellent so I'm assuming you have never left either.'

Joan was pleased that her Global life didn't show in her accent. When she had returned home just over two weeks ago, she had been concerned that she wouldn't be able to communicate with her parents properly. They had managed over the years but it had been basic communication using "virtual time" as and when her parents had been able to access the internet via a computer in their town hall. But as soon as Joan had heard her mother, father and sisters' familiar voices speaking in their wonderful, warm, endearing language, she had been transported back in time; before Global, GSW and Stephen Law. She was a child again, then a teenager, then a young adult, home with people she loved and who loved her; with her language that endorsed who she was and where she belonged. Joan sensed that Global and all she had longed for before GSW was slowly being removed from her as each day passed at home.

Joan put up her hand to cover her eyes and looked once more in the direction of the voice. As she did so, the sun moved upwards, allowing her to see his face, which looked intent, as he baited his rod.

'No, I've never left either. Why would anyone ever want to?' she replied, ashamed that she had chased after the Global dream and that she was lying to this stranger.

'So why have I never seen you in town? The Mayor usually knows everyone,' he said, smiling.

Stumped by his question and not expecting the angler to be the Mayor, Joan said the first thing that came into her head.

'Well I did leave I suppose, if you call living in the mountain village, nursing my grandmother, leaving.'

'I'd call that sacrifice,' he said, sympathetically, 'it can get very lonely and cold in the mountain village. Is she well, your grandmother?'

'No, she died, but she had an enjoyable life. She was well loved.'

'What was her name?' he asked, caringly.

Joan was stumped again. She thought back to what Phoebe had said about the story of her grandmother being shunned for voicing her opinion in favour of Global replacing their Mother Tongue.

'What was her name?' repeated Joan.

'Yes, my predecessor often visited the older generation in the mountain. I know he loved spending time up there. He told me a while ago they are the real language upholders. They would die to protect our heritage.'

'Not this old grandmother,' thought Joan, hoping a name would come to her.

Just as Joan was opening her mouth to impart a fictional name, the fisherman began reeling in his line, 'Here we go,' he said, obviously expecting a big fish to be dangling on the end. He got to work while trying to hold his balance.

'Would you mind holding the net so I can drop the wriggler straight in?' he asked, pleased with his morning catch.

Joan carried out his request, relieved that he had not asked her grandmother's name again. His prize had sent him totally off track. It was at that moment Joan realised her place was in Global City. How could she live a lie in her hometown? How could she expect her parents and sisters to invent a fabrication about the years she had spent living away. Besides, she needed to get back for Phoebe. But before she returned, she would reassure Phoebe's parents that their daughter was well. But as for their other daughter Georgia, she couldn't give them any news concerning her whereabouts.

31

Stephen's father's papers about Global replacing Mother Tongue in his own country formed a blanket on Stephen's bed as they had done so all those years ago, on his first night at the International School.

'There's your area of resistance,' thought Stephen, clinically, recalling Norman's comments. 'Baby steps. You are not the law. Global is not law. You are not the law. People are still free to speak whatever language they choose.' Norman's words vibrated frantically around Stephen's head.

Stephen unpinned his father's original map from his wall and placed it on top of the papers. When Stephen, as a teenager, had first looked at his father's map, he hadn't understood what it had meant. He wasn't aware that Apollos had tried to stop his father following his Global ambition. He didn't know that Apollos had spoken with his father about the future consequences of replacing their Mother Tongue with Global.

When Stephen studied the map as a teenager, he hadn't comprehended what the abbreviated codes and colours meant. But years later, Stephen's understanding of his father's vision for Global was so clear; it was as if he had written the plans himself. Stephen looked at the five countries on his father's map that were colour coded black and labelled GL. Stephen observed that his map labelled GS – Global Standard showed the same five countries. He looked proudly at his map, which emulated his father's desire for Global. He had achieved phase one of what his father had been denied. The "pocket of resistance" that fell within a region of Motherland and was colour coded orange on his father's map, had overnight become Stephen's focus. He remembered that Norman had colour coded this area blue, despite Stephen ordering it be coded orange. These "blue people" who were refusing to become Global citizens; these people who would rather die than give up the right to speak their own language, they WOULD conform to the only recognised language of Motherland – Global Standard.

Stephen put the GSW world map on top of his father's map and lined them up perfectly. To his delight, the transparent material of which both maps were made, when placed one on top of the other, the blue on top of the orange, created black – the colour of GS throughout the planet. Stephen smiled to himself, believing this to be concrete proof that this region would conform or bear the consequences. These language traitors were undermining GSW and the GSPC. This "small pocket of resistance" would be his test case – it would be his pilot scheme from which he would conquer all other Mother Tongue areas.

'Tell Rod Jones to come to my office immediately,' bellowed Stephen at a very anxious Phoebe as she fumbled at the buttons on her communication device. Being Joan Marsh was more difficult than she ever deemed possible.

'Mr Jones,' muttered a very timid Phoebe, as he picked up his office phone. 'Mr Law is requesting that you attend his office forthwith,' she finished, hoping she hadn't disconnected the line before she had completed transmitting the message.

A few minutes later, Rod was knocking at Mr Law's office door, which gave Phoebe the reassurance she needed that she had completed her task successfully.

'Mr Jones,' boomed Stephen, 'enter.'

Rod looked at Stephen who was hovering over the maps on his desk.

Stephen looked up; his eyes were bloodshot, suggesting that he hadn't slept properly in days.

'I have your first task as my language warrior,' he continued, eyes cast down, pointing irately at the maps.

'Meet me in your office tomorrow morning at six am sharp for your briefing. Pack a bag. You may be gone a while,' said Stephen, commandingly.

***

'But how long will you be gone?' asked a concerned Angelina.

'I don't know. My orders are to pack a bag because I may be gone a while.'

'Where are you going?'

'I won't know until I meet with Mr Law tomorrow morning.'

'Should I come with you?'

'No. That's out of the question. I don't need a babysitter. This is my job. If Mr Law needs me in a different region for a while then that is what I must do, without question.'

'So what am I going to do while you are away?'

'Explore, make friends and find a job. You have a lot to offer.'

'Maybe I'll ask Mr Law for a job,' said Angelina, thinking that could be an ideal means of keeping her eye on his movements.

'That's a great idea. Now let me pack so I can get on with my task,' grumbled Rod annoyed that, even though he was an adult, Angelina still treated him like the lesser sibling who needed guidance.

'Mr Law and I seemed like old friends at the launch party. Did you notice?'

'Yes, actually I did. It was a little weird to see him so amiable with a stranger.'

'Maybe he felt like our paths had crossed before,' she let slip, longing to tell her brother the truth.

'Just be careful. He can be very ruthless if you anger him,' he warned. Rod still didn't understand how Mr Law had been so smitten with Angelina. After all, as his sister, Mr Law was fully aware that she had the same Mother Tongue heritage. 'Plus, his grandfather is obviously not a Global native,' he thought further, still unaware that the old man he had met at the launch was in fact Norman's father.

'Don't worry about me. If I can deal with teenagers, I can deal with Mr Law,' she declared, leaving Rod alone to finish packing.

Rod got to his office to find Mr Law already there. He was immaculately dressed as usual; the perfect mannequin.

'Have you packed for your journey?' Stephen enquired.

'Yes, sir. Everything I need is in my car.'

'Very good,' said Stephen, handing him a new mini pc.

'My device is in working order sir,' said Rod, wondering why he was supplying a new one.

'Your instructions concerning your task are available on this device. Do not lose it as it contains everything you need to know to make your assignment a success. Your destination, appointments, objectives … it's all there. You may spend the next hour looking at the information. You will leave at precisely seven thirty am and follow the satellite instructions to get to your destination. You will be making the whole journey by car. It is not complicated. It will take you approximately three hours. During the time you are away on GSW business, you will not have contact with any other employee or family member – that includes your sister. Your task is covert and you will only speak with people I have made appointments with. Do you understand?'

'Yes sir,' Rod replied, unquestioningly.

'Remember, you are "the face of GSW". You will conduct yourself with passion, conviction and, above all else, loyalty to the GSW vision, which is …'

'One language, one version, one vision,' Rod repeated passionately.

'Very good,' said Stephen, pleased with who Rod had become in the name of Global Standard.

'I will leave you to prepare. There is a direct link to my mini pc. You may contact me day or night.'

'Thank you, sir,' Rod responded.

Stephen stood up to leave. He headed towards Rod's office door but then turned around to face Rod and said convincingly, 'You are my language warrior and I am expecting great things from you. Do not let any opposition to our vision get in the way of achieving your task. Do whatever it takes.'

'Yes sir,' nodded Rod, not fully understanding to what he was agreeing.

***

Norman crumpled another sheet of paper and threw it into the bin along with the other sheets. His resignation letter was proving more difficult to write than he had thought. He knew it was the right thing to do; he wasn't uncertain about that. It was letting his old friend David down that he was struggling with. Even though David had badgered him into accepting the Director's role, he knew that his long-standing friend had his best interests at heart. Norman's letter needed to be strongly constructed; his argument and evidence for resigning had to be unquestionable to ensure that David did not talk him around.

He began writing once more:

"Dear David,
Please accept this letter as confirmation that I wish to resign as the GSPC Director. Believe me when I say this, is not a decision I have taken lightly and I appreciate the belief and confidence that you placed in me to undertake the Director's role.

However, the decision to resign my post is purely based on family circumstances. My father's health has deteriorated over the last few months and Linda, as you know, needs extra support. I need to ensure that both my wife and father have the provision and care needed at this extremely stressful time in our lives.
I wish you, the GSPC and GSW every success.
Your friend and colleague
Norman."

He re-read the words, deciding they were acceptable, took a photocopy for his personal file and then placed it in an envelope. As he was addressing the envelope, his office telephone rang.

'Hello,' he began.

'Norman, he's gone again,' began a very shaky Linda.

Norman sighed, realising that despite his real reason for resigning, he was truly needed at home.

'Okay, don't worry. I'm sure he will come here as usual.'

'I was on the phone and then he'd gone. I don't understand how he even knows the way to your office. He forgets where the bathroom is but can make his way through the city. It doesn't make sense.'

'I know, none of it makes sense, but don't be anxious … he's here. I told you not to worry. He's here … Dad, what are you doing here? Linda is worried sick,' Linda could hear Norman scolding her father-in-law.

'Norman, don't be angry with him, just be glad he's okay,' said Linda, trying to calm her husband down. 'I'll go off the phone so you can sort him out. I'll see you when you get home.'

'Dad, sit down. Don't touch that. Just sit down for a minute and then I'll take you home.'

'Home, why would I want to go home? I've only just got here. I like it here. Where's my secretary gone? I need to dictate a letter,' he rambled.

'Dad, sit down,' said Norman, firmly. His father sat down like a naughty child. Norman handed him the *City Finance Daily* newspaper to read. His father opened the broadsheet, straightened his posture and held it at its usual upright position, so all Norman could see of his father was his bottom half. Norman knew the newspaper would keep him occupied for a while and then he would have to listen to an abridged version of everything that he had digested.

With his father occupied, Norman set about tidying his desk and placed a few belongings into a GSW carrier bag. He had never really "moved in" to his office, not like some people whose office was their second home. He placed his resignation letter on the centre of his desk so it would be easily found by David. He didn't want a fuss; he would phone David when he got home, which he felt was the least stressful way of leaving. He knew David would try to convince him to stay but he needed to be firm and just tell him that he is sorry but the letter explains everything.

'Ready Dad?' said Norman. 'Dad, are you ready?' he asked again, knowing that when his father started to concentrate on something, he was easily transfixed. 'Dad,' he said once more, walking over to him, pulling the newspaper away. 'Dad,' he cried out in anguish as his father sat motionless, eyes closed and his complexion ghostly white. Norman prodded him and to his horror his father toppled lifelessly to the left, his arms still in upright newspaper position – he was dead.

Norman stood looking at his father who just a few minutes ago had been so alive. Yes, his illness had made things stressful but, despite his father's confusion, he was still humorous, intelligent, loving, everything that a father should be. 'Dad,' Norman pleaded, 'come on Dad, I'm listening, tell me the old, old story. You know, about how my …' he broke down, unable to continue, realising that he was talking to a dead man.

'Linda,' Norman sobbed over the telephone, 'Dad's gone.'

'He's getting too good. How could he leave your office without you knowing?' she asked, bemused.

‘No, I mean, he’s gone. He’s gone for good. Dad’s dead. He was just sitting here, reading the paper, I thought he was concentrating, you know, like he usually does, sitting in silence, concentrating and then he would chirp up and give me an edited report … but I was busy and then I was ready to go and called him and called him again and then and then … Oh Linda, it was awful. Oh Linda, he’s just lying here on my settee …’

‘Norman, try to calm down. I know you’ve had a terrible shock but you must hang up the telephone and phone an ambulance. No. Don’t worry about that. I’ll phone an ambulance and the police will probably come too. Go and tell Claudia what has happened and wait with her until I get there.’

‘But I can’t leave him alone … just hurry,’ he said, sobbing.

‘I’m on my way,’ she replied in disbelief that her father-in-law was gone.

Norman locked his office door. He couldn’t bring himself to tell Claudia, his secretary that his father was dead. He would unlock it for Linda or the paramedics but no one else. No one else was coming in. Norman sat next to his father waiting for Linda to arrive. He didn’t know if she would get there before the ambulance. He hoped so. Time stood still. Norman tried to put his father into a more natural position. He looked so odd. His fingers were still crunched up as if he was holding the newspaper. His arms were bent at the elbows. Norman managed to get his father’s whole body onto the settee. ‘That’s better, you look more comfortable now Dad,’ he said softly. Norman sat perched on the end of the settee, waiting. He heard a knock on his office door. ‘Linda, at last,’ he thought, thinking there would be a lot more commotion if it was the paramedics or police. He knew he should have told Claudia what was going on but things would soon be self-explanatory. He unlocked his office door, longing to embrace his wife, longing to be comforted by her. 'Stephen, what are you doing here?' he blurted out, not expecting to be face to face with Mr Law. He was the last person he expected to see in his office unannounced. Norman could hear Claudia apologising, saying that he barged straight passed her and that he wouldn't take a seat. Norman just nodded so Claudia took that as acquiescence. Norman took a few steps backwards, dazed by Stephen's appearance. As Stephen barged his way in, Norman backed away further and stood by his window. Stephen, who hadn't turned his head to the right or to the left, was unaware that behind him lay Norman's dead father.

'You no longer have to worry about Mother Tongue area blue,' Stephen began, 'I have sent Rod Jones, my Operations Director, to take care of the situation. He will succeed where you failed. He will not be so easily intimidated. In fact, I am interested in hearing why you did not secure a meeting with the Education Minister for the region because when I spoke to him he very openly told me that the upkeep of their Mother Tongue is costing tens of thousands of pounds which could be better spent elsewhere. He couldn't recall you at all. Neither could he remember you contacting him to discuss Global Standard. In fact, he had never heard of the GSPC. What's the matter Norman? Cat got your tongue? No catchphrases to throw back at me? No glib retort? I'm waiting for an explanation, I'm …' Stephen stopped as he heard a commotion behind him and turned around. 'Papa?' he muttered, as he caught sight of an old man, lying down on Norman's settee; an old man who could so easily have been his grandfather. The hair colour, the tie and the walking stick that lay next to him, 'Papa?' he said out loud again, causing Norman to look at him with curiosity.

The paramedic looked at Stephen sympathetically and said, 'I realise this must have come as a massive shock. Would you like to step out of the room while we take a look at your grandfather?' Before Stephen could explain, Norman said angrily, 'This man has no business here. Please ask him to leave. I am the son.'

The paramedic apologised profusely and said, 'My sincere apologies. It's just that when I heard him calling out, distressed, I assumed he was his relative.'

'Sir, I think you should leave,' said the paramedic turning to Stephen.

Stephen walked slowly out of Norman's office, looking back one final time at the man who could have easily passed for Apollos; the hair colour, the suit, the paisley tie and the walking stick. This must have been the man Rod was referring to on the launch evening. Stephen shivered as memories of Apollos' death at the museum came back to him. He paled as he realised that his grandfather was not watching over him or looking out for him at all – but that his grandfather was dead. The invisible stranger was not Apollos reincarnated as his guardian angel. His grandfather was in the grave, along with his grandmother, father and mother.

As the paramedics took Norman's father away in a body bag, Norman thought about the audacity of Mr Law, that even in Norman's grief, he had made it about himself. What Norman had failed to digest was that Mr Law, in an unwitting moment, had called out in his Mother Tongue.

What Stephen had failed to realise was that the sight of Norman's dead father, lying there, a double of his own grandfather, when past grief engulfed his whole being, he had cried out in his Mother Tongue; a language that he hadn't heard or spoken for nearly twenty years. A language that he believed had been eradicated from his mind, heart, soul and tongue. But he could not remove the unresolved grief for his grandfather; the unresolved grief that subconsciously forbade Stephen to fully let go of who he truly was – Nastan Popov. Norman looked at his resignation envelope on his desk, retrieved it and put it in his jacket pocket.

'As long as I am Director of the GSPC then I will secretly do all in my power to limit Mr Law's spread of Global Standard. As long as I am Director of the GSPC I have the authority to halt any new laws concerning the language. I will ensure that Mr Law's vision is quashed. I will ensure that Mr Law is stopped from passing any new acts in Mother Tongue area blue. I will do it in honour and memory of my father and my great, great, great-grandfather and for Mother Tongue citizens all over the globe,' he thought, full of revenge.

***

Stephen arrived home feeling perturbed that he had allowed his emotions to be on public display, yet again. He replayed the scene in his mind unable to get rid of the image of Norman's father, lying dead on the settee. Stephen shuddered as he thought about the body that had lain just a few feet behind him, whilst he had been laying down his law to Norman. He thought back to Norman's expression, which had been vacant and uninterested in what Stephen had been saying. Stephen recalled the scene but did not realise that he had audibly called out for his grandfather in his own language. The paramedic, like so many other illegal Global citizens, had been surprised to hear his own dialect. But he knew better than to admit that he'd understood. He'd had to think quickly which was why he'd said 'calling out' when Stephen shouted in distress. He did not acknowledge the use of an endearing term that only a son or grandson would use in his unique culture. The paramedic was unaware of the irony that the speaker of such a tender word was the leader of the free Global world, who, supposedly had eradicated all traces of his Mother Tongue from his very being – or so he thought.

Stephen plotted calculatingly, 'Norman will need time off to plan the funeral, comfort his wife and so on… what better opportunity for me to hand pick who will oversee Global Standard in Norman's absence? This incident has provided me with the perfect reason to ask for a meeting with the real director – Norman's superior. By the time Norman comes back to work, I will have convinced the real director that Norman's role is redundant and the money that will be saved from his salary can be used to spearhead Global Standard in Mother Tongue areas who will then purchase the new translation technology.' Stephen knew the greed of men. He had seen nothing else since he had been in Global City. So, he realised the best way to approach the real Director was via the financial route as the GSPC was run based on profit margin alone. However, money was not Stephen's concern. He did not care about money. Taking Global Standard to the corners of the earth in memory of his father; that was his concern.

Stephen stood on his balcony. He looked at the GSW and GSPC neon sign which reflected "One Language,

One Version, One Vision" vibrantly around the city. Stephen stood perfectly still, with his arms outstretched. Without even whistling his usual call, the mourning doves flew and perched in his hand, one in each, looking for seeds. Stephen breathed in slowly through his nose and exhaled through his mouth, trying to rejuvenate his body. He felt a slight chill engulf him which caused the doves to fly back to their perch.

'Stephen, Stephen, Stephen,' he heard a voice whisper in his ear.

He swung around but nobody was there.

'You are right not to grieve for Norman's loss. You are right to see it as an opportunity. But, be careful you do not get lost in your own grief for your grandfather. Be careful you do not expose yourself by muttering words you cannot take back.'

'What do you mean?' Stephen asked, confused.

'Just be careful or everything you have worked for could be undone in seconds. Think before you allow your mouth to speak.'

'Papa?' said Stephen, longingly.

'That is what I mean. You need to eradicate that word from your very being or that one word will reveal to the world your true identity.'

'But if you are not him then who are you? If you are not my grandfather sent as my guardian angel to watch over me, then who are you?'

'Did I ever tell you that I was your grandfather?'

'No,' replied Stephen, falteringly, wondering why he had allowed himself to think it.

'Have I not given you everything that your heart desires to achieve your Global dreams and more?'

'Yes,' said Stephen, looking once more to the neon sign.

‘Norman’s father’s death has provided you with the perfect reason to meet the real leader of the GSPC. Tomorrow, you will go to Norman’s office and you will not leave until you have persuaded his superior that Norman’s role is redundant. Do you understand?’

‘Yes,’ said Stephen compliantly.

Stephen felt a dark shadow whirl around his body. Still unable to see from where the voice hailed, he asked, ‘If you are not my guardian angel, then who are you?’

The voice emitted a hollow laugh, ‘I am an angel Stephen. Am I not watching over you?’

The voice fell silent leaving Stephen alone on the balcony with his faithful friends.

Feeling cold, Stephen made his way back inside. As he approached the patio door he saw a reflection that was not his own. He recognised it to be the stranger’s silhouette but this time he was not wearing a red paisley tie or carrying a walking stick. This time he was dressed, all in black. Stephen was still unable to see his face.

***

David knew the moment Stephen entered the GSPC building. The biometric video entry device, situated in David’s office, alerted him to all GSPC employee activity which unknown to Stephen, included him. The biometric technology to which only David had access, showed Stephen sitting, uninvited, at Norman’s desk.

‘It’s okay Claudia, I am fully aware that Mr Law is in the building,’ said David, before she’d had a chance to express how disrespectful it was that Mr Law was in Norman’s office. Claudia, like Joan, would have felt that she had failed as Norman’s gatekeeper and was glad that he was not in work to witness such a cold boldness, dishonouring a lovely man who was grieving the loss of his dear father.

'He may be the leader of the free Global world at GSW headquarters, but he has no jurisdiction over me,' thought Claudia.

Stephen opened the closed blinds in Norman's office and observed Claudia at work. He was impressed by her tenacity and her loyalty to Norman. He was also bemused that she didn't seem intimidated by the status he held within the city. Claudia reminded Stephen of Joan and how she would be totally absorbed by her tasks, ensuring that everything was one hundred per cent. 'Maybe Claudia could be my new constant if Joan doesn't return?' he thought.

Stephen sat and waited; something that he wouldn't usually tolerate. But if waiting meant he would meet the real director and sort out his "Norman" problem, then on this occasion he would tolerate being treated like a lesser person. Stephen unpinned the GSPC world map from the wall and placed it on Norman's desk. Stephen looked at the "problem area" that for some reason, unknown to Stephen, Norman had colour coded blue, despite Stephen's instruction that it should be orange, as his own country. Stephen looked at his watch; his patience was now beginning to dissipate.

'Two hours,' he said to himself, irately, 'nobody keeps the leader of the free Global world waiting.'

Deciding that the person he needed to meet with must be situated on the top floor of the building, Stephen marched out of Norman's office, taking the map with him.

'Good riddance,' whispered Claudia, under her breath, assuming he was leaving the building. 'He's leaving,' she informed David, immediately.

‘Yes, I am aware,’ replied David. Claudia wondered how he could possibly know this when his office was on the top floor?

Stephen stepped into the lift and pressed the button for level six – he couldn’t see one for a higher floor. The lift started climbing slowly upwards, which reminded Stephen of his own elevator, except here he didn’t have a panoramic view. The lift continued steadily but it seemed to be chugging rather than moving slowly out of choice. Then the movement was accompanied by a high pitched, scraping sound as if the mechanism was having problems coasting along the metal. Stephen covered his ears and waited for the screaming noise to stop. ‘At last,’ he thought gladly, as the lift resumed its slow crawl skywards, free of the noise, which had previously suggested it was about to break down. Stephen waited for the lift to pick up pace, not thinking for one moment that this was its usual speed. His lift was unique and had cost him handsomely to programme it to his satisfaction. As he looked at his watch he realised that he had been at the GSPC for nearly three hours. The lift began to move faster. ‘At last,’ thought Stephen, wanting very much to get out. He didn’t hold much confidence that the lift was working properly. ‘Good job,’ said Stephen, as the lift worked up to a normal speed. But, without warning, it jerked to a sudden stop, then plummeted downwards, coming to another abrupt halt. Clutching onto the silver rail that ran around the perimeter of the lift Stephen steadied himself and pressed the “open door” button. He pressed it a few times but nothing happened. ‘Unbelievable,’ he thought, annoyed at the inadequate technology within the GSPC building. He pressed the button a few more times but the doors still did not part. Next, he pushed the emergency switch hoping that someone would provide him with an explanation about why the lift had failed with him trapped inside. When he pushed the emergency button he could hear the static of an open communication line.

'Hello,' he barked, 'is anyone there?' No one responded. 'Hello. This is Mr Law. Please assist me at once. I am trapped in the lift.' But still, no one answered.

'Hello,' he continued, pressing the button, 'I demand assistance. This is Mr Law …'

As Stephen issued his orders, the lift door began to open slowly, accompanied by the awful high-pitched scraping sound. As Stephen stood facing the door, covering his ears to try and keep out the disturbing noise, he heard a voice come through the intercom. The voice made him shudder and gave him an instant chill.

'Stephen, Stephen, Stephen,' the voice echoed, patronisingly, as the lift door continued to creak open.

'Stephen, Stephen, Stephen,' he heard again, unsure if the voice was coming through the intercom as it also seemed to echo around the lift. As the elevator door opened to about half way, all Stephen could see beyond was complete darkness.

'Stephen, Stephen, Stephen,' the voice carried on relentlessly, but this time it seemed to be coming from the intercom inside the lift and from outside within the darkness.

'Who are you?' Stephen shouted, frantically, feeling very unnerved.

'Don't you recognise me Stephen?' the voice replied.

'No! Who are you?' he yelled once more, desperately wanting to know who was taunting him.

'Come, come Stephen. Surely you recognise the loving voice of your guardian angel…?'